GUARDING THE BILLIONAIRE

THE JUSTIN TRAINER SERIES
BOOK 1

JANE HARVEY-BERRICK

HARVEY
BERRICK
PUBLISHING

Guarding the Billionaire

Copyright © 2019 Jane Harvey-Berrick

Cover design by Lee Ching / Under Cover Designs

Harvey Berrick Publishing

DEDICATION

To Justin
who inspired this more than he knows ♥

CONTENTS

PROLOGUE

Billionaires. Don't ya just love 'em?

Money coming out of their asses. They get their people to call your people, and that's just to schedule time to take a piss.

I should know. I'm one of the 'people' that gets called. Since I left the Marines, I've worked for a lot of millionaires, billionaires, gazillionaires. I've guarded European royalty and Saudi princes. I've stood next to politicians who've had death threats, and boybands who get mobbed by women wanting their babies. I've seen every vice and virtue, found every flaw, watched the shadows that darken lives.

And now, I'm working for the darkest, most twisted fucker that ever wore an Armani suit. Probably.

I work close protection.

I'm the silent bodyguard at the back of the room.

I'm the eyes watching you.

I'm the ears listening to you.

And I'm the foul-mouthed grunt with the gun who'll take a bullet for you. Although I'd prefer not to, and if I do my job right, it'll never come to that.

Intel is everything, so if anyone got the lowdown on my new

boss, the media would have a field day. Why? Because the guy who signs my paychecks is a sick fuck, into bondage, domination, sadism and masochism—and that's before breakfast—with a drawer full of files on his fuck buddies, submissives, who get tied up in his attached dungeon. Usually one at a time, but you never know. Still, at least he's honest about who he is.

He's a billionaire.

And I'm the man in black, guarding the billionaire.

Chapter One

HIGH SCHOOL MUSICAL

Six months earlier, October...

There's a certain technique to handling a naked girl—and I mean that in a strictly professional way.

This one looks about sixteen and she wasn't expecting to see me. Probably because she's hiding in the closet of Russell Vassal, lead singer of chart-topping boyband *Rock Boys*. You've never heard of them? Yeah, well, count yourself lucky. I hadn't heard of them either until I joined their world tour a month ago.

I grab a quilt off the bed, bundle her up and hand her off to a female security officer, hoping that when the kid sees her idols aren't as squeaky clean as she thought, she's not traumatized.

But at least she won't lose her virginity tonight, because it's my guess that's what she's offering. Jeez, she looks so young.

The blond kid, the drummer, is snorting coke off a pair of tits belonging to a red-haired groupie when my phone rings.

I see my wife's name and my sphincter tightens. Against my better judgement, I answer.

"I'm working, Carla."

3

"I want a divorce."

"I thought you'd never ask."

"Asshole."

"Bitch."

These days, it's what passes for a conversation with my wife of eleven years.

She takes a deep breath and I can hear the venom in her voice.

"And I'm going for full custody of Lilly. It's not like you ever see her anyway."

The call drops and just like that, my evening is officially fucked.

Then the drummer, Derrick, comes in his pants while motorboarding Colombian marching powder.

Sighing, I signal one of the other bodyguards to take him to the bathroom and clean him up, or at least get the evidence out of sight. I've already confiscated every cell phone in the room, but I can't afford to be too careful. There's money in celebs making asses of themselves, and the person who has the evidence is gonna make some serious moolah.

I'm paid the big bucks to stop that from happening.

Milton, a heavyweight dude covered with tattoos and a scar down one cheek, throws me an annoyed look as he walks toward me, but he doesn't argue. Instead, he grabs the kid by his collar and manhandles him out of the room.

The groupie stares at me with huge brown eyes, the pupils shrunk to pinpoints. She strokes her tits and offers them up to me, her head cocked on one side.

What, no hello?

I'm not tempted in the slightest. Sloppy seconds from a groupie who's serviced every guy on the tour bus including Jerome the geriatric driver? No thanks.

Besides, I wasn't lying to Carla—this is my work. Currently, I'm on tour with the hottest boy band on the planet. At least, that's what their marketing whizz kid tells me. All I know is that each day I have to listen to their crappy pop music that makes my ears bleed, and each night I have to watch them partying it

4

up with groupies, hookers, and assorted suppliers—meaning dealers.

Their big hit is *Strolling with Rocks*. No, I'm not making that up.

I'm strolling with rocks
My life full of knocks
Gonna stick that shit
In a damn big box.

Teenagers love it because it's deep.

The world is doomed.

But if I was in charge, I'd clean out the pushers and the whores, and hope the kids make it to 21 with most of their brain cells functioning and without a stint in rehab. Instead, they're surrounded by yes-men, and living every teenage guy's fantasy. Except it's killing them and they don't even know it.

I'm so tired of this gig, but it pays the bills and I need the money.

There are pros and cons to both short assignments like this three month tour or longer ones: time away from home versus money earned. Generally speaking, the longer the operation, the better opportunity to tailor the protective effort to the needs of the principal and according to resources—and these resources are more likely to increase over time. And generally speaking, the more time spent with a principal, the better the rapport and greater the trust. Although not on the current job.

Last month, my job was guarding some minor European royalty. Great-great-grand-nephew of Queen Victoria and the Kaiser. Yeah, gotta love that gene pool. But at least Archduke Klaus-Ferdinand was discreet about his addiction to male prostitutes and weed.

As long as the dudes he hired weren't underage, it wasn't my business. I ended up kinda liking the old guy. But then he died, which was a slight setback to my career, even though it wasn't my fault. Okay, maybe I should have known that a party with five guys wearing leather from a Berlin club might be too much for a ninety-three year old with a weak heart, but I like to think that he died with a smile on his face.

Unfortunately, the Polizei were involved, which meant I lost my 'anonymity guarantee' bonus.

Which is why I'm currently on tour with this bunch of musical misfits.

Carla's angry words allow a moment of emotion to filter through. When I think of my baby, six year-old Lilly, I suspect that she's about to become the bargaining chip in what's ramping up to be a bitter divorce.

I knew this was coming—I'm not a totally dumb grunt. I put two and two together a year ago when she told me I couldn't come back to the house I'd bought for us. The only reason she didn't serve me the papers immediately was because she couldn't afford a divorce lawyer. Which is why I can't leave this gig or any other job —we both need the money. Oh, the fucking irony.

I don't give a shit. I'm paid to keep the fuckers safe; I'm not paid to wipe their asses.

In this life, there are two kinds of bodyguards. There are the big brawny ones, the obvious ones, the ones with muscles up to their eyeballs and steroids shrinking their dicks. They keep things from getting too rowdy and are there to cut a swathe through crowds of fans, but also act as gofers and procurers for their clients. And sometimes they have to wipe their asses, too. Milton, poor bastard, comes into this category.

Then there are guys like me, paid to do the risk assessment and threat triage. I scope out venues and hotels, plan driving routes and escape routes. I'm the one who nixes the rooms that are vulnerable to snipers because there's another skyscraper across the street. I'm the one who knows the emergency protocol in the event of a fire, flood or plague of locusts. I'm the one who has to think the unthinkable to keep my client safe. I stay in the background, blending and anonymous. Guys like me, we're almost all ex-military and we're paid to make sure shit doesn't happen, and to keep the client alive if it does.

My co-worker for the night is all muscle and weighs 300 pounds, but I know that I scare him. I can see it in his eyes. He sees the killer in me: trained by Uncle Sam, honed by all my adult years in the Marines, and finished with a decade of those years spent fighting a guerrilla war against the Taliban, Al Qaeda, Boko Haram and a number of other nameless assholes who have personally threatened my right to exist.

Along with the Brits, the US provide the most coveted CP operatives in the world. I'd say that's because we champion the balance of soft skills like organization, planning and liaising with third parties, as well as the hard skills such as immediate action planning which are the emergency measures in reaction to emergent circumstances. Like royalty protection in the UK or the US Secret Service—layers of security from a well-dressed CPO standing next to the President, through to the more heavily armed counter assault teams operating in vehicles or marksmen on roofs hundreds of yards out of sight. The finesse on the surface, with the nastiness to back it up when it matters.

But right now, I'm nanny to a bunch of horny, tone-deaf, teenage rock stars. Still, it pays better than the Marines and there's less chance of getting my ass shot off.

Anyone in the public eye wants to be able to project their image and presence to fans. To quote the textbook, 'this may cause them to prioritize actions or activities incompatible with meaningful protection'—in other words, act like dickheads. Also, in the controlled chaos of a club or festival environment, there aren't necessarily well established rings of security on which the personal protection operation can rely. And many celebrities will have managers or other sycophantic individuals surrounding them, who definitely don't appreciate the close working relationship that a CPO requires with their principal, and may resent the protection team. Fucktards.

As Milton comes out of the bathroom looking pissed and giving me the evil eye, an unpleasant aroma follows him into the party room.

"Stupid kid shit himself. I'm not paid enough to clean that up."

"Did he throw up?"

"Yeah, he managed to get that in the shitter." Milton screws up his face. "I've put him in the recovery position with a towel under his head."

"Okay. Check on him every 15 minutes. Any change in his breathing or pulse, let me know. Fucker can clean himself up in the morning."

Milton gives a quick grin, flashing his gold incisor.

"You got it, T."

I give instructions to wind the party down. Yeah, I could have stopped the dealers and hookers from getting in the hotel suite in the first place, but the band's management likes the bad-boy publicity it generates. Before their taste of stardom, they were just five kids from Idaho—their management wants them to show a few rough edges, not too white-bread. But I can already see that they're getting addicted to this lifestyle, and it's a slippery slope from here all the way to rehab. But no one wants to hear that. Not from me.

The other guys in the band give me some attitude, getting in my face because I'm spoiling their fun, but I've learned how to read people over the years, and I know that they're pretty damn happy that they don't have to live up to this shit anymore tonight. They would never admit it, but they're missing those boundaries that they left behind when they went on tour.

They're not bad kids, just young and dumb. Then again, when I was their age, I'd already faced my first insurgent and seen friends die. You're not young after you've experienced shit like that. Sometimes being 32 feels ancient.

The hotel suite is a mess: drinks spilled and dubious substances drip from several surfaces. The hotel will tack on a grand to the bill for the deep clean, plus we'll have to pay out another to the cleaning crew to keep them mostly silent. Like I said, the band's management likes to keep them in the headlines; I think their philosophy is that there's no such thing as bad press. Stupid fuckers. These kids are just fodder to them. As long as they keep selling records.

Among my other responsibilities is to keep it secret that one of the kids is gay. Poor Gareth is so far in the closet that he's probably seen Narnia. The group's management plans to keep that piece of juicy gossip out of the news. Personally, I think they should worry more that he's tone deaf. One of the sound engineers told me that they switch off his mike and he lipsyncs. But he's a pretty boy and can dance his ass off, so they keep him.

Only one of them has any talent as far as I can see, but he's horseshit ugly with bad skin, so they hide him behind the keyboards and take all the credit for his work.

Cynical? Me? You ain't seen nothin' yet.

I supervise the clean-up, keeping an eye on who's entering and leaving the room, hand out wads of cash, then finally head to my room for a cozy three hours sleep before doing it all over again. Milton, the poor bastard, is on vomit-watch. Until Derrick wakes up enough to get to bed, the bodyguard will have to stay with him.

I wake at five with the thought I'd better get lawyered up if I ever want to see my baby girl again.

Another month touring Europe, then I can go home.

$$\sim\gamma\circ$$

"Trainer, I've got another job for you when you've finished with the Rock Babies."

"Not interested," I reply, wishing I hadn't answered my boss's call.

"Why the hell not?"

Mason is the guy who sends work my way. Technically, I'm freelance, but habit has me biting my tongue to stop myself calling him 'boss'. He was my C.O. in the Marines. When he retired two years ago, he set up a security company, saying there'd be work for me when I'd had enough of being a Leatherneck. I hadn't figured it would be this soon, but knowing my marriage was in trouble, I'd tapped out. Too late.

"I need to be stateside to see my baby girl. Carla served me papers."

"In Europe?"

"Yep."

There's a long silence on the other end of the phone.

"Shit."

I don't answer and Mason sighs. He's been married and divorced twice with two families on either side of the country, so I know he gets it.

"You'll want to take this job, Trainer. Pay is off the charts. Look, another month won't make a difference now, but what the client is prepared to pay you will."

I can read between the lines: I'm gonna need all the money I can get to make sure I have the best lawyer.

"The pay is that good?"

He names a figure that makes my teeth ache, it's so sweet.

"Great. What, when, where and why?"

Mason laughs.

"You're a funny guy, Trainer."

Yep, laugh a minute. That's me.

"Close protection for a Saudi Prince in Riyadh. He's on the liberal side of Old Testament and he's had some death threats."

"Yeah? How come his own team with local knowledge isn't his first pick?"

"He thinks there's a traitor and he's running scared. He wants someone with no prior connection to him."

"So, I sit around with my thumb up my ass waiting for the traitor to blink first?"

"Pretty much."

"That could take months."

There's a long pause and I know what's coming next.

"There's a big race happening at the end of the month in Rumah, 120km northeast of the capital. He says everything will be resolved by or at this meet. So it's three weeks max. This isn't a job you turn down, Trainer. The money will solve your immediate financial problems and for a couple of years to come."

I won't lie—it's really fucking tempting, but I shake my head even though he can't see me.

"I need to see my daughter."

And I'm worried that a clever divorce lawyer will twist my absence into something that makes me look bad.

"Wrong. You need to save up the dough for your daughter's college fund."

"She's six."

"Your point?"

Shit, he's right. I'd do anything for Lilly. She's the only sunlight in a very fucking dark, ugly world.

He knows he's gotten to me, and I can hear his smug smile over the phone line.

I spend my final night with the *Rock Boys* at another party. This time, I'm a guest—an unwilling one.

It's the end of tour party, and in their *lets-play-rockstar* way, they think they're being mighty bad. I've been to an Afghan wedding, and the fun doesn't start until you've eaten the week-old air-dried goat meat and blasted off a few dozen rounds from your AK47. These pansy-ass kids have no fucking clue.

I sit nursing a beer, a dark brooding presence. No one comes near me and I wonder if the words 'Fuck Off' printed across my forehead has something to do with it.

The drinking and dancing—well, grinding and twerking—goes on for the whole night. I just want to go to my room and sleep.

Then Derrick Dickhead staggers over, drunker than a Halloween skunk, spilling his beer on the expensive carpet.

"Hey, Mr. T!" he slurs.

The kid thinks it's hilarious and laughs loudly, sounding like a constipated donkey.

Besides, I look nothing like Mr. T. You won't see me in ironic leisure wear, or sporting a Mohawk, or pointing my finger at someone and calling them 'Fool!' (even though I'm thinking it), and all that jewelry—the pimp look is so 80s—not that I'd tell him that to his face, being the sensitive type. All in all, I look nothing like Mr. T.

Oh, and I'm not black.

But just to keep the client happy, I laugh my ass off at his little joke. I exaggerate. Nope, not even a facial tic.

I stare back, not a flicker of emotion in my eyes.

"Joke!" the kid mumbles lamely, starting to fidget.

I lean forward and he takes a step back, his eyes widening with fear.

"Ha. Ha."

He blinks, not knowing what to do, then staggers off in the opposite direction.

Milton has been watching the play-by-play and walks over, heaving his bulk into a chair next to me.

"You trying to make the kid piss his pants again?"

"Nope. Seen one piss-stain, seen 'em all."

"You got that right, brother," he sighs. "I can't wait to get home."

This is the most personal conversation we've had in three months of working together. We really are counting down the hours now, and I wish like hell that I was catching a plane back to the good ole USA.

"Where's home?" I ask, just to be polite and all.

"Little Rock. You?"

And isn't that the question? Where the fuck is home now? For 13 years it was wherever the Marines told me was home. Lilly lives with her mom in Connecticut. A place I use to call home but not anymore.

"Heading to Saudi tomorrow for another job."

It's an answer of sorts.

"Wow, that sucks, man. I thought you were heading stateside?"

"Change of plan."

He hears something in my voice and decides not to ask more questions. Just as well—he wouldn't have gotten any answers.

I finally get an hour's shut-eye when the party winds down. No lives lost or hospitalizations, so I call that a win.

Once we get to Schiphol airport, I'm officially off the clock.

Derrick, the little shit, surprises me by handing me copies of the two *Rock Boys* CDs, all signed by the band.

"Thanks for everything, Mr. Trainer," he says.

It still feels weird not to hear myself being called 'Sergeant' anymore.

"Thanks, you know, for not letting me choke on my own vomit. Or anyone else's."

I raise an eyebrow. Did the little runt just make a joke?

"Anyways, so me and the boys wanted to thank you. If you don't want the CDs, you can sell 'em on eBay. You'd get a couple of grand for them."

He holds out his hand, his eyes wide as if he thinks I might shoot him anyway. But I do remember how to act like a civilian, so I shake his hand and nod.

"Thanks. Stay out of rehab." *Ah hell, now he's making me all sappy.*

I walk away, mentally prepping myself for the next client.

Chapter Two

LARRY OF ARABIA

The vintage Rolls Royce Corniche is sparkling white with a creamy leather interior. It's $200,000 worth of auto and it belongs to Prince Talal's fifteen year old son. Good to know.

The Little Prince is sitting in the air-conditioned waiting room with a trio of bodyguards. I'm outside, standing in the shade, but feeling the hot tarmac slowly cook the soles of my feet. We're all waiting to meet his father who's flying in from Dubai.

I'm still on European time and feeling wiped. The blazing sun of a Saudi winter sucks the moisture out of my body as I study Riyadh in the distance, a huge modern city sprawling across the desert, punctured with minarets in all directions.

It's my first time working for Saudis, but not my first time working with Muslims. Back in Afghan, I helped train the ANA— Afghan National Army—and got to know and like many of the guys.

They were poor, honest about the corruption at all levels of government, and simply wanted to make things better for their families and country. They were young and broke, and I understood that.

Here, it's a whole different ball game, and I'm still learning the ropes. That makes me edgy.

His Royal Highness arrives on his private Boeing 747 that reputedly comes with its own gold throne. I don't know about that since I'm not invited inside, but the nose-cone has Talal's name on it.

I can tell you that those born into wealth can be disconnected from the real value of money and hard work. If they're famous, they see a need for guys like me, but if they're not well known, there could be a lower threat against them from general crime and they may not see the value in a protection operation. In other words, a guy like me is a hindrance.

Let the dice roll.

The Prince is a couple of inches shorter than me, with a Burt Reynolds mustache under a large nose and piercing black eyes. He's dressed in a Western business suit and a red checkered *ghutra* headdress, every pore in his body exuding power.

If it weren't for the fact I don't give a shit, he'd be intimidating. But I've faced down terrorists with RPGs and my soon-to-be ex-wife when she's PMSing.

"You come highly recommended, Mr. Trainer. My treasure must have the best."

I still don't know what the fuck this treasure is. Mason mentioned death threats? Maybe the guy is talking about his wife? Well, maybe his favorite wife...

I guess we must be thinking along the same lines, because what he says next concurs with my train of thought.

"You have a family, Mr. Trainer? A wife? A man needs these things in life."

I don't reply because I know he's had me checked out and a security clearance has been secured, otherwise I wouldn't be here. Hell, he probably knows my inside leg measurement and the date I had my appendix out.

I've done my research, too, and I'm trying like hell not to be impressed by the serious money this guy has.

As well as the $130 million mansion in Riyadh, the one with 371 rooms and 500 TVs, the one filled with fresh flowers flown in weekly from Amsterdam; he has a 250 acre estate a few miles away that has its own zoo. He also owns five-star hotels all around the world and more than 300 cars, several of which are copies to act as decoys when he travels. I'm talking Porsches, Lamborghinis, Ferraris, Maseratis, Bugattis—a gear head's wet dream.

I scan the surrounding area, never taking my eyes off the people around us or the buildings from where a sniper could take aim.

"Sir, I'll be frank."

"Please do," he says, raising a bushy eyebrow.

"I can guard you or I can guard your son. I can't guard both of you and do a good job."

He stares at me, those fathomless black eyes analyzing, calculating.

"Sons are more valuable than gold, Mr. Trainer. But that's not why you're here."

He gives a small, subtle smile.

"I will introduce you to my treasure."

We drive from the airport in convoy. I'm still no wiser about this so-called 'treasure' that I'm supposed to be guarding.

Talal's road captain leads in an armored car that's identical to his boss's, which follows behind. Then comes the kid in his white Roller, accompanied by *his* personal bodyguards. I'm in a limo with a driver who doesn't speak English, and since my Arabic is restricted to "Hello", "Goodbye", and "Infidels love Santa", conversation is limited.

Another armored car brings up the rear.

The further we drive from Riyadh, the further we drive into the past. Donkeys pull wooden carts along the sleek, dust-covered highway, eyes half-closed as we breeze past in air-conditioned luxury. Men and boys wearing headscarves and long robes in pale colors, sell fruit and vegetables at the roadside. I haven't seen any women yet.

Finally, we enter some sort of gated compound heavily guarded by black-dressed security teams armed with sub-machine guns.

A boy of about fourteen rides past on a camel, leading three more behind him. Camels? Definitely makes me look twice.

Before the country found oil, wealth was measured in the number of camels you owned—for the roaming Bedouin, it still is, to some degree. And maybe, as the oil wells begin to run dry, that will be the case again. Although if this was a place I called home, I'd be investing in solar energy. Just sayin'.

The House of Saud, the Royal family and rulers of Saudi Arabia, have an uneasy peace with the Bedouin. It goes back a few hundred years. I looked it all up on Wikipedia, but then I fell asleep.

Whatever.

What I need to know is that Talal has a lot of enemies among the Bedouin, traditionalists, and even a number of his own cousins. Since the Royal Family numbers some 15,000 people, that's a lot of people pissed at him. Although luckily, King Salman is also a reformer. Saudi women have been allowed to drive since 2017. Woohoo.

The cavalcade stops in front of a long line of stables. But it's not beautiful Arabian horses watching our arrival, it's camels, lots and lots of camels.

My door is opened by a uniformed servant, and the hot air rushes in as I step out into a strange world.

I watch as Talal greets all the workers by name, speaking swiftly in Arabic then listening to their reports. I don't know what they're telling him, but he seems pleased.

His son, Prince Nayef, doesn't speak to anyone and spends the whole time playing with his phone as he follows his father.

Guess teenagers are the same pretty much everywhere.

"Mr. Trainer, if you please."

Talal's English is better than mine. Must be the three years he spent studying at Oxford and post-grad at Harvard. I read that Nayef goes to Eton.

I step forward, keeping an eye on my surroundings as Talal

sweeps his arm toward a stable in the middle of the front row. It's slightly larger than the others and a puff of cooler air spills out as the door is opened.

"This is my treasure," he says proudly. "Her name is Nabila. It means happiness. Isn't she beautiful?"

He sounds like a proud parent and I briefly wonder why he keeps his woman in a stable when I finally realize that my bodyguarding duties are required by a large, dun-colored female camel.

A tawny head on a snake-like neck peers out, making a noise like a frat-boy puking his guts.

"Look! She's calling to you!" Talal says happily. "She likes you!"

He rubs the camel's long nose, cooing to her in Arabic. The camel's eyelids droop and she snickers softly.

"She's worth more than ten million dollars," he states.

My jaw hits the floor.

"Nabila has won me more than three thousand Dirham, or twenty million of your US dollars in races."

Now, I get it. That is a fuck-ton of money.

Talal continues proudly.

"And her brood mare fees will significantly increase if she wins the *Mazayen Al-Ibl* next month. Her offspring will be very valuable. There have been threats from my rivals," he says darkly. "Twice, ground-up glass has been found in her feed. But it was found in time, *Inshallah*."

I look up at the security cameras and the armed guards, and understand what Mason meant about it being an inside job. And I'm the biggest outsider Talal could find.

"You, Mr. Trainer, will watch Nabila around the clock. You will keep her alive. You will keep her safe."

Nabila puckers up her hairy lips and comes towards me for a smooch. I back away, but not fast enough, and she sends a stream of saliva dripping down the front of my best suit.

Talal claps his hands, a huge smile on his face.

"This is a good omen, Mr. Trainer!"

Yup, lucky me. I'll be sleeping in a stable for the next month.

What the hell, I've slept in worse places for a lot less money.

"Hey, Princess!"

I've managed to get a free half-hour to Facetime Lilly. I thought Carla might fight me on this and I wouldn't be able to do fuck-all about it, but she passes over her phone to the cute little bundle that is my reason for living.

"Daddy! When are you coming home? I have a new Elsa! You want to see her?"

Something in pale blue and pink flashes across the screen.

"Isn't she pretty?"

"Not as pretty as you, Buttercup."

"Where are you, Daddy?"

"I'm in the desert, baby. There's sand everywhere, but there's no ocean."

Lilly's face scrunches up and I know that she doesn't understand, so I pan the camera around to Nabila who peers into the lens, and I can hear Lilly shrieking with surprise and laughter.

"This is daddy's special friend. Her name is Nabila and she's a racing camel."

We spend the next five minutes talking about camels, but I suspect that Lilly doesn't have much clue what a camel is, since she keeps asking me if Nabila has a horn like a unicorn and where she keeps it when she's not wearing it.

Lilly giggles and it's the best sound in the world.

Followed by the worst.

"Bye, Daddy!"

"Wait, sweetheart, I..."

But her mom has taken the phone back.

"It's her bath time," she snaps. "Try to remember that if you bother to call again."

Bitch.

I'm left holding a silent piece of plastic. I really hate it when that happens.

Nabila nudges my shoulder and I pat her nose.

"Just you and me tonight, hot stuff. I sleep on the left, right?"

"Baaaaaaaaaaaaaaaah!"

I'm not sure if that means yes or whether I've just struck out.

My room in Nabila's stable is, in fact, a rather snazzy two-room suite with an attached bathroom. It's got AC and Wi-Fi, and a very nice arsenal of weapons, including an anti-tank missile launcher which I'm really hoping that I won't need.

I plug in my phone and Google the shit out of *Mazayen Al-Ibl*. And then my eyes do that weird bugging-out thing when I realize that I've been oh-so wrong.

The *Mazayen Al-Ibl* isn't a race—it's a beauty competition.

For camels.

I shit you not.

Last year, King Salman was the chief guest at the closing ceremony for the month-long King Abdul Aziz Camel Festival held outside the city of Rumah, 70 miles northeast from here.

Partly to appease the Bedouin, and partly to celebrate Saudi culture and traditions, this weird-ass beauty pageant brings together 1,400 camel owners and ten thousand camels from different Gulf countries.

Nabila is the front-runner, so to speak, among the one-humped supermodels, judged by a panel of all-Bedouin camel-rearing experts.

It may sound comical, but the stakes are high. Twice already, someone has tried to kill Nabila. Ground-up glass in her food would be a cruel and painful way to die. I'm not going to let that happen.

I'm somewhat stunned to read that the US Army considered having a Camel Corps back in the 1850s to serve the states of Texas, Mexico and So Cal. Well, how about that?

I also learn that a racing camel is as fast as a thoroughbred horse, able to run up to 40mph. And Nabila's breed is said to have mad skills of desert survival that would shame a Marine

Sergeant—being able to survive for a month without water, eating thorns and living off of their own fat. Camel fat, that is. Not a Marine Sergeant's. They don't have much fat. Speaking from experience.

Moving on.

I'm less happy to hear that up until recently child jockeys as young as six years old were used in racing up, and that practice is still legal in some countries. It's linked with people trafficking and twenty-first century slavery.

Fucking people. Give me camels any day. Although I wonder how many times I'll have to dry-clean my suit to get the stench of eau de camel out of it. Nabila stinks like a goat. Or camel.

I spend another hour reading up on my latest client until exhaustion takes me. I fall asleep dreaming of big brown eyes fringed with long lashes and a strong propensity to spit.

The next morning, I'm up before dawn, but still later than most of the men working here. I guess they get going when it's slightly cooler, and by that I mean 70°F instead of 89°F. In the summer, the mercury regularly tops 110°F.

I'm wearing my desert camos, civilian style, but I'm still armed. Mason got permission for me to bring my favorite Smith & Wesson M&P with me as a side weapon. Not that I need it here, but we all like what's familiar. One guy in my platoon used to take his own pillow with him wherever he went. Said he slept like a baby with that piece of foam.

I take a peek at my en suite arsenal and pick out a newish AK-103. Not a bad weapon.

With Nabila's handler on duty grooming her, and the black-clad bodyguards standing outside the stable, I have a free hour to go down to Talal's firing range and make sure I know everything there is to know about my AK-103.

None of Talal's men seem to speak English, or if they do, they're not practicing their linguistic talents on me. But that's fine. I watch and I learn, picking up the rhythms of stable life.

One of the ANA guys I got to know when I was in the sandbox, said that Allah gave us two eyes, two ears and one mouth, so we should watch and listen twice as much as we talk. Smart guy.

I follow in an ATV as Nabila is exercised and pampered. Her trainer is a young guy of about 18 who seems terrified of me, backing away whenever he sees me. But he's kind to Nabila, encouraging her and talking to her. I kinda hope the kid goes with Nabila to her new home or he's gonna be joining the Lonely Hearts for Camel Lovers website.

Even so, I watch him closely as Nabila's post-exercise food is weighed out, then I examine it carefully through a magnifying glass. Then there's a test for common poisons, and, finally, it's fed to a chicken that's specially brought in for the occasion. When the bird is still scratching around in its cage after 15 minutes, the food is given to Nabila. I'm pretty happy about that, because I was wondering if my next job was to be official taste-tester to a camel.

Nabila is *not* happy to be kept waiting. I have to say, she's kind of a diva.

It's been a long day, and Nabila and I are ready to hit the sack, or straw, in her case. The stable is locked and the alarm set, but I also have a code number that overrides all the systems in the event of a fire or armed attack.

I'm therefore more than a little surprised to see a beautiful woman standing in my bedroom, her dark eyes watching me dispassionately.

I don't think she's armed since the silk robe she's wearing doesn't cover much at all, but I draw my Smith & Wesson and point it at her, just in case. Women are weapons of mass destruction all on their own.

"You don't need your gun, Mr. Trainer," she says in a husky voice. "But you might need your ... weapon."

I'm not seeing the funny side. How the fuck did she get into a high security facility ... into my *private* space.

"Relax," she says, slinking over to the bed and taking a pose right out of a high-class porn movie. "His Royal Highness sent me. He thought you might need some company."

She could be telling the truth. The Prince could have hired her to check how much I have my mind on the job. On the other hand, she could also be something much more lethal.

Either way, I want her out of here.

"I'm calling bullshit, lady. I'm also calling security."

"You seem tense," she says, her voice only slightly accented. "I can help you with that."

Her eyes widen as I reach across to press the stable's silent alarm that will bring security running.

"Don't! Please!"

I pause, my hand hovering over the button.

"Talk."

"His Royal Highness really did send me. I'm ... a gift."

A gift or a test?

She pulls open her robe. Nope, not even slightly interested. I prefer my women uncomplicated these days.

I press the button and her lips turn down, a look of fear on her face.

The guards arrive quickly and guess who else? It's not Talal, but the Little Prince, malicious intent darkening his face. The woman shouts something at him, her tone begging. He gazes at her dismissively as she's dragged away still begging for his help. They definitely know each other.

Now why would the little shit want to harm Nabila? And what's Big Daddy going to say about it?

But I'm left in the dark. After the woman is taken away, no one comes to tell me what's happening. I can't leave the stable in case someone takes it as a gift-wrapped opportunity, and I don't know who to trust.

Finally, Nabila falls asleep. I'm wide awake, on edge and pissed. I message Mason with an update and a request that he finds out what the fuck is going on.

The next morning, I'm tired and gritty-eyed, feeling mean as shit and possibly feral. All the guards avoid me as if I've suddenly contracted plague or a severe case of unpopularity. Nabila's handler starts to pray when he sees me, which is slightly unnerving. I don't see Talal or the Little Prince, and I'm left to carry on with my duties.

Eventually, I hear back from Mason. It's all being hushed up, but Nayef has been sent back to school in the UK and his *mistress* has been banished. Yup, the fifteen year-old with the Roller and bad attitude has a mistress on the pay roll. Well, ex-mistress. Turns out that wasn't enough for the little asswipe, and he'd wanted Nabila, too. When Big Daddy finally said 'no', he decided to get his own back.

I'm stuck in a half-world where Talal can't stand the sight of me because his son's betrayal has shamed him, and I'm the lucky asshole who knows the truth. But he still wants me around to ensure Nabila's safety. He obviously doesn't trust his spawn not to take revenge anyway.

I spend a lot of time thinking about that, how sometimes your family turns out to be your worst enemy.

Chapter Three

JARHEAD

I'm contemplating the meaning of life. Philosophical questions. You know, deep shit that you only find at the bottom of a cold bottle of Bud.

It's the kind of peace that comes at the end of a long, tough job, and being able to relax for the first time in months.

I've only been back in New York for a few hours, and I'm fully appreciating the cool temperature and the cooler beer. These things matter when you've been working in an alcohol-free desert state. After Nabila won *Saudi's Next Top Model*, I had three days to visit Lilly, then it was another top-paying job in Qatar for a month. Well, it was supposed to pay top dollar, but the op didn't work out too well, or to use the official Marines term, it was completely FUBAR—fucked up beyond all recognition. I'm ready for some down time, but not too much.

Time to think doesn't suit me—too many bad memories.

I did twelve years with the Marines before I decided to call it quits. It was another year before I was allowed to leave: lucky-thirteen. Joined the day I graduated high school and never wanted to do anything else. I did tours in Iraq, Afghanistan, Germany and

Hawaii. That last one was really dangerous—a lot of hot women in bikinis could be considered a temptation to a married man.

But I never cheated. Not once. And leaving the Marines was supposed to be the start of a new life for me and Carla, a.k.a. Super Bitch.

The day I got home was the day she tossed me right back out again. I didn't even get to kiss my daughter hello before I was kicked to the curb.

It was a good thing I had Mason on speed dial, because what else was I going to do? Get some night security job and bore everyone with stories about firefights I've known and loved?

The work is varied and rarely as dangerous as being a Marine. Pays a lot better than being a Jarhead, too.

So the target, um, client might change, but the job is pretty much the same in any country in the world, and there are only four lines in a bodyguard's job description that matter:

1. Ensure the safety of the client.
2. Ensure areas are kept secure and all personnel have been approved.
3. Provide crowd control.
4. Observe location and situations for potential dangers.

To be good at my job, I need organizational skills, attention to detail and patience. I have two out of three of those.

I've been asked to score drugs and hookers. It's easy to find out who's providing that particular service: hotel concierges always know. I might not like it, but it comes with the territory.

Memories scroll across my brain, some better than others, none that I want to revisit.

I twist the cap off another bottle and get more comfortable on the hard hotel mattress while I watch a ball game.

I've also got a postcard next to me that I was planning to send to Lilly. It's got a picture of a goofy-looking camel that will appeal to a six year-old's sense of humor. I didn't get to mail it before I flew home, but I think I'll still send it.

I've been sending her postcards since before she could read. I just want her to know that wherever I am in the world, her old man is thinking of her.

The phone rings in the last innings of a Yankees game. I consider leaving it, but old habits die hard. I check the number and withhold a sigh.

"You checking up on me already, Mason? I'm touched."

"I might have something for you."

I sit up straighter. I could really use a new job. Lilly's latest dental appointments, ballet classes, karate classes and upcoming summer camp costs have diminished my bank account, since most of my wages from Saudi are now padding out Lilly's college fund. At this rate, she'll be going to Harvard. But the last guy, the Qatari businessman went and died on me—natural causes—so Mason didn't get paid which means I don't get paid, and I'm out of work until something else comes in. I'd rather take an interesting job, but right now, I'll consider almost anything. As long as I get this weekend to see my baby.

"What's the job?"

"A new client. A businessman who's just made his first billion. Hotshot entrepreneur, operating out of Manhattan. There have been some non-specific threats against him recently, to do with redundancies at a factory he bought in Michigan. Nothing serious, but now he's in the super-rich league, he'll need 24/7. You interested?"

Yeah, I'm interested. The Big Apple is only a couple of hours from where Lilly and the soon-to-be-ex live. I could see my baby more often. I'm certain Mason has that in mind, but no way I'm admitting it to him. If it sounds too good to be true, it probably is.

"What's the catch?"

Mason laughs.

"You don't change, Trainer."

Not true. I tried crunchy peanut butter. Once.

"Well, I don't know that there is a catch. I'm still doing some deep background checks on him, and apart from some normal hijinks when he was a teenager, and the fact that he dropped out of his expensive private college—no reason given—I'm coming up empty. His name is Devon Miguel Anderson, single, twenty-nine years old, gay. That a problem?"

Shit! A baby-sitting job?

A guy that age with more money than everyone except Bill Gates and God—maybe. It's a recipe for disaster. I can guess what's coming: fast cars, fast dates, drugs and debauchery—all the kind of shit that is dangerous and difficult for the poor slob who's hired to keep the fucker safe.

"It's not what you think, Trainer," says Mason, guessing my thoughts. "He needs personal protection and someone running point on security at his homes and office building. Just meet the man, then make up your own mind."

Fair enough.

"Okay, give me the time and location."

"Seventeen-hundred hours at his office on Monday. And you'll need to sign an NDA before you speak to him."

I shrug. The type of people I work for spit out Non-Disclosure Agreements like old chewing gum.

"Wait till you hear what he's prepared to pay—plus dental and health for you and your family."

Mason gives me a figure, and I whistle. It's fifty percent more than I got working for Saudi royalty, and that was tax free. But the amount makes me nervous, too. Someone who pays that much must have something to hide. Is he trying to buy my silence?

Mason emails the NDA, gives me a downtown address and hangs up. I go back to the Yankees game. They've just lost. Again. Maybe this won't be their year.

I check my watch, staring at the date. April 1st. Is it a sign?

But tomorrow, I have a few hours with my baby girl.

When Lilly sees me, she half runs, half skips down the driveway yelling, "Daddy! Daddy!"

It's a bittersweet moment, seeing my gorgeous girl and also knowing that I'm just a peripheral part of her life.

I kneel down, and she throws her chubby arms around my neck so I can bury my face in her soft curls. I can't get enough of that.

"Hey, baby girl! I think you grew again. Got a kiss for your daddy?"

She plants a loud, wet kiss on my cheek then wrinkles her button nose.

"Ugh! Prickles, daddy!" and she rubs one finger cautiously over the faint stubble that's grown since this morning.

I look up when I feel eyes watching me.

"Justin."

"Carla. How are you?"

"Good. You?"

"Good."

She sighs.

"Still the great conversationalist, Justin."

I ignore her and take Lilly's hand in mine.

"Ready to have some fun, Princess?"

She grins up at me and my day is a thousand times better.

We drink milkshakes, eat burgers, go to the park and play on the swings. Well, Lilly plays—those tiny ass seats definitely aren't made for adults.

Carla is always saying that Lilly is like her, a girly-girl who loves nail polish and hair clips, glittery shoes and frou-frou dresses, and that's all true; but Lilly is also *my* daughter, and she's brave and strong, and always wants the swings to go higher and faster, climbs trees and jungle gyms, and gets her knees muddy and her clothes messed up. See, *my girl*.

The day is too short and when I take her home, I tune out Carla's complaints.

I'm still getting used to leaving. Carla and I bought that house together, made dreams, lived and loved there. Well, one of us did.

Now, I'm on the outside, unwanted like a stray dog that can't take a hint; definitely unloved. I suspect there's someone else, but she's never admitted it. I don't care anymore. I only care about seeing my baby girl.

If I have to work as close protection for some billionaire asshole just to be near my Princess, then that's what I'll do.

On a dull Monday afternoon, I'm booted and suited and on my way to meet this Devon Miguel Anderson kid. Jeez, that name is a mouthful-and-a-half. Poor kid learning to John Hancock that.

I Googled him last night and found a lot of fluff stories, but not a single serious interview. All the usual stuff: so rich, so young; some about his family—upper middle class—his mom is a homemaker and his dad's a stockbroker—figures; he's got a sister who's a freshman in an expensive private college. Sure, he does. These rich types keep the money in the family.

But there was nothing about his private life, nothing about who's he's been seen with or dated. Reading the reports, I wouldn't even know that he was gay, and I wonder how Mason got that intel. I could ask him, but I doubt he'd tell me his source.

The twenty-story construction of DMA Solutions is almost new enough for me to leave handprints in the concrete, and I admit I'm impressed to see that Anderson owns the whole building. A classy receptionist in a tight-fitting gray suit gives me a security tag and sends me up to the top floor. From what I can see of the security guards and CCTV in the foyer, it's a pretty tight ship.

Anderson's assistant is waiting for me when the elevator doors open. Also in gray.

"This way, Mr. Trainer. I'm Ryan Parker, Mr. Anderson's Personal Assistant. May I offer you refreshments? Tea, coffee, water?"

"No, thanks."

He shows me into a large office, and I get my first look at the kid.

He's taller than I expected, and I can tell by looking at him that he's built of hard muscle. He obviously works out. His eyes are cool and assessing me as thoroughly as I'm assessing him. When he shakes hands, I can feel calluses.

His suit looks expensive. Hell, everything in his office looks expensive, from the original art on the walls, and a landscape that could be a Monet or a Manet or something that begins with M.

It's subtle, no bling, but it's there—the wealth and power. And the Lower Manhattan address overlooking Battery Park is worth a mint.

He points me to a seat and I take the chair opposite his desk. He may be young but I was wrong to call him a kid: there's something about his eyes ... they remind me of men I served with in Iraq, men who'd seen too much.

Interesting.

I wait for him to speak.

"Mason tells me I need personal protection and that you have experience in that area."

"Yes, sir."

He hasn't asked me a question yet, but he's watching my expression. I keep it parked in neutral. I can keep that shit up all day.

"My schedule is busy and it can change very quickly. I need someone who can be flexible. I understand you're separated from your wife?"

"Yes, sir."

"So 24/7 wouldn't be a problem?"

"No, sir."

"Good. There'll be a month's trial."

He pauses, measuring my response. I don't give one.

"I have live-in accommodation for employees at Wolf Point, and I spend most weekends at the Farm on Long Island."

I'm guessing that by 'Long Island' he means The Hamptons.

31

"Any questions?"

Where the fuck is Wolf Point?

"No, sir."

Yeah, I have a shit ton of questions, but none that people ever answer honestly. So I'll wait to see for myself who the new client really is; what's behind the businessman's façade.

"When can you start?"

"Immediately, sir."

"Good. Ryan will give you the details."

He presses a button on his desk, and the assistant escorts me out.

That must be the quickest, goddamn job interview I've ever had. And now I'm really curious to see where the dude lives.

I'm relieved that I won't be going back to the crummy motel room, not only because I already packed my bags. I wasn't sorry to say goodbye to that dump. I thought I'd be living on the cheap for a while to save money for Lilly. And her mother who has champagne tastes on a beer budget. But I can admit that she's a good mother and I loved her once, so I don't complain. Much.

I drive my rental over to Wolf Point, having learned that it's what the real estate websites describe it as a 'Tribeca Urban Mansion'. Or what I'd describe as another charmless glass and chrome building, also new. I figured him for one of the old Brownstones, but no, he hasn't chosen anything where other people have lived before. Anderson has made his money very recently and seems keen on spending it, especially on expensive real estate.

I punch in the entry code that I was given for the underground garage and park in the allocated bay. I can't take my eyes off the Aston Martin DB9 I park next to. I *really* hope Anderson is going to need me to drive that some time. I also cast my eyes over the SUV that's in the adjacent bay. Looks like it's up to light-armored level and has bulletproof windows. So far, so good.

The elevator code takes me to the Penthouse which in reality is the entire top four floors of the building. There's an older woman in a dark skirt suit. *What is it with Mr. Anderson and all the gray suits? I* wonder if he's like the original Ford cars, "Any color, so long as it's black." This assistant is maybe five or six years older than me. Great legs and a warm, friendly smile.

"Mr. Trainer? Welcome. I'm Rachel Smith, Mr. Anderson's housekeeper. Let me show you to your room."

Housekeeper, huh? I'm happy Mason told me that Anderson was gay, otherwise I'd have to worry about him fucking the help—it just makes things much more complicated.

The main room is huge. Christ! You could play ball in here. The floor is white marble, half an acre of it, and there's what I'm guessing is more expensive art on the walls, plus a grand piano sitting in one corner. I wonder if he plays it or if it's just for show.

The staff area is on the first two floors, with its own access and elevator. I follow Ms. Smith inside, and as the doors close, I'm trapped in a small space with a hot blonde who smells like sunshine. As the doors slide open, I find myself appreciating the way her tasty ass fills out her stylish, pencil skirt. *Shit! Mind on the job, Trainer. You're here to work and earn a fucking fortune!*

I let out a slow breath when the doors reopen, and Rachel walks me past the CCTV room where I see a bank of monitors. I'll have to look at that thoroughly later.

The rest of the staff rooms are more modest than Anderson's, but that's to be expected. And it beats sharing with a camel. Sorry, Nabila.

When Rachel shows me my bedroom, I nod with approval. It's large, light and airy, tricked out like a five star hotel, which I guess is what this whole building is, because it sure doesn't feel like a home.

But I'm definitely not complaining when there's a state of the art curved screen TV with sound bar, and a large leather sofa that's just made for lazy days. Not that I'm expecting many of those.

Even the drapes are made from heavy raw silk and hide a top quality wall safe where I can leave my spare ammo. The best of everything for Mr. Anderson—and his employees.

"I cook for all of us," says Rachel, breaking into my thoughts.

"We eat our meals in the private staff dining room, and Mr. Anderson eats upstairs. He has his own dining room, but he prefers to eat in his kitchen or in his office."

"Does he have any other employees? At all?"

She laughs softly.

"Not live-in. I know that's unusual, but Mr. Anderson values his privacy more than his convenience. A cleaning service comes during the day while he's out, and there's a laundry service that also dry-cleans. The pool man comes every two weeks and Mr. Basqiat, his personal trainer, comes several times a week—usually early evening. Occasionally, they train at DMA Tower at lunchtime. There are more people out at the Farm, but the estate manager, Mr. Van Sant, is in charge of them."

She pauses.

"I'll be serving supper in an hour if you're hungry?"

"That would be great, thank you."

She smiles. It's such a sweet, kind smile that I can't help but smile back.

As a rule, I don't smile a lot. My face nearly cracks.

"I'm sure you'd like to look around the rest of Mr. Anderson's home," she says. "If you have any questions, please don't hesitate to ask me."

"Thanks. Where is Mr. Anderson now?"

"He's in his private gym on the third floor next to the swimming pool. Mr. Anderson's rooms are kept private from house guests— well, only his family that I've seen—but he has weekend guests on occasion. I don't work weekends so I don't really know. Oh, you'll need this additional access code."

I nod, make a mental note, and watch as she leaves. I throw my bag on the enormous king-size bed and wander off to have a look around. As well as the staff rooms, which are bigger than most ordinary apartments with five bedrooms and six bathrooms, Anderson has six guest bedrooms and seven bathrooms, an impressive library with a competition-size pool table, and a TV room that looks like it's hardly used. Not that it's dusty, but it's too neat—no books or magazines laying around, and the remote controller is lined up at a precise right angle to the coffee table.

Tidy.

Soulless.

That's my gut reaction as I walk around the building, and I wonder who this Anderson guy really is. He doesn't act like any twenty-nine year-old that I've ever met. I sure as hell wasn't like that at his age. But then again, I was on Sergeant's pay and sitting in the sandbox waiting to get shot by Taliban insurgents. Nope, nothing in common at all.

Anderson's private rooms are on the top floor of the penthouse, separated from the guest area and living room. I take the elevator and use the access code Ms. Smith gave me.

There's a large home office with views of the little people on the streets below, three computer screens, a closed laptop and an iPad, lined up on top of a huge slab of white oak desk. One chair.

Anderson's bedroom is equally large and empty—a huge bed, walk-in closet that looks as if a GQ photoshoot threw up in there. Does one man need a hundred different suits, fifty pairs of shiny shoes?

The tub in the attached bathroom could almost double as a second swimming pool, and it's got those fancy jets that turn it into a Jacuzzi.

Holy crap, I have tub-envy.

I find a wall safe behind the painting in his bedroom—good quality, hard to crack. The safe, not the painting.

There's only one door that I can't get access to. Probably storage—I know Anderson recently moved in here. I'll have to ask Rachel about that later.

The painting is interesting. It's an abstract landscape and very restful to look at. But again, the kind of picture a much older man would have.

Heading back to the staff area, I check out the CCTV room that will be my office. It's everything I could want and more. Top quality comms unit and surveillance: sound and vision from four cameras external to the garage as well as inside, in the elevator and freight elevator, on each floor, and in all the main rooms in the house. No cameras in the bedrooms, the staff quarters, or Anderson's home office, although there is one at the Penthouse's foyer.

If I can work for this guy—which remains to be seen—technically, the job will be a breeze.

I spend forty-five minutes checking it out, but it's all adequately secure. I have a few suggestions, but I see signs that tell me Mason's team has already been out here.

Eventually, I make my way back to the employee kitchen. The aromas coming out of there are mouth-watering. It'll make a change from take-out pizza or halal lamb with yogurt.

"Hello, Mr. Trainer," says Rachel, when she sees me. "Everything to your satisfaction?"

"It's just Trainer. One question: there's a locked room that I haven't been able to access. Do you have a code for that? I'd like to check it out."

She lowers her eyes, a look of distress on her face. I don't know what put that expression there, but I can tell that she's not going to share.

"That's Mr. Anderson's meditation room. He keeps it locked because ... well, he keeps it locked. But yes, I have the access code: 6669."

Meditation room? Like a yoga studio? Why lock it? What sort of 'meditation' are we talking about?

I head back to the top floor and key in the code. When I open the door, my jaw hits the fucking floor.

?!!!?*

I don't even want to walk inside, but I do because that's my job and I'm a professional.

But this room ... it's definitely not for yoga. Kama Sutra maybe, but in any case, definitely an Aladdin's cave of twisted fuckery. There's equipment here that I haven't even seen in porn movies, and when you're on a boring-ass deployment in the sandbox, you watch *a lot* of porn.

Whips, belts, canes, paddles, floggers, a cat o' nine tails, even what seems to be a whipping bench with polished leather upholstery. But as I make a mental inventory, I realize that's it what I *don't* see. No cuffs or restraints, no bed, nothing that invites ... participation. The emphasis is on self-flagellation.

There are no windows, no daylight, just one bare bulb glowing a sickly yellow, and the dry-walling has been painted an institutional gray.

Nailed to every square inch of wall are pieces of paper, some handwritten, some printed from a computer.

I move closer to read the words.

Now the works of the flesh are evident: sexual immorality, impurity, sensuality, idolatry, sorcery, enmity, strife, jealousy, fits of anger, rivalries, dissensions, divisions, envy, drunkenness, orgies, and things like these.
Galatians 5:19-21

You shall not lie with a male as with a woman; it is an abomination.
Leviticus 18:22

Do you approach males among the worlds. And leave what your Lord has created for you as mates? But you are a people transgressing. Indeed, I am, toward your deed, of those who detest it.
Quran, Sura 26

There's more of the same from various religious texts, most of them fire and brimstone, denouncing the sins of the flesh, several of which I personally enjoy a lot.

But my eyes are drawn to a piece of paper above the whipping bench and I peer through the gloom to read it.

The mass of men lead lives of quiet desperation.

I don't know who this Henry David Thoreau dude is, but I wouldn't invite him to my party.

As I turn to leave, I read the largest banner, strung together with several pieces of paper:

For sin, seizing the opportunity deceived me, killed me. It is no longer I that work it out, but sin that dwells in me.
Romans 7

And in foot high letters, scrawled in red paint:

DEVON : DEV-ILL

I stand in that dark, dismal room, a cloud of misery clinging to me. This lair out of place in Anderson's bright, white building and yet, I suspect it's the room that matches him the most. And that is very fucked up.

So that's it. Anderson feels guilty for being gay. Maybe his parents are religious types, although Mason didn't mention anything. But whatever has caused it, this guy is a twisted son-of-a-bitch who gets off on his own pain. No wonder he's prepared to pay top dollar for me to keep his secrets.

I knew men like that in the Marines: guys who'd stub out cigarettes on their skin. They'd say it was for a dare, or that they were testing themselves, but those were lies. They did it because they needed it. Like Anderson, I'm guessing. But if I'm wrong and he's bringing other people in here, I'm going to have to get one thing straight: if there's anything illegal or underage going on, I'm out of here.

Obviously, Rachel knows and it definitely seems to bother her. *Shit! Maybe she and Anderson...*

No, Mason said he was gay, so I try to drive the thought out of my head. I can't imagine the prim and proper Ms. Smith in here, although everyone has secrets. No. I have to talk to Anderson himself about this.

I return to the kitchen.

"It's not what it looks like," Rachel says softly. "Well, I suppose it is ... Mr. Anderson has a lot of ... issues. He seems to be a pleasant young man, but, well. I really don't know what to say."

Her voice drops to a whisper.

"Sometimes he whips himself until he bleeds." She swallows and looks away. "That's not normal, is it? But ... I think other things happen when he goes to the Farm."

I'm trying to keep up, but she's not making it easy.

"The farm?"

"That's Mr. Anderson's weekend retreat in Sagaponack on Long Island. I don't go there."

"You don't?"

"No."

"Never?"

Her cheeks turn a delicate shade of pink and she shakes her head.

"Never."

Hmm. Why wouldn't Anderson send his housekeeper to his weekend home?

"I haven't had anything to do with the Farm or Mr. Van Sant."

Discreet, Rachel, very discreet. She's told me everything and yet nothing. But something about the boss's farm bothers her.

I'll know more when I check it out for myself. I could ask Anderson, but I'd prefer to come to my own conclusions, especially given Rachel's odd reaction.

I had a client once who was into pothead male prostitutes and dives on the wrong side of town. No way I can do close protection for someone like that, someone who likes the danger.

Anderson's addiction is of a different kind, but that doesn't necessarily make it any safer or easier for me to do my job. Does he go to S&M clubs? Are there boyfriends? Because all of this makes him a target for blackmail. Okay, so he doesn't have a wife to worry about, but he does have a family; and even though he doesn't have shareholders, he still has customers who buy his products. And in the competitive world of business, reputation is everything.

I wonder who else is in on his secret lifestyle? Ms. Smith, obviously. But his family? Maybe. Anyone else? The more people who know a secret, the more likely it is to be discovered.

I rub my forehead—this job just became a whole lot harder. I'm beginning to understand why Anderson needs to pay the big money to his CP team.

I go sit in the CCTV room and think about what I want to say to him. I see on the monitors when he's on his way, so I'm waiting, standing to attention when he walks into the Penthouse's foyer.

"Trainer."

"Sir."

He's ringing with sweat after what must have been a punishing workout.

"Debrief in ten minutes," he says.

"Sir."

He pulls off his t-shirt as he strides towards his room and wipes his face with it. And I stare—I can't help it. Because his back is crisscrossed with scar tissue: dozens and dozens of raised, painful-looking welts, on top of paler scars. They're on his back and chest. I'd guess that they were caused by a leather belt—one with a buckle. But they're old, healed for a long time. The fresher ones are pink and slightly puckered, newly healed. Shit. The guy really likes pain ... or needs it.

It gives me another piece of the puzzle. I shake my head. I'm finding Anderson too interesting. I just need to do my job.

I wait a few minutes and then head to his office. I stand with my hands behind my back, head up, eyes front. When Anderson enters, he's casually dressed in jeans and a loose shirt, and his hair is wet from the shower. His feet are bare, and the message is clear: I-don't-give-a-fuck-what-you-think-of-me.

I'm older than him by three years, but he's going to be my boss. Maybe. So it's a power play of sorts. But in the Marines, you take orders from your C.O. even if he's a wet-behind-the-ears dickhead, right out of officer candidate school.

He points to a chair, and I sit while he positions himself behind the enormous desk.

"You've had a look around the place?"

"Yes, sir. No access points of concern. I might need to adjust a couple of the CCTV cameras for better coverage and I'd like one more camera in the garage, and two external ones at the rear of the property."

"Fine. Anything else?"

He raises an eyebrow. The bastard knows what I'm going to ask him. He's waiting for it.

"Your meditation room, sir. I have to know that what goes on in there is legal and consensual."

"It's for personal use only. Occasionally ... very occasionally, I'll invite a ... special friend to join me."

Can I take him at his word? I think I'd rather see for myself. Well, not all of it and not in use.

He pauses again.

"Any more questions?"

"Mason said you'd had some low level threats: were any of them trying to blackmail you?"

He hesitates, considering my question.

"No."

"But blackmail is a possibility," I state.

He sighs and leans back in his chair, his eyes tired.

"Possible but unlikely. My sexual partners all sign NDAs and..."

I interrupt for clarification.

"All?"

He gives a cool smile.

"My tastes are specific, so I have a mutually beneficial arrangement with those who share those tastes. They all sign NDAs. I've had no problems."

So far.

"Other than that, you, Mason, my housekeeper and one friend, Frederick Landon, are privy to this information."

"And at your farm, sir?"

He nods quickly.

"It's managed by Mr. Van Sant. He, too, has signed an NDA."

If he's being honest and no one else knows, it's not that long a list. But if he really thinks NDAs will protect him, he's being naïve. But I suspect he knows that. And he said 'all', plural. How many men?

The questions are piling up.

"I'll need a list of any prohibited visitors, as well as those who have permitted access."

"You'll find those in a file on your desk," he says, cool as ever. "Any more questions?"

"No, sir."

"Good. If you wish to use the gym or the swimming pool, the entry code is 6668. I won't need you again tonight, Trainer."

"Sir."

That was unexpected. Normally the people I work for don't like me using their facilities, and definitely not at the same time as them. But I don't get that feeling from Anderson. Strange.

If this is his version of foreplay, I'll have to persuade him that he's not my type. Crap, if he hits on me, I'll be so fucking fired.

Rachel passes me with Anderson's meal. It sure smells good.

"Are you ready to eat, too?" she asks pleasantly.

"Yes, thank you."

"I'll just be a moment."

When she returns, I follow her into the dining room ... *our* dining room. Chicken chasseur with green beans and potatoes. Suddenly, I'm mouth-wateringly hungry.

It's our first evening together and could be awkward, but she's surprisingly easy company.

"How long have you worked for Mr. Anderson, Ms. Smith?"

"Please, call me Rachel. Just a few months now. It's been ... interesting."

I bet.

"Anything I need to know ... from a security point of view?"

"He doesn't go out of his way to make himself liked," says Rachel, carefully. "But I believe he's a good man. A troubled man, but a good one, nonetheless. Mr. Anderson works very hard, a punishing schedule, I'd say."

This interests me: I know she's using it as a metaphor, but Anderson is punishing himself for something. But what?

It's not the question I ask.

"What's a typical schedule?"

"He goes for a run at 5:30AM in the morning, sometimes earlier unless he has a business breakfast. He'll leave for the office about 7:30AM and I usually don't see him again until the evening. Mr. Basqiat, his personal trainer, comes several nights a week as I said, and then Mr. Anderson is usually in his study until late unless he's gone to the Lincoln Center. He's a patron of the New York Philharmonic. I work Monday to Friday, because most weekends, he's at the Farm, so I don't really see him as much as you'd think."

No, I imagine not.

"Does he go out? Friends, drinking buddies?"

"He visits his parents and sister in Scarsdale; one grandparent living in Florida."

"Anything else?"

"Fundraisers, occasionally; business dinners."

Is this guy twenty-nine or fifty-nine?

"Friends?"

"Well ... there's Mr. Landon. A friend of his father, I believe."

The one in on the big secret is a friend of his father?!

"No other friends?"

"Not that I've seen. Mr. Anderson is something of a loner. Now, can I offer you dessert? We have vanilla ice cream, or cheese and fruit."

Rachel has given me a lot to think about. It's obvious that she likes Anderson, in a maternal sort of way. At least, I'm not picking up any attraction between them, but I'll be keeping an eye open. It's a need-to-know basis, and I need to know.

I'm good at reading people—I have to be in this job. Anderson has been upfront about his *special interests*. He wasn't trying to shock me or be gratuitous, he was just stating a fact. But he's clever, so I'll be watching.

And Rachel is no one's fool either, so I can't help thinking that someone like her, a decent person, wouldn't work for Anderson if he was a really sick fucker. But I'll just have to make up my own mind about that; after all, Rachel isn't around on the weekends. And I'll be very interested to see what goes on at his farm.

About midnight, I decide to call it a day. Night, um, day.

Anderson is still working, just like Rachel said. When I knock and enter his office, he's poring over spreadsheets. Just looking at all those tiny figures gives me a headache. But then I suppose that's why I'm breaking my ass as close protection to a sick fucker who has whips in his meditation room, and he's the bastard who's paying me.

"Will that be all, sir?"

I'm polite as fuck.

"Yes, thank you, Trainer," he says distractedly.

"I understand you like to go for a run in the mornings, sir?"

He frowns and looks up at me when he realizes what I'm saying: that I intend to go with him. If he refuses, I'm out of here. I can only work with people who let me do my job.

"Of course. I leave at 5:30AM, Trainer."

"Sir."

I figure this guy must be one of those people who doesn't need much sleep since it's already late. Luckily, I can survive on five or six hours, so it doesn't really bother me. I was in the Marines long enough not to worry about long hours and broken sleep.

My bed smells wonderful, and the sheets are clean and crisp. *Thank you, Rachel.* There are certainly fringe benefits to working here. Gratefully, I slide under the covers and fall asleep immediately.

About three in the morning, I'm wide awake. Bad fucking dreams of places that I have no interest in revisiting.

I pull on sweatpants and a t-shirt and pad out to the kitchen to make coffee. Java in hand, I head to the CCTV room. May as well do some work as I'm awake.

I'm surprised as hell when the cameras show Anderson prowling through his private rooms. He's pacing, agitated and tugging at his hair. He pauses outside his meditation room and a shiver runs through me when he enters. I wait, watching, but he doesn't come out.

Feeling unnerved, like a sick voyeur, I take the fire escape stairs to his private floor and enter unseen and unheard.

But then a shrill scream has the hair standing up on the back of my neck, and I reach for a weapon that I don't have.

What the fuck was that?

Another scream—louder—someone in pain. The scream comes from Anderson's meditation room. I grab a heavy bronze statue and burst through the door, gripping my improvised weapon with both hands and scanning the dark room quickly. There's no one there— just Anderson, soaked in sweat, his breaths coming in short gasps. He's kneeling on the floor, naked, and holds a flogger in his hands. The skin on his back is bright red and a trickle of blood seeps from one of the raised wheals. My entrance has stopped him mid stroke. His eyes dart around the room, confused, wide with fear, and I can see from the way his chest is heaving that his heart rate is dangerously fast. Then his eyes fix on me, and I see awareness flood back. He shakes his head as if to clear it.

"Everything okay, sir?"

I speak tentatively, lowering the statue.

He drops the flogger in his hand and looks away.

"Yes, thank you, Trainer."

His voice is gravelly, but turning cool. He doesn't like that I've seen him this way: weak, vulnerable.

"Sometimes I need ... release," he adds grudgingly.

He doesn't say anything else, but I can see that he's shaken.

I walk back to my room slowly, my thoughts heavy. I've heard those sorts of screams before, from men who've seen too much. I think of the older scars I saw on his back, and realize the ones I can't see are even deeper.

I look at my hands and see that they're shaking slightly. I was dreaming about my buddy, Aiden King. Anderson isn't the only one who has nightmares. PTSD is no respecter of age or status: anyone can suffer—and Anderson is on the list.

Chapter Four

MEET THE PARENTS

I set my alarm for 5AM, but never get back to sleep after my weird encounter with Anderson.

I don't know fuck-all about self-harm. I've never been into any of the that BDSM shit. I'm not even that keen on tying up a woman I'm with. I prefer them fully responsive. I do know that someone who flogs themselves until they bleed doesn't have all their dogs barking. Although there are worse methods of coping with life. I knew a guy in the Marines who used to cut himself— said it helped. But then one day he took his AK-16 and swallowed a bullet.

I shit, shower and shave, then grab a pair of sweatpants and my running shoes. They're looking pretty worn. I'll replace them when I get my first pay check.

I pull on my shoulder holster and check my weapon. The holster is an X-project style: I find it the most comfortable to wear for hours at a time, and it's definitely the best for going running. My weapon is the most valuable thing in my life, other than my daughter Lilly, of course. The gun is my Smith & Wesson M&P, custom made, and it goes where I go. It has a Trijicon RMR red dot sight, AmeriGlo suppressor height sights, surefire XH55 G weapon laser. And it's also been one of the best investments, the best decision I've ever made. You could call it a lifesaver.

I've got a light, cotton jacket to wear over my t-shirt when I'm running. It conceals the Smith & Wesson pretty well.

I'm standing in the foyer seconds before Anderson. These rich types don't do waiting, and I'm not sensing that patience is one of Mr. Anderson's virtues.

He frowns when he sees me.

"You're armed?"

Of course! "Yes, sir."

"I don't like guns, Trainer."

Nobody *likes* guns: they're a tool like a spade or a shovel—as good or bad as the man using it. I remember my old man telling me that, but I have a feeling he took the line from someone else. I want to roll my eyes at Anderson, but I don't. That would be a quick way to get fired.

"It's how I do my job, sir."

Make or break time: if he tells me not wear my weapon, I'm walking. He frowns again, but doesn't say anything as we move to the elevator. I break the stony silence first.

"What route do you usually take, sir?"

"South to Battery Park, then through the East Village. It's a six mile circuit."

"May I suggest, sir, that we vary the route each day?"

He sighs.

"Sure."

He sets a fast pace once we're outside—it's the illusion of freedom. Unlike some of the people I've worked for, I can see that he's not doing it to impress me, that's just the speed he goes.

The streets are still pretty empty at this time and there's very little traffic. That's good because it makes it easier to spot a tail.

To anyone watching, we'd probably just look like two buddies out for a run. But the whole time we're running, I'm scanning the surroundings and assessing the situation: parked cars, anyone with overt interest, anyone acting suspiciously. I'd liked to have run the route by myself to assess it, but didn't get the chance. It would make my life simpler if Anderson used a treadmill, but I get why he wants to run outside. The threats against him have been mostly low level, and Mason's daily updates will pick up any change in that status.

Forty-five minutes later, we're back at Wolf Point. It's been a pretty good work out. In some jobs, the client expects me to sit on my candy-ass 24/7 and still maintain peak fitness. So you could say that some clients just sit with their thumbs up their asses when it comes to intelligence. But not this week and not this client.

I take another quick shower and head to the staff kitchen.

Rachel is standing at the stove. Boy, she looks good: starched apron, immaculate white blouse. I wouldn't mind helping her crease it.

She's set two places at the small breakfast bar instead of in the staff dining room. It's more intimate, and I like that too much.

Everything smells great. I could get used to this.

"Good morning. What would you like for breakfast? There's a variety of cereals, oatmeal, fruit, eggs, bacon and pancakes."

"That all sounds good, Rachel. Whatever is easiest."

"Mr. Trainer," she says with a tone of mock severity, "you and I will get along swimmingly if you tell me what you do and don't like to eat." She smiles warmly, to take the edge off her words.

Not that I'm offended. Far from it.

"I'd like bacon and pancakes, please, Rachel."

"Excellent choice!"

"And it's just Trainer."

"Does that come with a first name? I can't keep calling you by your surname," she says sweetly.

"Trainer works."

"Humor me."

I sigh, rubbing a hand over my hair. I really don't like my given name, but seeing as she's asked...

"Justin," I say, at last.

"Justin..."

She tries the name, and you know what? It sounds damn fine coming from her beautiful lips.

"That's a nice name. So, maple syrup, Justin?"

I shake my head. I can't face that much sugar in the morning.

She pours some pancake batter into a pan, and two minutes later I'm tucking into delicious buttermilk pancakes and crisp pieces of bacon. Damn, her coffee is good, too. I note that she takes Anderson a plate with an egg white omelet and a small bowl of blueberries with yogurt.

She returns quickly.

"Mr. Anderson says he will be ready to leave in twenty minutes."

"Thanks."

I drink my coffee and watch as she moves efficiently around the kitchen. If my gaze bothers her, she shows no sign of it. She's clearly at ease with her work and very professional.

I'm ready and waiting in the Penthouse foyer when Anderson appears. He looks preoccupied and tosses me a car key.

"You drive."

"Yes, sir."

The key fob says 'Range Rover', and I remember seeing the brand new SUV in the garage. *Niiice.*

Rachel enters the foyer, and it reminds me of my mom seeing me off to school. The thought amuses me, but you'd never know it.

"I won't be back until late this evening, Mrs. Smith, so if you could leave out something cold, please."

"Of course, Mr. Anderson. Have a good day, sir."

Shit! Mrs. *Smith? She's married?*

I'm surprised by the surge of disappointment I feel.

We travel down to the garage in silence. I sense that Anderson doesn't do polite chat. Fine by me. I'm not here to be his friend.

But when he goes to exit from the elevator first, I stop him.

"Excuse me, sir."

He takes the hint and lets me go before him. Yep, all clear. Nothing unusual to worry about. But the day you don't check, that's the day you're gonna get fucked. And not in a good way.

I point the fob at the Rover and the lights flash once. I open the rear passenger door for Anderson and he gets in without speaking. As I slide into the driver's seat, I note with approval that he puts on his seatbelt without me having to remind him. Careful Mr. Anderson. I like that in a client.

It's 7:15AM and we're barely out of the garage before his cell rings.

"Pam? What? Yes. Ten minutes. Tell Ryan to set it up."

Mr. Anderson insists that I drop him off at the front of his building. I'd rather have taken him into the underground garage where it's more private, safer, but he's in no mood for waiting. He tells me to come to his office once I've parked.

That's the crappy thing about being close protection—you can only offer advice; the idiot paying you doesn't have to take it. It can make things more stressful, if you let it.

There are only two other vehicles already in the underground garage. Probably the woman he spoke to on the phone and his P.A.?

Security checks me out as I enter the building: they know who I am so introductions aren't necessary, but they do their job carefully, knowing that I'm their new boss. I make my way to the top floor as I did yesterday, and the same guy as before is just leaving Anderson's office.

"Good morning, Mr. Trainer. We met yesterday. I'm Mr. Anderson's Personal Assistant. He's asked me to explain his schedule for the week. You'll liaise with me or my assistant Tessa for the day-to-day timings."

He points at a skinny blonde who looks as if she's about to cry. Isn't it a bit early in the day for that?

Still, the organization and clear lines of communication should make things simple. Anderson certainly likes to be in control.

"Tessa!"

I hear Anderson yelling from his office. He sounds pissed about something.

"Where's Trainer?"

"You'd better both go in," Ryan whispers to Tessa, who looks alarmed.

I head into Anderson's office and see that he isn't alone. He's frowning at a tall, strong-looking woman with short brown hair.

"Pam, this is Trainer. Trainer, Ms. Russo."

"Hello, Trainer."

"Ma'am."

I know from Mason's notes that Pam Russo is Anderson's number two guy, um, woman, um, colleague.

Tessa enters with a notebook. When she looks at Anderson, she flushes and her hands shake. *What?* I catch Pam rolling her eyes and she smirks at me.

Okay, I get it. The assistant's assistant is panting for billionaire Mr. Anderson, and apparently no one sent her the memo that he bats for the other team, so she's getting nowhere fast. Ms. Russo, I would guess, isn't interested in Anderson for similar reasons—she prefers broads.

I remember the speculation I read about him on some gossip websites—which women celebs he'd dated.

Besides me, doesn't *anyone* know the dude is gay?

And yeah, keeping up with the gossip websites can be part of the job. Especially when it comes to who the boss might be dating. Because dating a celebrity can get you on a lot of hate lists.

The thought takes me back to Rachel. I haven't figured that one out either. *Married.* So where has she been hiding Mr. Smith?

"Trainer, we'll be flying up to Williston, Vermont this morning. A change to the schedule: I have a meeting at the University. Leaving in five. Tessa, reschedule my morning meetings for later in the week."

Flying?

I'm not happy about sudden changes of plan because I don't get the chance to check up on security first, but I guess that's why Anderson's got me now so I roll with the punches.

On the move, I learn that Anderson occasionally hires his own private whirlybird for transport, currently perched on the roof of DMA Tower.

During the 20 second elevator ride, Anderson doesn't take a break from the constant stream of phone calls on his cell. If I had that many calls while I was driving, my safety record would be considerably dented.

Most of the calls are short as Anderson makes decisions quickly. The only person he seems to have longer calls from is Pam.

We're met on the roof by an older guy who seems pleased to see Anderson.

"She's all ready for you."

For the first time since I've met him, Anderson smiles and his eyes light up. For a second he looks his age, then the barrier slams down again, and he's talking wind speeds, air quality and visibility.

Please tell me that this doesn't mean my freaky boss is going to be responsible for flying me in an aircraft that resembles a fucking flying brick?

The flying brick is a trim-looking Eurocopter X3—a cool four million bucks of metal parts attached by a single bolt to the rotor blades.

Did I mention that *I fucking hate helicopters?* The memory of being shot at while airborne in a Chinook, a.k.a. another flying brick, and being able to do fuck-all about it, has never gone away.

Thankfully, it's a real pilot who runs through the final pre-flight checks, not an eager amateur. Thoroughness should be reassuring. It's not. I try very hard not to grip onto my seat. It's not good for the hired muscle to show white knuckles.

Ninety minutes later, the chopper touches down on a tiny helipad just outside the Agriculture College of Vermont University. Pam tells me that Anderson has a business interest here and paid for the helipad to be installed.

I unhook my clenched hands from the seat and manage to refrain from kissing the tarmac.

Another old-timer ambles over to Anderson, welcoming him.

"Thanks, John. We'll be back in a couple of hours. Maybe later."

"Yes, sir. Have a good day, Mr. Anderson."

We're on our way to UVM in a rental, a Tesla S electric car, when Anderson's cell rings again. I see his eyes flick up to me in the rear view mirror.

"Mason, I'm going to put this on speakerphone so Trainer can hear."

He taps a button and my old C.O.'s voice fills the car.

"An impromptu demonstration has been organized outside the Agriculture College building. Not serious, but could be messy."

"Oh, for fuck's sake!" Anderson snarls, running his free hand through his hair.

This is the first time I've heard him lose his temper. I can't tell yet if it's a regular occurrence.

"What do those fucking students have against feeding fucking developing countries?"

Mason's reply is calm, pragmatic.

"They don't like research to do with genetically modified crops, Mr. Anderson."

"Ignorant fuckers."

"The administration has advised that you use the rear entry, sir."

For some reason, his words make Anderson smile, and immediately, he's calm again.

"Fine. Consider me advised."

He cuts the call, his equilibrium apparently restored.

"We'll enter around the back, Trainer," he says evenly.

As we approach UVM, I can see small groups of students beginning to congregate and I check that the car doors are locked. I know the rental has automatic locking but usually I turn it off since I don't want to drive with locked doors in case there's an accident—emergency services lose time forcing locked doors—but in this sort of situation, or slow moving traffic, I do.

Anderson doesn't speak, he just watches me, his face impassive. He doesn't seem particularly fazed at the thought of being a target for an angry student mob.

The rear of the facility is quiet: clearly the students aren't that well organized because none of them have considered that a billionaire mogul might be smart enough to find an alternative to using the front door.

Anderson stalks inside to be met by an anxious-looking professor type.

"Mr. Anderson, I'm so sorry that you've been inconvenienced. I can assure you that the ... um ... demonstration is not the opinion of all our students. I do hope it won't influence your decision adversely. The team is very excited to meet you ... you've taken such an interest in their work."

"Thank you, Dr. Greenberg. After you."

"Yes, of course, of course! This way."

I'm slightly puzzled as to the reason for our visit. I don't need to know, strictly speaking, but I'm interested. And, if I have to justify myself, it helps that I know a little about the client's business.

Mason's file described interests in satellite comms and green technology, but more recently agriculture, buying up farms in Minnesota and Iowa in large numbers.

From the current meeting, I assume that Anderson is also involved in agrichemicals of some sort, but as Dr. Greenberg chats away, showing us around a series of dull looking laboratories and into some hothouses that have desert-like temperatures, and others that are cool and damp, I begin to understand that Anderson is a benefactor. This surprises me. I'd assumed that being so rich so young, money was his only motivating factor. But apparently not.

Yet another Anderson-shaped mystery.

He waves away offers of coffee, which is a pity. After the disrupted night and early start, I could really use another shot of caffeine. But my job is to be wallpaper, until I'm needed.

Finally, we're led into a meeting room. I stand by the door while Anderson takes a seat. Every other person is at least twice his age, but there's no doubt he commands the room with quiet authority.

"Is there anything else you'd like to ask us, Mr. Anderson?" wheezes Dr. Greenberg, cleaning his glasses and staring myopically.

"Your grant application isn't viable, Dr. Greenberg," says Anderson.

The expectant, hopeful faces of the assorted academics and scientists are suddenly bereft.

Dr. Greenberg crumbles, disappointment showing clearly as he repositions his glasses on his nose.

"May ... may I ask in what way?"

"You'll need a larger student body to meet your goals," says Anderson dispassionately, "and you need to accelerate the plans for crop rotation to pre-empt changes to the statutory research guidelines. In short: you need considerably more capital than you have budgeted for."

A distressed silence fills the room.

"I propose that you increase your budget to $8.5 million on an annual basis for the next seven years if you wish to achieve your stated research goals."

The good professor gapes at him, wringing his hands.

"Mr. Anderson! We have little hope of raising a tenth of such a sum. Our fundraisers are all volunteers. Our work doesn't attract many sponsors, especially since there is little financial incentive for businesses to do so. Not that your business, I mean..."

He looks distraught, and I feel sorry for him. Clearly he's passionate about his work.

A small frown of irritation flickers across Anderson's face.

"You misunderstand me, Dr. Greenberg. I'm saying that DMA Solutions will fund your work here: $8.5 million annually for a term of seven years, to be reviewed in thirteen months."

Did I just hear right? Anderson is planning to give away almost $60 million dollars? From the expressions on the faces of everyone else, I'm not the only one wondering if they have a problem with earwax.

"You ... you wish to ... *proceed?!*"

"Indeed, Dr. Greenberg," says Anderson clearly. "I'll have my lawyer send over the paperwork."

He stands suddenly, and the professor jumps.

"I ... we ... can't thank you enough, Mr. Anderson. This is most generous ... most generous indeed!"

"I look forward to seeing the positive results of your team's research, Dr. Greenberg. Thank you for your time."

"No, no! Thank *you*, Mr. Anderson. I'm sure the university's public relations team will be delighted to..."

Anderson scowls, and the professor visibly quails.

"No publicity."

"No ... no publicity?"

The professor looks confused, his gaze flickering to his equally bemused colleagues.

"None," says Anderson with finality.

He shakes hands with the professor who is looking rather limp, and then stalks from the room, business concluded.

I really don't get this guy. He's just given away a formidable chunk of his own capital and he doesn't want anyone to know?

Why?

Could it be some sort of money laundering scheme? Mason's checks haven't uncovered any dodgy dealing, but life has taught me to be cynical. For once, I wouldn't mind being proved wrong.

It's late by the time we finally head back to Wolf Point. I'm looking forward to seeing what Rachel ... I mean, *Mrs.* Smith has made for dinner. But we've barely exited the elevator from the underground parking garage when a skinny girl with short spiky hair throws herself at Anderson.

The sudden ambush has me reaching for my weapon.

"Surprise!"

Surprise?! She nearly gave me a heart attack.

"There you are, darling!"

I look away from the girl and see an attractive older woman walking towards us. I recognize her from Mason's photographs: same dark eyes, same black hair, she's Gloria Anderson née García, the boss's mother. So the girl must be his sister. She's cut her hair since the photo Mason has on file.

I relax immediately.

"Who's he?" asks the girl, looking at me.

"Trainer. He works for me, Abigail," says Anderson. "Trainer, this is my mother, Gloria Anderson and my sister Abigail."

"Hi, Trainer!" says the girl. "Nice to meet you."

She holds out her hand.

"Ma'am."

She giggles as we shake hands, peeking up at me through her eyelashes.

"Do you have a gun?"

I'm taken aback.

"Abigail!" says her mother, shaking her head.

"I was only asking!" says Abigail, pouting. "Do you?"

"That's enough, Abigail," Anderson snaps, clearly irritated.

To my surprise, she completely ignores him.

"Don't be so bossy, Devon," she says rolling her eyes, then turns back to me. "I bet you do have a gun. Everyone disapproves of that, you know. Dad supports more gun control."

I don't know what to reply that would be considered polite, so I make my escape to the staff quarters.

I haven't counted on the tenacious Miss Anderson following me.

"I think it's cool that Devon has a bodyguard," she says, eyeing me up and down.

"I use the term close personal protection, Miss Anderson."

"It's the same thing though, isn't it," she says giggling again.

Fuck, that's annoying!

"Devon's a lot of trouble, you know. He drives everyone crazy. But I think he likes you ... I can see why."

I don't know if it's particularly warm in the kitchen, but I'm suddenly feeling rather hot under the collar. I walk around the breakfast bar to give me some distance from the force of nature that is Abigail Anderson.

She follows close behind like a small, irritating dog.

Or possibly a bitch in heat.

"You look very strong, Trainer. Do you work out? I bet you do. What did you do before you started working for Devon? Were you a soldier? I bet you were. My friends are going to be so jealous when I tell them I've met a real bodyguard."

She follows me around the kitchen. I feel like I'm being stalked. *Shit!* I don't have an escape route unless I actually climb over the breakfast bar. Believe me, I'm considering it.

When Rachel walks in, I have never been so fucking happy to see backup.

"Hi, Rachel!" Abigail shrieks, like a cheerleader on helium. "I was just asking Trainer all about himself. Don't you think he's a hottie?"

She probably is a cheerleader. I wonder if Anderson confiscated her pompoms. Every sentence is screeched as if she's at a pep rally.

"Good evening, Miss Anderson," says Rachel calmly, although she her cheeks look a little pink. "Mr. Anderson has asked to see you in the main room."

Abigail pouts.

"Devon's always spoiling my fun. Never mind, Trainer, I'm sure we'll be seeing lots of each other. Bye!"

She blows me a kiss, hugs Rachel, and hurtles back to the main room.

"Are you alright?" asks Rachel sympathetically as I loosen my tie and try to regulate my breathing. "Miss Anderson can be a little ... overwhelming."

Oh, fucking yes!

"I thought I was going to have to fight my way out of here," I manage to croak. "You are a sight for sore eyes."

She laughs, but I can see that she's blushing, too, and I realize how else my words can have been interpreted.

I blame little Miss Anderson. I suspect she has the power to freeze men and turn them to statues like the Ice Queen in ... some kids' book. I'm sure I've read that story to Lilly.

Rachel serves dinner to the Andersons while I take a quick shower, then settle down in our shared living room to write Lilly a postcard. It's a pretty boring picture, a bird's eye view of Yankee Stadium. I promised I'd take her one day.

"You're a Yankees fan? Oh dear!" Rachel teases with an amused smile.

"Yep, for my sins. You're not?"

"I'm from Pennsylvania—Phillies all the way."

"Nice part of the world."

"Yes, it's lovely—not the sunniest place though."

"You prefer somewhere warm, preferably with beaches, for vacation?"

Rachel's eyes light up and she smiles.

"Oh definitely! I went to Florida once and I loved it."

"Yeah? I've been to Florida a bunch of times because I have friends who live in Montverde, just outside Orlando. Great climate … if you don't mind the occasional hurricane."

"I think you missed your calling as a vacation planner," she laughs. "Ready to eat now?"

"I could definitely eat."

My stomach agrees by rumbling loudly.

Rachel returns to the kitchen and I finish writing my postcard but I don't have any stamps. I'll have to buy one tomorrow.

When Rachel serves our dinner, it takes every ounce of self-control not to scarf it down.

"Hungry?" she asks, raising an eyebrow.

I guess I was eating quickly after all.

"You cook too damn well," I admit, taking a long drink of water.

"Thank you very much," she laughs, then gestures at my postcard. "Would you like me to mail that tomorrow while I'm grocery shopping?"

"Yeah, that would be great, thank you. I meant to send it today but I didn't get a chance to buy a stamp. It's for my daughter."

"Oh, you have a daughter? What's her name?"

"Lilly, she's six, nearly seven."

"That's a pretty name."

"Yeah, she's gorgeous. I'm probably biased."

"Probably," she smiles. "Do you have a picture?"

Only about a hundred on my phone, not that I'm going to admit that. I choose one where I'd taken Lilly for milkshakes and she has a chocolate mustache. I've always liked that one.

"She's beautiful, Justin! She looks a lot like you."

I raise an eyebrow.

"Yeah?"

Rachel flushes slightly.

"I meant, she has your eyes and your chin, I think."

"Good to know."

"Where does she live?"

I sigh, my smile falling.

"With her mom in Connecticut."

Rachel nods slowly.

"It must be hard to be away from her."

I nod, then wonder if she's fishing for information on Lilly's mom.

"I'll mail your card tomorrow," she says after a short pause.

"Thanks."

"No problem."

It's a civilized way to finish off a weird ass day. But I like it.

Chapter Five

YOU'VE GOT TO BE KIDDING ME

Anderson has ditched his evening workout for a boxing lesson with his personal trainer. If I had to look at all those business reports he reads before breakfast, I'd want to beat the shit out of something, too.

I've heard of Enrico Basqiat: he's very choosy who he takes on as a client. He's not interested in soft executives who eat too much and drink too much then think they can stave off a stroke by raising their heart rate once a week.

He's a former Light Heavyweight National Amateur Champion. He's the real deal. He has a three-year wait list for blue bloods wanting him to be their personal trainer.

He and Anderson are well matched: focused to the point of fanaticism, hardcore. I watch for a while as they try to maim each other, then wander back to the CCTV room which has become my second home. I've got some reading up to do on Anderson's employees. There are 3,209 at DMA Tower, all with potentially close access to him. Mason's firm has already done background checks, but I like to be thorough—my client's life and my life could depend on it.

I'm surprised to see an envelope on the desk with my name on it in Anderson's handwriting. It makes me frown. He hasn't said anything. If he's going to fire me, surely he'd have the balls to tell me in person?

But when I open it, two things fall out: a thick wad of paper that turns out to be a permanent contract, and a check for a ridiculously large amount of money. It's far more than I'd agreed with Mason. I don't get what's going on. Is he paying me for several months in advance? Is it a mistake? That seems unlikely. Anderson doesn't make mistakes. I decide it must be a test. He wants to know if I'm honest and that I'll point out the error to him. I'm slightly disappointed that he'd try such an obvious tactic. Usually, clients test me by leaving out their fucking Rolexes.

I can see from the CCTV monitors that Anderson's workout with Basqiat has been concluded and he's soon strolling through the foyer. I decide to wait until Rachel has fed him before I ask what's the story. I've already figured out that feeding the beast puts him in a slightly better mood. It's not saying much—the guy smiles less than I do.

Thinking about Rachel irritates me. I still haven't asked her whether or not she's married—still married, separated, divorced, or *it's complicated*. We've talked some and I know she's got a sister somewhere outside of Philly, but she hasn't mentioned a husband. I know that I could just look her up in Anderson's files, but somehow that seems like an invasion of her privacy. I'm getting soft.

When Anderson heads for his office after dinner, I wait a moment then knock on his door.

"What?" he snarls.

So much for him being in a better mood after eating.

I show him the check.

"I wanted to ask you about this, sir."

"Well? What about it?"

"It's more than we agreed."

He frowns.

"For your daughter's schooling."

He turns back to his computer screen as if that's obvious enough.

"Could you explain that, sir?"

He runs his hand through his hair in irritation, a gesture I've become familiar with over the last week.

"To pay for your daughter's elementary education, Trainer."

He hands me another piece of paper.

"A list of the three top elementary schools in your ex-wife's district. Choose whichever you think is the best fit."

And I'm lost for words.

"But ... I haven't signed the permanent contract, sir."

"Will you?" he frowns up at me.

"Yes, sir," and I see an expression that I can't identify pass across his face.

"Thank you, Trainer."

He turns back to the screen again. I'm being dismissed.

"Thank you for the tuition, sir."

"Okay."

He doesn't turn to look at me, but carries on studying columns of minute figures.

I'm ... surprised. It's not just the money—although I really appreciate that—it's the fact that he's researched and printed out a list of suitable schools.

I'm about to sign the contract when I remember what Rachel said about his weekend habits. I think I'll hold off signing until I've been to his farm, although not this weekend apparently. Still, I'm a cautious man.

"Justin?"

Rachel's soft voice interrupts my dour thoughts. She's not wearing her usual uniform of skirt and white blouse. Instead she's dressed in blue jeans and a long-sleeved t-shirt—and she looks damn fine, the way the denim clings to her hips and...

"I'm going now," she continues.

Shit! I forgot she doesn't work here on the weekends.

"I've left some cold cuts in the fridge and a list of frozen dishes by the microwave if you want a hot meal. And there's a bunch of menus from places nearby who'll deliver take-out if the microwave proves too much of a challenge." Her teasing smile takes the sting out of her words. "I'll be back Sunday evening. You have my cell number?"

"Oh, sure, Rachel. What about food for Mr. Anderson?"

"I think you'll find that he'll take care of anything he wants," she says kindly. "*Le Bernadin* delivers."

"Really?" A three-star Michelin restaurant does takeout?

"Well, they deliver to Mr. Anderson," she smiles, raising her eyebrows.

I'm impressed that there's no hint of condescension in her voice. Whatever she thinks of Anderson, it doesn't affect the way she does her job, or the way she talks about her employer.

"Okay, see you Sunday."

She waves and leaves, and I find the thought of rattling around the soulless mansion, with just Anderson for company, an unpalatable prospect. If I liked being stuck alone with a weirdo, I'd have been a spotter for snipers. But I'm not paid to enjoy myself. So I pull some more personnel files and go to work.

But my mind wanders. I keep asking myself, what is it about Anderson that makes him beat the shit out of himself until he bleeds? What kind of person *wants* to hurt?

I wince, thinking of the blood I saw on Anderson's back, but then again, there were guys in the Marines I knew who liked to push the limits of what their bodies would take physically, believing literally in 'no pain, no gain'. Even so, real masochism is not something I've thought about before. If that's what this is. I wonder if the boss gets off on the pain—or was my first guess right: it's punishment?

I've certainly never met any women into BDSM or who would agree to do exactly what I tell them when I tell them. Although having been married to the bitch, I'm kinda wishing ... but, no, not even then.

It's a long, boring weekend. We go nowhere and nothing

happens. Seeing Rachel return on Sunday evening is the highlight of my week. She's surprisingly pleased that we didn't visit the boss's farm this weekend. Strange.

Monday morning, my phone buzzes, interrupting my thoughts.

"Trainer, I'm leaving in five minutes."

And the phone goes dead. I get with the program, and Rachel waves goodbye as I haul ass down to the garage.

Once we're at DMA Tower, Ryan gives me Anderson's schedule for the coming week. Jeez, could it get any more dull? More meetings, more business dinners, a gala night at the opera. Okay, that might be his idea of a good time as he's into that whole classical music shit, but come on! *The guy's twenty-nine!* And this week there's another fundraiser, this time at some other rich dude's house in Scarsdale. Anderson's family will be there and I groan to myself. I'll need a week to prepare for my next meeting with Miss Abigail Anderson. Full body armor, perhaps? She looked like she might tackle me at any moment. Are all the Andersons this intense?

I sit at my desk and read some more personnel files, then check out the schools that Anderson recommended. They really look amazing. I've no idea how to choose between them—the one where the kids are the happiest, I guess. I wonder when I'll get the chance to visit them. If the money's coming from my bank account, I'm not leaving it up to my ex to choose.

The only person at the office who stands up to Anderson is his number two, Pam Russo. From what I can work out, they've been together from the start of DMA Solutions and he relies on her, as much as he relies on anyone. She's good at calming him down when no one else dares go near him. Although Ryan must be tougher than he looks to have lasted nine months as senior assistant, or maybe he's just damn good at his job.

There's one other guy who seems to be part of Anderson's inner circle. But when I met him this afternoon, he looked more like one of those perma-students you see near campuses, always studying and never graduating. His shirt was untucked, his pants were halfway down his ass, and he walked around like a stoner in a house of mirrors.

When he wandered into my office, I thought he was lost.

"Dude, you're here."

"We haven't met."

"No shit! You're the man."

"Who are you?"

"I'm Howard."

"Great t-shirt."

"Yeah. The Lone Gunmen were soothsayers."

"Are you lost?"

"Philosophically, yeah, dude. It's the twenty-first century."

What? I'd better speak slowly.

"Do you have a job here?"

"Yeah, man. Epic. I'm head of IT: network security, upgrades and configurations, hacking."

Are you kidding me? This is the boss's brainiac head of IT for one of the most successful new energy and comms companies in the US? Or maybe I was just abducted and aliens are messing with my frontal lobes.

Howard scratches his ass while he stares at me.

"Great meeting you, T. Later, dude."

Then he walks out.

I pull up his file on the personnel system. Apparently Howard joined MENSA when he was six. He graduated high school at twelve and finished his education with a PhD from MIT when he was seventeen. He's worked for Anderson for seven years. Epic doesn't even begin to cover his brain power.

And suddenly, I'm feeling very much like a dumb grunt.

At 1800 hours on Friday, I'm waiting in the underground garage for Anderson. He seems more pissed than usual. I wonder whose head he's bitten off today. He needs to chill or the guy's gonna explode.

His phone rings for the third time on the short journey back to Wolf Point. I feel sorry for whoever's calling.

"Abigail. What do you want?"

Oh, the sister. *We should have sent her against Saddam Hussein, it would all have been over much more quickly.*

"No, you can't ... because I'm busy ... oh, for fu— ! Okay ... what? No, you can't ... No!"

I did some research on the sister after I met her. I haven't changed my opinion and I really pity the nineteen year-old guys she must meet. Carnage won't even come close.

Anderson ends the call obviously annoyed, but beneath the irritation I can see that he's fond of his little sister. Maybe she reminds him of him.

Rachel is already gone by the time we get back. She's been quiet all week and I'm not sure why. But because I'm me, and a bona fide idiot, I don't ask.

I don't sleep well either, but neither does Anderson. At some point during the early hours, he goes to 'meditate'. The thought makes me shudder. I roll over and try to ignore what he's doing to himself.

When the alarm on my phone goes off at 5:15AM, I'm tempted to hurl it through the window. Instead, I drag on my sweats and running shoes, shave so quickly I nearly cut my throat, and am standing in the foyer at 5:29AM.

Anderson appears on time, as usual, and apart from the fact that he's unshaven, he looks like he's had eight hours of blissful sleep in his mommy's arms, when I know for a fact his bed is barely on first name terms with him.

I wonder if this morning's run will be shorter than usual but no, the same punishing pace for six miles, this time north to Greenwich Village, then back through Washington Square Park. He hasn't made an appointment with his personal trainer for a few days.

I slink out quickly, then skulk around in the staff quarters having a shower, and eating a bowl of granola until I think it's safe to head to my office without being spotted. There's a knack to being invisible when you live with your employer. But Anderson is so unpredictable, it's harder than usual for me to achieve wallpaper status.

I'm halfway there when I hear the door of the meditation room bang shut. I mean, *slam* shut. *Again?* Un-fucking-believable.

When I slide behind my desk, I start scanning more personnel files.

Three hours and forty-seven files later, an alarm on one of the monitors indicates that the fire door on the second floor has been opened. I'm up the stairs two at a time with my gun in my hand, but there's nothing to see and the door is firmly closed. Knowing how recently Mason's team have been over the joint upgrading the security, I suspect it's faulty wiring. I holster my weapon and make a note to get someone to look at it asap.

I turn when I hear soft footsteps behind me. Anderson is wearing the same sweatpants from last night.

"Problem, Trainer?" he's frowning at me.

"The monitor showed an alarm going off at this stairwell, but it's secure. I think it's faulty wiring. I'll have it fixed."

He nods and stalks off down the corridor. And I see the scars on his back close up, this time decorated with long red marks. Fresh ones.

Poor fucked up bastard.

Chapter Six

THE FARM

"Trainer, we'll be going to the Farm this weekend. A private function."

"Yes, sir. I'd like to drive out there to do a sweep since I haven't had the opportunity before."

"No, Mr. Van Sant manages security at the Farm."

"Sir, as head of your personal security, I…"

"There won't be any trouble this weekend, Trainer. Do your sweep when you get there."

I don't like this. It's fucking stupid. Why hire someone like me and tie one hand behind my back?

"Yes, sir." *You asswipe.*

I'm still in the dark about the boss's farm. Maybe it has something to do with his interest in agricultural technology. I don't know. But it's strange, when I looked up Van Sant in the personnel files, the details were sketchy. I only know that he's paid some serious bucks to manage this farm out on Long Island.

It's been a busy few weeks with trips to offices, factories, farms and shipyards all over the US, as well as Canada, Mexico and Taiwan—all part and parcel of being the CEO of a multi-billion dollar business empire.

The overseas op required a lot of background intel and organization which Mason and his team take care of, and I'm the guy on the ground, liaising with local security. Anderson hates all of that, but the richer he gets, the bigger the target on his back. He knows it, understands it, loathes it. He tolerates my presence. Just.

I haven't gotten a chance to go out to his farm yet, but from the hints Rachel has dropped and the fact that Landon is in on the big secret, it makes me both curious and wary.

Mason tells me is that the farm produces around 500 tons of hay a year and also sells energy back to the grid from its solar farm and wind turbines. There's also a small desalination plant, making it self-sufficient for water, too. But the interesting part is that the farm manager, Aston Van Sant, seems to work as much for Landon as for the boss. Fifteen years ago when he was twenty-three, Van Sant was arrested for soliciting. And that fact was *very* well hidden. Mason wanted to look into Landon's background, too, but Anderson refused point blank—something else I find interesting. It suggests to me that Landon also has secrets that Anderson is aware of but wishing to keep hidden.

I doubt Mason obeyed that order, but if he found anything, he's not sharing. Yet.

One other little factoid that Mason did share, although the boss says he uses the farm for private functions, none of those expenses are passed over the business accounts.

Using my highly honed investigative skills, I track down Rachel in the kitchen, and don't even have to ask for a cup of joe before the bitter, black elixir of life is put in front of me.

"You have but face," Rachel says, turning back to her food prep.

"Butt face?!"

That stings. I've always been popular with the ladies—no one has ever asked me to put a bag over my head. Until now.

She laughs quietly, glancing over her shoulder.

"Not *butt face*, BUT face—like you want to ask me something."

"Oh, right. Yeah." I gather my straying thoughts. "What do you know about the boss's farm?"

Her shoulders tighten immediately and she looks away.

"I've never been there," she bites out.

Interesting reaction.

"Okay, but you clearly have an opinion on the place."

Her shoulders sag and her head droops.

"I overheard Mr. Landon talking about it. He *wanted* me to overhear. Mr. Anderson was very angry with him."

"And what did you hear?" I ask, trying to sound gentle as this is clearly upsetting her.

She sighs, her hands stilling.

"The Farm is used for entertaining—*special guests* of Mr. Anderson. Lots of *special guests.*" Her voice drops to a whisper and a faint blush creeps up her neck. "Sex parties."

I blink a couple of times.

"You mean orgies?"

Her cheeks turn scarlet.

"Yes."

Huh. Should have guessed. No wonder the place is shrouded in secrecy. But as the boss's wealth increases, so does public interest. He's playing with fire keeping up this lifestyle.

And then I remember something else that Rachel said.

"What was Landon talking about that made the boss angry?"

Rachel looks away, her lips pressed together in an unhappy line.

"He said..." and she takes a deep breath. "That Mr. Anderson should bring me along as I probably would enjoy a ... a threesome. He knew I was there—he looked right at me as he said it."

Fucking bastard! Landon was trying to embarrass and humiliate Rachel, and it sounds like it worked.

"I would have walked out, then and there, but Mr. Anderson apologized and said that he wouldn't tolerate me being harassed like that. It was quite a while before I saw Mr. Landon again. Now, he never speaks to me; he just watches."

Rachel looks up at me with her big blue eyes.

"Are you going there, Justin?"

I want to tell her no, but I can't.

"Yep, the boss said we were headed there this weekend."

She looks down again.

"Oh."

"Rachel, this weekend is work, that's all. I have zero interest in the boss's twisted version of relationships, if that's what you can call them."

She still won't look at me.

"I thought all men liked no-strings sex," she says sadly.

I don't know how to make her believe that I'm not interested in dipping my wick in anyone's sloppy seconds, and definitely not at a free-for-all. Free to catch STDs, and all for nothing.

"Rache, does the boss seem like a happy guy to you?"

"What?"

She faces me at last, her expression puzzled.

"Anderson. Does he seem happy? You know, singing show tunes, tiptoeing through the tulips, hell, I don't know, maybe even *smiling* on occasion?"

She thinks about it and shakes her head slowly.

"No, I guess not."

"Then what makes you think that there'd be anything about his lifestyle that I'd want? I've seen a lot of shit in my life, Rachel. Things I wish I could un-see, but I can't. I don't want the glitter, I want it real. With one person." *And I'd like it to be you and pisses me off that you're married.*

She gives me a tentative smile, but when I pick up the car keys to the boss's Rover, her eyes grow sad again.

"Be careful, Justin."

"Always."

The drive to the boss's farm proves interesting in a number of ways. I'm enjoying being out of the city and looking forward to seeing the ocean without a bunch of skyscrapers in the way. I'm also digesting the intel that Mason sent me this morning.

I'm heading for Sagaponack, a village in the Hamptons, or as Mason put it, 11962 is the most expensive zip code in the US. Not only does Anderson own a second home there, where the *average* house price is a cool five million, but he owns 120 acres of the most expensive real estate in America, nearly a square mile.

It takes some time to get my head around that. And I have more questions.

I don't usually interrupt him when he's working on his laptop, but I'll make an exception today.

"Sir?"

"What is it, Trainer?"

"This weekend's private function—what should I expect?"

I glance at him in the rear view mirror and see him frown.

"Pull over."

Surprised, I ease the Rover to the side of the road and leave the engine idling, but when Anderson gets out, I turn off the engine, follow him, locking the car behind me.

I have no idea what the fuck's going on. I unbutton my jacket and loosen my Smith & Wesson in the holster.

He turns to face me suddenly.

"What do you think happens at the Farm?" he asks abruptly.

I don't miss a beat as I answer.

"Sex parties, sir."

He frowns again then gives a resigned sigh.

"It's a place where invited guests, consenting adults, come to enjoy a weekend of freedom: no restrictions, just mutual pleasure— mostly along the lines of my special interests. We don't define what we do."

I stay silent. Always best when you don't know what the fuck to say. I'm also wondering why we can't have this bizarro conversation in the car and not with the dust from the road kicking up around us.

"Many of my guests have a certain level of prominence," and

when he looks at me his gaze is fierce. "They require discretion and I have considered increasing security. The Farm's manager, Aston Van Sant, assures me I have nothing to worry about. But my instincts tell me otherwise. My instincts are rarely wrong."

"What does Mason say?"

His mouth twists.

"I haven't involved Mr. Mason or his team."

Yeah, well, it's a good thing I'm shit at taking orders because I've already made my own investigation and I'd say the boss has good reason to be concerned. But that still doesn't answer why he hasn't involved Mason.

I wait a beat but he doesn't explain further.

"May I ask why?"

Mason is the best at intel, and he still has a lot of contacts from his time in Military Intelligence, and yes, I know that's an oxymoron.

"I have no reason not to trust Mr. Mason or his employees," he says carefully.

I want to laugh in the dude's face. Is he for real? Mason knew about the take-down of Bin Laden before the President. You don't get higher security clearance than that, and Anderson is worried about his goddamn orgies? Since I'm a professional, I keep a straight face. Just.

"Mason hired *me*," I point out, my tone flat.

He doesn't answer directly.

"I'm aware," he says slowly, "that NDAs afford only a small amount of protection to ensure my continuing privacy. Suing someone after the fact doesn't stop the information about my ... predilections ... becoming public knowledge. A scenario I am anxious to avoid." He meets my unimpressed gaze. "I have had the opportunity to observe your work, Trainer. It's convinced me that you're the right man for the job."

I'm growing impatient at the way he's beating around the BDSM bush.

"What is the job, sir?"

He nods briefly as if he realizes that he's been rambling.

"I'm concerned about security at the Farm. There have been two occasions when I've suspected a leak, but I need any investigation done discreetly."

"What made you suspect that you have a leak?"

"One of my regular guests suddenly stopped coming. I reached out to him ... but he's blocked my calls." His jaw tightens. "I don't know for sure that he's being blackmailed, but his behavior is out of character."

"Anything else?"

"I don't want to believe it, but it's the only scenario that fits." He shakes his head.

The guy just told me his instincts are never wrong, and bearing in mind he became a multi-billionaire before he was thirty, I'm thinking he's right about not being wrong.

Huh, I'm sure there's a sentence in there somewhere.

Whatever.

"I'll keep my eyes open, sir."

Holy shit—I've just promised to keep my eyes open at an orgy. Definitely not something I thought I'd be saying when I woke up this morning.

I think I see a flash of relief on his face, but then he turns and walks back to the car. I start to follow and then have another thought.

"Sir?" I call after him.

"Yes?"

"Are you concerned that the car is bugged?"

His lips flatten again.

"It's possible."

I add *sweep the car for bugs* to my to-do list, irritated that I had to pump his stony heart to get this information. We've been working together for weeks—at least I thought we'd been working together— turns out I'm still in the dark about a lot of shit—and I'm supposed to be his fucking head of security. Jeez, and I thought *I* had trust issues.

As we continue to drive, the number of properties grows fewer and driveways become longer until I'm only catching a glimpse of houses from a distance.

When my GPS tells me to turn, it's at an entrance that's so discreet, I almost miss the tiny signpost that says 'The Farm'. There's no mailbox.

We drive a hundred yards inside around a curving, paved road, and have to slow down in front of ornate gates made of marine steel —either that or some poor bastard has to clean off rust every few months seeing as we're by the ocean.

I'm assuming the gate is programmed to recognize the Rover's license plate, because they swing open soundlessly. But I also notice a camera cleverly hidden in the ironwork, so maybe we're being watched already.

From a distance, the house looks like a simple two-story building in the traditional Hamptons' style with pale blue weatherboarding and white trim. It's only as we get closer that I realize how huge the place is.

I pull up to the double front doors and a short, stocky man with a soul patch—seriously annoying facial hair—appears. He's wearing Chinos and boat shoes with no socks. Dickhead.

"I didn't know that you were coming this weekend, Devon." His eyes flick to me. "And with a friend."

The boss gives him a chilly stare. The boat-shoe-wearing dickhead is behaving like this is *his* house. That's not gonna fly with Anderson.

"Debrief in my office, ten minutes."

"Okay," says the asshole, shrugging his shoulders. "And should I show your *friend* to the master bedroom or a guestroom?"

Now I'm pissed, as well.

"Be careful, Aston," the boss says in a voice so cold it could freeze oxygen. "Being Frederick's godson isn't the guarantee you think it is."

Landon's godson? That explains a few things.

Van Sant's cheeks are quickly stained with red and I can see the humiliation and fury that he's trying so hard to hide.

"I only meant..."

"I know what you meant. Show Trainer to a suite in the staff quarters."

Then he stalks away through the house, leaving the sound of icicles dripping. Oh wait, no, that's just Van Sant's blood thawing.

"So, you're the bodyguard," he sneers.

I somehow don't think we're going to be buddies.

"Yep, and you're the asshole. I think we've gotten acquainted now."

Swearing under his breath, he turns on his heel and storms through the building.

Gee, bad manners and cussing? Fucktard.

As I follow, I take a note of the general layout of the place, intending to do a full recon at the first opportunity.

My bunk is pretty nice. It's a room at the back of the house on the second floor, but the wide balcony gives tantalizing glimpses of the ocean. I know from looking at a map of the Farm's location (and I guess I have to give it a capital F now), Gibson beach is to the southeast, and Sagaponack pond to the west. With water on two sides, the property is as private as you can get.

I toss my bag on the bed—yep, all settled in.

I haven't been formally invited to the debrief the boss has set up with Van Sant, but I decide to show up anyway, just to piss him off. I'm professional like that.

Van Sant frowns when I finally find my way to the boss's office —hell, I just follow the sound of laptop keys clicking. He badly wants the boss to throw me out of the meeting, but Anderson barely acknowledges my existence.

"How many guests this weekend?"

"About twenty."

"*About* twenty? How many *exactly*?"

Van Sant shifts in his chair.

"Twenty-one, but Judge and Mrs. Dwyer are expected but haven't confirmed yet."

Shit! Judge Dwyer?! Associate Justice of the Supreme Court Judge Dwyer?

I can see why Anderson has his panties in a bunch about security.

"Why hasn't the guest list been messaged to me?"

"Freddie said that you wouldn't be attending this weekend and..."

Anderson leans forward, his elbows planted on the desk.

"*I* pay you to manage things here, Aston, not Frederick."

There's a long silence as Van Sant squirms under the boss's hard gaze.

"Have you hired security for the weekend?"

"Of course. I always do."

"Cancel them. Trainer will be in charge of security from now on."

"What the fuck, Devon? I *always* hire the security! This guy shows up and suddenly you're kissing *his* ass? I mean, what the actual fuck?!"

The boss's nostrils flare and his body stiffens, but he speaks quietly, dropping each word like a bullet from a silencer.

"I'll make things very clear to you, Aston. You work for *me*. You're paid by *me*. You live here rent-free because I allow it. Frederick asked me to provide you with a job. That doesn't give you carte blanche. So don't fuck me around."

"Dev, come on! I'm not just some paid lackey! You and me—we go back!" His eyes flick to me again. "We have history!"

"Yes, Aston, history. In the past."

Let's just say that after that the meeting goes to hell in a handbasket. Van Sant gets his ass handed to him and slinks out of there with balls the size of lentils and his tail between his legs.

Then after that fun start to the weekend, I check out the rest of the place. The house has 12 guest bedrooms upstairs, a separate wing for the employees, and Van Sant has his own cottage on the estate.

There's a large, well-equipped kitchen at the back of the house and another in the staff wing.

Downstairs, there's also a TV room, a movie theater, and a large indoor/outdoor pool with a retracting roof.

So far so normal—for a rich dude.

There are also several *meditation rooms* on the ground floor. I'm guessing this is where the orgies take place. The four, large rooms have wooden shutters covering the windows, and each one has a different theme. One looks like a Vegas whorehouse that I may or may not have visited once, tricked out in red velvet, gold brocade, and the soft end of BDSM: fluffy handcuffs, feathers, cute little whips, that sort of thing. Another room looks like my idea of a medieval dungeon or a gimp's paradise, depending on your point of view, with torture contraptions: cock rings, anal plugs, clamps, ball gags, strap-ons, bondage gear, restraints, dildos, vibrators, weird fleshy-looking anatomical body parts made out of silicon.

I wonder who has the stella job of sanitizing them after usage, then wish I hadn't had that thought.

Room three has a cage and a swing. I crane my neck trying to work out how they're used together, but I guess necessity is the mother of invention.

The fourth room has a bed big enough for six or seven people— no guesses needed for what goes on there, and a quick look in the closet shows a load of clothes, wigs and masks to play dress up.

The rooms don't appear to be soundproofed and there are even little minstrel galleries where you can go and watch the action, if you're more of a voyeur than a do-er. Every vice is catered to, as far as I can see.

I want to do a complete sweep of the whole building before the first guests start to arrive, but it's not possible.

I hear tires crunching on the gravel and know that the party is about to get started. What the hell is the boss thinking? There's no way one man can provide adequate security with this many rooms and twenty-plus guests. Why the hell hasn't he briefed Mason? Why haven't I been given time to do my job? What the fuck is going on?

The boss has a long game, but he's not sharing the rules or naming the key players. It doesn't make sense. Nothing about the Farm makes sense.

We're all fucked—and not in a good way.

Chapter Seven

FRIENDS IN LOW PLACES

I didn't go to college, but I have a PhD from the University of Life. You think frat boys can party? Try hanging with a gnarly group of grunts after nine months in the sandbox without a beer in sight. Now *that's* what I call a party.

Before I got hitched, I was known to party some, and I've enjoyed a threesome now and again. But I have to admit that Anderson's orgy has me whipped, I mean stumped, um, beat. Oh hell.

At first, it's like one of those upscale cocktail parties Anderson goes to, but then the gloves come off, along with the dresses, pants and shirts. Leather seems to be the go-to fabric of choice. Although Anderson has stripped down to black silk briefs. Even with the lights dimmed, I can see the scars on his back. But nobody else blinks an eyelash—they've seen it all before and it doesn't bother them. This is sick shit.

I'm surprised to see that he's sexing it up with a couple about his age—a male/female couple. A married couple. When he kisses the woman hard and starts working her clit through her panties, I'm more shocked by this than by anything else I've seen in this house of horrors. He's into women? Or is he just getting her prepped for her husband to bang her? I have no idea. Do gay men get off watching hetero sex? Jeez, not a question I thought I'd ever need to ask.

I'm also reassessing Mason's assertion that Anderson is gay. I'm beginning to think the dude might swing both ways. And if he does, he'd sure as hell better not try anything with Rachel.

The hairs on the back of my neck stand up and I turn my head a fraction to see Van Sant watching. Only he's not watching me, just the scene going on next to the fireplace. He also has his junk in his hand. He's getting off on watching the boss getting off. It's creepy as hell.

Van Sant stands to one side, his gaze flicking between me and the boss when he becomes aware of me. But I don't miss the longing in his expression. And it's definitely not for me.

The 'history' that he spoke about makes me think he still has the hots for the man who signs his pay check. Never a good position to be in.

After Anderson leaves the room with the couple, presumably to find a bedroom, hands all over each other, the remaining guests get down to the nitty gritty, which means they start fucking, but Van Sant has disappeared. I bet I can guess where's gone. He's definitely got some twisted obsession with the boss.

Security is pretty much non-existent. Anderson dismissed Van Sant's hired help and left everything to me, but one person can't see everything in a house this size, never mind the grounds.

The only thing I could do was insist that cell phones were left at the door, but without searching anyone, I can't be sure. Although naked people don't have many places to hide a cell phone.

I walk the rooms, a silent presence in the shadows.

I'm somewhat in awe of a woman who has the skills of a contortionist as she manages a triple-penetration. Although if I was the guy with my dick in her mouth, I'd be nervous about her gag reflex.

Yep, I've seen enough. Enough to know that anyone filming here could make the dough to be set up for life. And Anderson hasn't had the place swept for bugs. I didn't figure him for a fool. Live and learn.

I step outside to walk the perimeter and for such much needed fresh air, but the sounds of flesh slapping against flesh comes from the bushes, and the splashing in the pool puts me off the idea of taking a swim later. I don't care how great the purification system is.

I patrol the boundary, catching glimpses of heaving bodies. It's strange how tedious it all becomes. The exhibitionism does nothing for me. I guess I should be relieved. At least no one's asked me to join in.

"Hello, Mr. Tall-dark-and-disapproving. I'm Ellie."

I spoke too soon.

The woman is a beautiful redhead and completely naked. Although the curtains don't match the rug. She's the woman who left with the boss a couple of hours ago. I force myself to keep my eyes on her face.

"Good evening, ma'am."

She gives a quiet, silvery laugh.

"Very formal. Very fit." She runs her hand down my chest until I take half a pace back. "Are you Devon's new ... friend? Why don't you join us?"

She slowly parts her legs and starts touching herself.

She knows I'm not a guest but she seems to think she can taunt me and get away with it.

I lean forward, watching her lips part as her eyes dilate.

"I'll tell you what I am ... not interested."

I step back and see surprise and understanding turn to fury. I doubt she gets turned down often. But I've had enough ice cold bitches to last me a lifetime.

"You don't know what you're missing," she calls after me.

I feel like yelling back, *Get a life. And some clothes.*

But I don't.

A second later, I almost trip over the boss. He's sitting in one of the Adirondack chairs by the pool. His chest is bare, criss-crossed with new red welts that turn my stomach, but at least he's put his pants back on.

He glances up at me, probably having overheard the whole exchange.

"What is your assessment, Trainer?"

I shoot him a hard look.

"The place is wide open. I'm amazed you've only had one person blackmailed so far. Because the rest ... it's going to happen."

He nods, his gaze shadowed in the moonlight.

"Do what you need to do."

I don't even consider sleeping. The place has me on edge and I have the same feeling that I used to get before an op: brain on high alert, body tense.

I message Mason's team to send over the equipment I need asap or sooner: wifi jammer, night vision goggles and some fucking backup to keep an eye on the perimeters.

They arrive within an hour from the waterside in a small RIB, and I brief the men quickly, then I continue to lurk inside the house, unseen.

The orgy goes on until the early hours. I don't get it. I seriously don't get it. All the other people there enjoy swinging, sometimes literally, for the audience. The boss isn't like that. When he wanted to get it on, he went to a guest bedroom. Why does he let Van Sant continue to call the shots at the Farm? He's obviously indifferent to Van Sant's crush, so what the hell?

At dawn, Mason's guys fade into the half-light, and then I take a moment to check out the spy-guy goodies they left with me. I look over the merchandise, pleased with what I've got to make a start on some real security.

I think everyone else has gone to bed so I check out the four sin-gym rooms, because, let's face it, with a senior judge on the mailing list, any images or footage would be worth a politician's ransom.

When I search a room, I look for anything that seems out of place: pictures on the walls in illogical locations, lampshades that don't look normal; smoke detectors and loud speakers are always good places to hide recording devices, too. I also look for wires that appear to go nowhere, but in this box of delights, everything looks weird, so that's pretty much a non-starter.

I listen carefully as I enter the room because small, motion-sensitive cameras will make an almost inaudible buzz or click when they start operating.

And just in case I'm dealing with amateurs, I turn off the lights and stand in the dark, checking for any small red or green LED lights—a pro would deactivate these, but it's worth checking. So far, zilch.

I use the flashlight on my phone to test the mirrors—bingo. One in each room has a spyhole camera behind it. Although as Anderson encourages voyeurs, I'll have to check whether or not these are legit.

Finally, I use a top military RF spectrum analyzer that Mason just happened to have on hand. Listening devices use multiple radio frequencies in a spread spectrum that a basic RF scanner won't pick up.

This one picks up feeds in every room. Now I know for sure that someone is watching, listening, and probably recording.

I wonder why the fuck Anderson hasn't had these rooms properly swept before. Why hasn't Van Sant? I can't check the guest bedrooms as they're all occupied, so I jog across to the boss's office and am not at all surprised to find him awake.

I give him the good news.

He listens but doesn't speak, then nods slowly like I'm just confirming what he's suspected.

"Can you tell where the feed is going to?"

"Could be anywhere, sir. But I'm guessing there's a relay device somewhere on the property."

We're probably both thinking of Van Sant's cottage.

"Sir, I can sweep for bugs and I can set up an RF shield that will block the signal, but that can only do so much."

It's a version of the safe sex talk we had in middle school—abstinence is the only 100% safe method.

"I need to inform Mason."

He sighs.

"Fine. Do it."

I head back to my room to make the call. Mason answers on the first ring.

"Trainer, what is it?"

"Mason, this job is protecting Gilligan's Island for the very rich and very twisted."

My voice is indignant which makes the bastard laugh.

"I know. How's it going?"

"You gonna give me the full sit-rep this time? No more need-to-fucking-know?"

"Anderson didn't want me involved with the Farm, for reasons that are still unclear. I've been keeping an eye out, unofficially, of course. But a previous bodyguard was hired by Van Sant and joined in. He was planning on posting the footage on the internet."

"The fuck?! When was this?"

"Three months ago?"

"And you're telling me *now*? Does Anderson know?"

"Yes. It was after that that he brought us on board at Wolf Point and DMA Tower."

"And no one thought that was information I should have had?" I'm pissed. "So why hasn't he had the Farm secured?"

"He said that his manager would take care of it."

"Van Sant. Shit! You buy that?"

Mason gives a cynical laugh.

"Hell, no. I warned Anderson, but he told me to stay out. Like I said, it makes no sense.

"So how come I got the short straw and landed this gig?"

"I knew that you wouldn't be affected by ... anything that you saw."

"You're hurting my feelings."

"Bullshit! You don't have feelings, everyone knows that."

It's true.

I tell him what I've found.

"I need RF shields to block the signals, and a mobile one to use with the boss's car. Ditto wifi connections. I'll tell his data security people to increase the scrambling level on all of Anderson's personal devices."

By the time I've organized all of the above, a cleaning crew has taken care of the rec rooms, poolside and living area, the husband and wife team that provide the breakfast buffet are cleaning up in the kitchen, and the guests are starting to leave. Their limos arrive with precision timing. For some reason it makes me angry. Nothing ruffles their serene pool of wealth and power; nothing penetrates their bubble of self-importance. They don't care that the hired help —that would be me—has seen them in abandoned fucking with strangers. They don't notice the people who make their beds or shine their shoes.

My brothers-in-arms died to protect these assholes in their pristine lives. And this is what they choose to do.

Don't get me wrong, I'm usually a chilled, laidback kind of guy, but this weekend has rubbed me the wrong way.

Wow, that sounds bad. Touched a nerve—yeah, that's it.

On the journey back to Manhattan, Anderson senses my irritation but ignores it. All he cares about is that it's business as usual.

Rachel seems tense when I arrive back, but she pastes on a smile.

"How was your weekend, Justin?"

"Eye-opening, Rachel. But definitely not my scene."

And I stand by what I said before I went. *There's only one woman that I'm interested in.*

This time her smile is genuine.

"Oh, some mail arrived for you. I left it on the counter in our kitchen."

I like the sound of that: 'our kitchen' not the staff kitchen.

My light feeling disappears when I open the envelope. It's from my lawyer. It's a letter informing me that our divorce has been finalized. I gave the ex- pretty much everything she asked for, hoping that she'd play nice on visitation rights to see Lilly. Yeah, well, I didn't say I was smart.

But I'm officially a free man.

Chapter Eight

DEAD CALM

Some nights I don't sleep so well. Bad memories, bad dreams. It's the same for a lot of ex-servicemen and women. But it's nothing compared to how I feel at the thought of an afternoon on a small yacht with Miss Abigail Anderson.

I've been working at Wolf Point for a while now, and have had to avoid her five more times. I heard Anderson ask her why she keeps coming around. She said I was 'more fun' than college guys.

She's his little sister and I'm an employee trying to hold onto my well-paid job without pissing anyone off. It's a tightrope act and not always easy.

And this day is turning out to be pure torture.

For a start, I'm not a great sailor. *Yeah, I know, former Marine, ought to have seawater in his veins*, but there's a helluva difference between being transported on a 40,000 ton Naval destroyer and being trapped in a fucking fifty-three foot canoe with a nineteen year-old whose hormones are more rampant than an armored tank division, and whose come-to-bed eyes are going to get me very fucking fired.

"Hi, Trainer! How are you?"

"Fine, thank you, ma'am."

"It's going to be so *fun* to go sailing, isn't it? Do you like sailing? I *love sailing*. It's one of my favorite things in the whole world. Devon loves sailing, too, don't you, Dev?"

Anderson doesn't bother to reply.

This is the first time I'll be meeting Anderson Senior. The family knows not to come to Wolf Point or the Farm on weekends. I wonder what they think he's doing? Working?

Each Friday night, ravishing Rachel leaves, and Anderson goes to his meditation room to beat the shit out of himself.

I guess it works though, because nothing seems to shake that intense focus Anderson has the other 167 hours a week. Guess that's why he's a twenty-nine year-old billionaire, with a swanky mansion in Manhattan's ritziest zip code.

And now I'm fending off Abigail Anderson and contemplating a family day of forced enjoyment. Which is not my idea of fun. Well, not since I've been emancipated from my marriage, but the Andersons seem to get along well enough. In fact it's kinda weird to see my boss unwind to such an extent. I swear I actually saw him smile today, although it could have been gas.

I did a quick check of the family sailboat moored at Orienta Yacht Club just to make sure there was nothing obviously awry and it all looked shipshape. But Anderson figured out that I wasn't a-okay with the whole set-up.

"Problem, Trainer?"

"I think I'd better stay with the vehicles on land, sir," I say, nervously flicking my eyes towards Miss Anderson, who blows me a kiss *while my boss is watching, for fuck's sake!*

His eyes narrow, and I think he's got every right to fire my sorry ass, but instead he says,

"Good point, Trainer. I'll see you in a couple of hours."

Abigail pouts at him, actually pouts, and I can see her mother having words with her. If I was her father, I'd buy a ball and chain and a shotgun, then hire a 24/7 bodyguard. A female, ex-Soviet, shot-putter bodyguard might do it. Just.

Anderson Senior comes over to chat with me. *I don't do chatting.*

But I'm polite and answer his clever-assed questions in a neutral way. *I don't care if you are my client's father, I'm still not telling you jack-shit.* Oddly, he seems pleased by my taciturn responses, and I sense I've passed some sort of test with him.

He obviously cares about his son, but I sense a wariness, a feeling that they walk on eggshells around him.

Although Miss Anderson seems to follow a different set of rules. No surprise there. She hugged the boss hard enough to take down a linebacker, but he just shook his head and almost smiled again.

Anderson Senior is an interesting character. There's no file on him, but Mason filled me in on the basic details. He's a successful stockbroker, but he also has personal investments in businesses to do with green energy. He's into all that environmental shit, solar panels and carbon-neutral homes. Probably where the boss gets his interest from.

Married for thirty-seven years and no extra-marital interests, but before he married, his weakness was women—lots of them. There's also an old rumor—one that Mason couldn't substantiate—that he may have shared his son's taste in sexual variety, orgy-style.

I used to be like him, dipping my wick wherever I could. But being married to a cold-hearted sister of Satan did a number on my desire to bed potential bunny boilers. The ones who look normal are the ones you have to watch out for. Except for Rachel.

Anyway, these days, I'd rather get to know a woman first.

I wonder what Rachel is doing right now.

But it's his father's quiet greeting to the boss that nearly has me passing out from shock.

"Hello, son. I saw Freddie a couple of days ago—he says he hasn't seen you in a while. He, um, he thought you might have met someone. Your mother would love to hear if you've met a nice girl at last ... or a young man..."

What?

"No comment, father," says Anderson, only mildly irritated.

"Devon ... son ... you've never even had a date. Your mother worries about you. We both do. People just aren't designed to live alone."

I can't help staring at my client as it becomes obvious that his family has *no fucking clue* about his lifestyle. His own father thinks he's a virgin, and from the sound of it, not entirely sure if he's gay or straight either.

Wow, this is taking secrecy to a whole new level. How has he managed to hide the fact that he has a *dungeon* in his Manhattan mansion and holds orgies at his vacation home? I can't believe little Miss Anderson hasn't been over either place like a wrecking ball through a wet paper bag. But I guess not. It's an eye-opener.

From my peripheral vision, I can see that Anderson is watching me but my face is still at the neutral setting: *no siree, I ain't giving nothin' away*.

He lets his father talk to him about dating one day. I don't get that *at all*. He just screwed several fuck-buddies for an entire 12 hours straight, no pun intended, and he doesn't have one word to say to his father who thinks he's a *virgin?*

It doesn't add up. No one just starts out having S&M relationships, do they? But for all I know, private colleges have S&M frat clubs. Didn't he ever date? Obviously not, or his family would have known. There's something weird here. I mean *more* weird. It's obvious he cares about his family, and I can see that they love him, but you couldn't say they were close—they don't know anything about him. Hell, I've known him for nine stinking weeks and I already know him better than they do. Not that it's any of my business, except how it affects the way I do my job.

Once the yacht slips the moorings and sails from the jetty, I wander down through the small marina looking at the sailboats and gin-palace motor cruisers, then I sit out on the Yacht Club's deck with a coffee in one hand, newspaper in the other, and a clear view of the whole marina. The coffee isn't bad, but not as good as Rachel's. I wonder what she's doing this weekend. I wonder if she's with her *husband*.

The thought sours my mood, so I scan the sports pages and

wish I'd brought a book to read. I like John Grisham and Tom Clancy, but when I was a kid, I read all of Rider Haggard's novels. It's sort of why I joined the Marines—looking for more adventure than I could find in small town Idaho.

The happy family return a couple of hours later, and Anderson effortlessly arranges it so I'm not left alone with his sister. I wonder if he's going to chew me out about her in the car as we drive back to Manhattan, but he doesn't say anything. He seems preoccupied, lost in thought.

When we get back to Wolf Point, he gives me the rest of the day off. I assume he's going to the dungeon, sorry *meditation room*, but instead he heads for his office. It's like he's addicted to work. Boxing and beating the shit out of himself seem to be the only ways he has to let off steam. He doesn't drink much—a single glass of wine with his evening meal, he doesn't smoke, and I know his stance on drugs. All his employees have a one-strike-and-you're-out clause in their contracts, including me. I don't need drugs, I'm just high on life.

As I'm not needed, I decide to head out and grab a beer, catch a few games at a sports bar I spotted in the Village, do normal-Joe stuff.

I'm so happy to be out of here for the next few hours. When I return, the place is quiet. I check the CCTV out of habit, but there's nothing to see, nothing to notice—although I wouldn't say nothing to worry about.

Sunday passes uneventfully, although Anderson is in a foul mood, but that's nothing new. He takes it out on his spreadsheets and some poor sap I hear him yelling at over the phone. Seems like a pap got a photo of his family having dinner at the club house after we'd already gone—probably someone at the marina spilled the beans. Whoever it was used a long lens—those fuckers are hard to spot.

I've worked for a lot of wealthy people and the number one cardinal sin is talking about them. You don't get second chances for blabbing.

But even with all of that happening around me, the day drags.

So I sit in my office going glassy-eyed over more DMA Tower personnel files until the CCTV shows me that Rachel is back home. It irritates me that I'm so damn pleased to see her. For all I know, she's someone else who's been playing happy family this weekend. But I can't help myself, so I casually stroll out to the foyer to meet her coming up in the elevator.

She's surprised to see me, but beams a huge smile and I'm instantly smiling back.

"Hello, Justin! How nice of you to meet me. Did you have a good weekend?"

I know she's just being polite, but her voice is so warm, it feels personal. Then I remember that she's asked me a question.

"It passed, Rachel. It passed."

She smiles sympathetically.

"Well, I bet you're ready for a change from cold cuts, aren't you? How about risotto with chorizo for supper?"

"That sounds damn fine, thank you, Rachel."

She smiles that beautiful smile again.

"And how is Mr. Anderson?"

"Preoccupied."

"Oh, dear," she sighs.

And that's all she says.

Suddenly, the elevator call button rings: someone's on their way up. One of Anderson's family, perhaps? But I'd sure as hell better find out, so I jog back to my office and look at the CCTV. It's a white male, late fifties or early sixties, and not Anderson's father. I scan the very short list of permitted people who have access to the garage and elevator codes, and deduce that this is Frederick Landon: family friend.

That's part of the puzzle that doesn't fit. He knows about Anderson's kink but the family doesn't?

I pass Rachel on the way to the staff wing as I head to meet the elevator.

"It's Mr. Landon," I tell her.

Her mouth tightens slightly.

"I see," she says.

Rachel really dislikes the man.

I knock on Anderson's office door.

"What?" he spits.

What a laidback, happy-go-lucky dude—much like myself.

"Mr. Landon is on his way up."

"Oh for fuck's sake! What does he want? Fuck. Show him in."

He's obviously delighted.

The elevator doors open and Mr. Landon walks out. He's rail thin, silver hair, ice-blue eyes, pencil mustache, designer suit. Cool, clinical and ice cold.

His glacial expression chills further as he examines me from head to toe. The hairs on the back of my neck stand up. I wasn't a Marine for more than a decade without recognizing a predator when I see one.

His gaze never wavers. I don't think the guy has blinked in his life.

"Good evening, sir. Mr. Anderson is in his office."

"Trainer, I presume?"

And he knows who I am.

"Yes, sir."

He smiles, but his expression is reptilian and his eyes feel like they're trying to see all the way through me, assessing, evaluating, but also greedy and hungry. I don't get him and Anderson Senior being friends. At all.

"Divorced."

"Excuse me, sir?" *I think I saw a forked tongue.*

"Divorced. Ex-Marine." He gives an icy smile. "Devon's *body*guard. Lucky Devon."

There's a faint emphasis, as if it's a private joke. But he's read my file and he wants me to know it. He's pretending to be amused, but can't quite mask the irritation in his voice. For some reason, he isn't pleased by my presence.

Gee, and I'm such a little ray of sunshine. Maybe he wants to hurt my feelings.

Shame I don't give a shit.

I turn without replying and walk slowly to Anderson's office, keeping Landon behind me. I hear a small huff of annoyance, and that makes me smile.

I probably shouldn't be pissing off the boss's friends this early on the job, but sometimes it's the small things that make life worth living.

Besides, he reminds me of my ex. I think it's the charm of a snake-oil salesman.

I overhear the exchange as he enters Anderson's office.

"Good evening, Devon."

"What do you want, Frederick? I'm working."

The boss's response is childish, bordering on hostile.

"Just dropping in to see an old friend. I missed seeing you at the Farm the other weekend. If I'd known you were going to be there, I'd have put in an appearance. It's the first time you've been in months. I can't imagine work keeping you that occupied. Maybe it's your new bodyguard."

He smirks at me as I turn away.

"Are you going to offer me a drink?"

Seems as though Hissing Sid isn't intimidated by Anderson, unlike most people.

The boss mutters something under his breath, then leads Landon back to the main room.

"I could have found you a *bodyguard* if you really felt you needed one," he says in a sharp tone.

"Mason found him," the boss snaps back.

As I head to my office, I can hear the cadence of their voices, but not their words. Landon sounds like he's scolding the boss *and Anderson is taking it.* I'm intrigued.

I check through the files in the cabinet as well as the electronic files that I have access to for my work. There's no personal file on the Master Viper, but a reference to a business arrangement that Anderson has with Landon. I'm surprised to see that the boss has a considerable stake in the exclusive Saint-Mars Cigar Bars that pepper Manhattan and other wealthy East Coast enclaves, such as the Hamptons. It doesn't seem to fit in with the boss's no smoking stance or his other business interests. Maybe he's the silent partner. Or maybe I'll get a box of Cubans as part of my annual bonus. Dare to dream.

My stomach rumbles, reminding me of Rachel's offer of food. I wander into the kitchen, lured by the delicious smells that emanate.

But Rachel's demeanor is stiff, and she's crashing around in a totally noisy, un-Rachel-like way.

"I really can't stand that man!" she hisses between clenched teeth.

"Landon?"

"Who else?" she snaps.

I'm taken aback. Why is she mad at me? *Women!*

"Oh, sorry," she apologizes immediately. "It's just that he puts me on edge. He always looks at me as if ... I know, I know. It's none of my business who Mr. Anderson entertains, but there's something so cold and calculating about him. And the way he watches him, like ... like Mr. Anderson is his property ... pretending to be a good family friend, when really..."

She stops.

"Oh, just listen to me. I mustn't talk out of turn. Please forget I said anything."

"Your secrets are safe with me, Rachel." *All of them, whatever they are.*

She sighs.

"Thank you. I really shouldn't talk about his father's friend like this."

"Yeah, it's hard to imagine Anderson Senior and Landon as friends."

"Apparently, Mr. Landon taught the piano to their children. I think that's how they became friends..." She looks puzzled. "That's right, isn't it? Although maybe I'm wrong. I've never heard Mr. Anderson play."

"I've no idea."

"Mr. Anderson always seems ... different when he comes back from the Farm ... more distant."

She shivers.

"The way he watches Mr. Anderson all the time. It's creepy. I mean, he just stares at him, like ... like..."

Rachel's words grind to a halt, but I'm really curious to know how she would have ended that sentence. Is the getting a pedo vibe from Landon? 'Cause I know that I fucking am. Whatever she was going to say, she's changed her mind. Interesting.

Rachel frowns, and I fish around for a way to change the subject.

"How was your weekend?"

"Oh, restful, thank you. More so than yours, I think!" she says smiling and arching one eyebrow.

I decide to probe further.

"What did you do?"

"Relaxed, read some books, went for a walk in the park, shopping with my nieces. Nothing much."

"Sounds real nice, Rachel."

She smiles at me.

"Yes, it was."

She still hasn't mentioned her husband. Okay, time to pay or play.

"Were you with Mr. Smith?"

She blinks up at me, her lovely blue eyes clouding over. *Oh, shit!*

"My husband passed away five years ago. I would have thought you'd seen that in my file."

Not what I was expecting. And now I feel like a prick for asking her.

"I ... I haven't read your file, Rachel."

"Oh." She pauses, then smiles. "I see."

I realize I'm staring. Her smile fades slowly and her breath catches in her throat ... and then the fucking kitchen intercom buzzes.

Rachel blinks twice then answers.

"Yes, Mr. Anderson. I'll bring it through right away for you."

She busies herself over the stove, her cheeks pink. I shake my head. *What are you doing, Trainer? She's an employee! You're an employee! Do you want her to lose her fucking job? Do you want to lose yours and all those lovely benefits for Lilly?*

I head back to my office and pull myself together. It's a golden fucking rule: never, ever screw your coworkers. That wasn't really an issue when I was in the Marines. Although there was that one Sergeant in the motor pool: great rack, knew her way around an oil change.

To clear my mind, I think about what Rachel told me about Landon and what I've read in his file. He's a family friend, he's in business with Anderson, he's not intimidated by him, he scolds him; he has his private access codes, he's cold and authoritative, he taught him piano when the boss was a little kid; he's one scary bastard, he knows about the meditation room and joins in orgies at the Farm.

Rachel is right about one thing: Anderson Senior and Landon have known each other since before Anderson was married.

Mason's private report states that Landon worked as a private tutor and piano teacher in the homes of the upper middle classes on the East Coast.

Since then, he's become a wealthy and successful businessman, but only because Devon Anderson invested in his chain of Cigar Bars. Mason's file says that Landon has never been known to be in a relationship but is assumed to be gay.

I don't know when he started teaching Anderson piano, but they've known each other at least twenty years. He visits unannounced and knows the boss better than his own family.

And suddenly I'm wondering—the whole S&M thing, the reason Anderson has apparently never had a date, the reason his family knows nothing about his twisted lifestyle. It all adds up to one thing: Frederick Landon.

Fuck.

What are we talking here? Predator? Pedo? Or just opportunist?

But it still doesn't answer the question: why does Anderson call him a friend?

Chapter Nine

COSMOPOLIS

"Oh, Trainer! I'm going to ride you until you pop like warm champagne!"

I look up into Rachel's scorching blue eyes, my hands reaching up to touch her full, round, beautiful breasts.

We move together like we were made for each other and I know I'm close, so close...

A persistent ringing noise intrudes on the moment.

What the fuck? My fucking alarm has gone off.

And I wake up. Alone. And ... oh *what?* Sticky. A fucking wet dream? I don't believe this! Am I fourteen for fuck's sake?

I fight my way out of the knotted sheets and sit on the edge of the bed, calming my wild thoughts and ragged breathing.

Just a dream. But a damn fine dream. I haven't had a dream like that since ... I've *never* had a dream like that. I blame Anderson and all the kinky shit that goes down. No pun intended.

I stagger to my feet and into the shower, washing away the dream, the stickiness, the confusion. *This is not me. This is not how I behave. I am not so fucking stupid as to screw the help. I will not cause Rachel to lose her job.* No matter how much I might want her. *Stop this now, you asshole. Get a fucking grip.*

I trail back into my room feeling slightly depressed. The bed is a mess and, *oh shit*, just a fucking mess.

I dress quickly in my sweats and running shoes, then pull the sheets off and bundle them up to take to the laundry room, when I see...

Shit! Rachel!

"Oh, good morning! Did you sleep well?"

Yeah, too fucking well.

"Uh, yeah. Thanks, Rachel."

"You really don't have to do that, you know," she says, pointing to the sheets. "Let me take those from you."

Shit!

"No, that's fine, I can manage," I say slightly too emphatically.

Her face falls.

"Really, it's no trouble. It's nice to have someone to look after as well as Mr. Anderson."

I don't know what to say to that. Nobody has looked after me since ... well, my mom, I guess. My ex-wife certainly didn't. But maybe I'm not being fair—we were both so young, and I was away saving the world on behalf of the US Marine Corps and Uncle Sam.

I realize that I haven't replied to Rachel, and she's still watching, looking slightly hurt.

"Old habits, Rachel," I mutter, slinging the sheets into the washing machine and slamming the door.

She smiles at me cautiously.

"I understand. But please let me do that in future. You have enough on your plate with Mr. Anderson."

Her gentle reminder makes me look at my watch. *Shit! 5:29 AM —and the bastard doesn't do waiting.*

"Thanks, Rachel!" I call over my shoulder as I jog out to the main room.

I hear her laughing voice behind me.

"You're welcome!"

Anderson is walking into the foyer at the same time as I arrive. Made it. He gives me a curious look.

"Everything okay, Trainer?"

Shit, the guy really doesn't miss a thing.

"Yes, sir."

He nods, and we ride the elevator to the ground floor in our usual silence. Then he says,

"I've changed the schedule for this morning. I have an appointment at 8:30AM. The address details are on your desk."

"Yes, sir."

He seems more distracted than usual, but it doesn't stop him powering along at his usual rate for six miles, ignoring the glances he gets from other joggers, male and female. I suspect he knows that he's a good-looking bastard, but he doesn't give a shit. If I hadn't seen him at the Farm, I'd think he was asexual.

At 8:15AM, we're in the car and off to the first meeting of the day. I'm taken aback when I realize that it's an appointment with a shrink, specifically a sex therapist. I don't know what to make of this: it can only mean that Anderson knows he has problems and is trying to deal with them. And for a moment, I try to imagine what it must be like to have untold wealth and responsibility for over thirty-thousand employees at the age of twenty-nine, to be haunted by demons that cause him to want to abuse himself and other people. But my imagination isn't that good. *I have no fucking idea what all that shit must feel like.*

I've seen a shrink a few times. It's mandatory when you finish a tour, but I can't say it was particularly helpful and they're pretty much all the same and by the book.

- [*The Introductory Phase introduces the team and explains the process.*]

Shrink: So, Sergeant, my name is Major Hoffer and I'm here to debrief you after your last tour.

Me: Yes, Sir.

- [*The Fact Phase reconstructs events in detail in chronological order.*]

Shrink: We'll start with a timeline of your deployment.
Me: Yes, Sir.

- [*The Thought Phase is when you highlight 'thoughts' you had during key events.*]

Shrink: So you were in Kabul when seven of your team were blown up by an IED. What thoughts did you have on that occasion?
Me: Harsh ones, sir.

- [*The Reaction Phase is when you're invited to identify and ventilate emotions.*]

Shrink: And how did that make you feel?
Me: *I fucking hate that question.*

Yeah, *ad fucking nauseum.* Then the shrink 'normalizes and validates' your stress responses, although when I ask what 'normal' looks like, the shrink says it's not a word they use.

It goes on, or as the textbook says, 'transitioning back from emotional to factual' (the Symptom Phase). Then he (and it's usually 'he'), then he tells you that PTSD sucks and it could take a few centuries to feel normal again, which is the Teaching Phase.

And you know what? None of it stops the nightmares, but gee, it's okay to shit your shorts at night because you're so fucking terrified, because the shrink says that's *normal.*

I wonder what a sex therapist does.

As it's always useful to learn about a client, I Google 'sex therapy'—it covers a multitude of sins:

- Erectile dysfunction
- Premature ejaculation
- Sexual desire disorders
- Sexual identity, orientation and fetishes
- Sexual abuse or trauma.

My dumb smile slides right off of my face as I think back to my encounter with the uber-creepy Frederick Landon. I'm not liking the picture I'm seeing as the pieces in this jigsaw start to come together.

I close the search engine, not wanting to read any more.

So while Anderson is having his brain excavated, or possibly other organs, I wait, going over the rest of his schedule for the week. I'd really like to get an afternoon off so I can go check out those schools for Lilly and spend some quality time with my number one gal. I need something clean and good after my dark thoughts.

I'll see what sort of mood the boss is in when the headshrinker/dick-shrinker has finished with him.

He's in there for ninety-three minutes, but seems calm when he comes out. So on the way to the office, I risk asking.

"Sir?"

"Yes, Trainer?"

"I was wondering if I could take the afternoon off. I'd be back by 8PM to drive you to the fundraiser at the hotel."

He frowns. Oh well, it was worth asking.

"Fundraiser. Yes, of course, Trainer. Take the Range Rover, if you like. Ask Mrs. Smith to send my Tom Ford tux to the office and we'll go from there."

Once again, the bastard has surprised me: *Take the Range Rover.*

I fucking love driving this car. It rides high, so there's good all-around vision, and it's got every safety feature under the sun. Best of all is the fan-fucking-tastic sound system that Anderson's had installed. It's like having the musicians in the car with you.

I flick through his playlist: it's an eclectic mix including all the Rat Pack, Suzanne Vega, Red Hot Chili Peppers, Springsteen, Puccini, Chopin, and some modern classical music that I've never heard of and sounds like nails on a chalkboard. I put on *Californication* and turn it up LOUD.

I've texted the ex to let her know that I'm coming. We try to keep communication to a minimum to avoid starting World War Three. But first, I've got to check out these schools. As soon as the boss gave me the afternoon off, I made appointments to visit them all, but since I have no idea what I'm looking for, I'm just going to trust my instincts. And I'm really looking forward to doing this dad shit.

The first school is fucking awful. It's full of tiny kids who should be getting dirty, collecting worms and playing ball, but instead are wearing uniforms and sitting in rows, rote-learning the state capitals. They're *six*, for fuck's sake. The Principal is a real tight-ass, too, so I give him my best thousand-yard stare until the prick is quaking in his slip-on shoes.

The next two are much more to my taste: easy going, friendly, with happy-looking kids and great facilities. The last one perhaps has the edge, as they seem to do lots of field trips and outdoors stuff. I think Princess Lilly will like all that, and it sure appeals to her old man. Still, I can always play nice and let the my ex decide. It'll go easier if she gets some choice in the matter. I'll just tell her that the new boss will pay for one or the other. She doesn't need to know about the first school I visited.

I stride up to the front door and knock. Yeah, I still have my old key, but the locks were changed before she told me we were through. It was the opening salvo in a long-running war.

When she yanks the door ajar, she's got a face like a bulldog chewing on a wasp.

I try to play nice.

"I know it's short notice..."

"You didn't give me *any* notice, Justin."

Because you'd have conveniently been out.

"Can I take Lilly for a milkshake?"

"Mandy is coming over for a playdate. I can't cancel now, *since it's such short notice.*"

"Who the hell is Mandy?"

"Her friend from school. You'd know that if you'd been around."

I can't win.

So, I tell Carla about the schools I've seen. Naturally she's pissed that her choice is restricted to just these two.

"And what if I decide that a completely different school is the best place to send my daughter?"

Lilly is playing in the backyard, some complicated game with a set of plastic ponies.

"Our daughter. And you *can* choose—either of those two schools; whichever you prefer."

"What if I don't like either of them?"

"It's not about what you like, it's what's best for Lilly, and those are the best."

"Says who?"

"Look, Carla. They're good schools. Just go take a look."

"You're trying to bully me into doing what you want, as always, Justin."

"For fuck's sake, Carla, will you just go and fucking look at them!"

"Don't curse at me, Justin. And that's only one of the reasons I divorced you."

Thank fuck.

"They seem like great schools. Just go see." I decide to try a more conciliatory tone. "Please."

There's a pause.

"How's your new job?" she asks at last.

"Fine. How's your mother?"

"Fine."

"Good."

Silence.

"Do we have anything else to say to each other?"

"No."

"Good."

I walk into the garden and kiss my Princess. She's in the middle of her game so she waves me away imperiously. She's so like her mother. But I fucking love her anyway.

Improvise.

Adapt.

Overcome.

I learned that in the Marines. But it's not easy adapting to the constant current of guilt inside me, or improvising ways to spend the little time I have with my daughter. And I don't know how to overcome the dreams I had when I first held her in my arms, just a few minutes old.

No one can tell you how. But you have to learn anyway.

The fundraiser at the hotel is so tedious that I'm in danger of falling asleep with my eyes open. With the job I do, I've been to a lot of these highfalutin, dull-as-ditchwater speaker marathons: lots of rich folk flashing their cash. All worthy causes, but all so damn boring. From what Ryan tells me, Anderson usually attends two or three of these a month, although this is my first. I don't know how Anderson stands it. I don't know how *I'll* stand it.

There are 250 guests and seven have security. Like me, they hover at the back, eyes flicking around the room for anything out of the ordinary that could signal danger. I recognize one of them: Jim Rayment, Brit, ex-SAS, hard as fucking nails. He nods at me, and I nod back. We don't speak. Not when we're working.

I'm starting to be able to read Anderson's body language and I can tell that he's bored witless. He hides it well, but he's holding his body rigid and every few minutes he forgets and starts fidgeting;

then he remembers where he is and his spine stiffens, trying to hold it all together. I'd say the present speaker has about three minutes before Anderson is out of here.

I start counting. At three minutes and 45 seconds, Anderson looks over at me and gives a subtle nod.

Yeah, I'm gooooood.

He stands up, whispers something to the bald guy on his left, and strides away from the table. The speaker falters in her delivery as her eyes follow him from the podium, but Anderson is a man on a mission: he wants out of here.

I'm about to join him at the exit when Rayment tilts his head, sending me a subtle message. He taps his earpiece gently and softly lays three fingers on the sleeve of his jacket. I frown and nod back. He raises one eyebrow, asking a question, and looks toward the exit: *Do you need assistance?*

Probably not. I give a small shake of my head and he indicates that he understands. But now I'm on the alert.

Rayment has told me that there are civvies outside this room, unarmed, but here for some mayhem. This is probably the low level situation that Mason warned me about when I took the job. Rayment's also offering back up, and he's let me know that he has eyes and ears beyond this room, so I'm cool that whatever is coming our way is under control, as much as it can be.

Anderson is about to exit the room, but he glances over to me. I narrow my eyes slightly and shake my head. He looks pissed, but he waits for me to reach him.

"What is it, Trainer?"

"Three men in the foyer: possible interception in mind. We should leave via the fire exit, sir."

Anderson glances over to the nearest fire exit, but it's right at the front of the room. If we go that way, 300 people will see us leave.

Anderson shakes his head and starts to open the main door.

"If I could go first, sir."

It's phrased like a question, but it's not.

Casually, I unbutton my jacket and check my weapon, making sure that it's loose in the holster and won't stick if I need to draw it in a hurry. I don't want to pull it unnecessarily, and Anderson has made his feelings on guns clear, but if it means doing my job, I don't give a flying fuck what he thinks—and he knows it.

His frown deepens but he allows me to exit in front of him. I see the threat suspects right away and I'm surprised that hotel security hasn't already moved them on—fucking amateurs.

Two are sitting pretending to read newspapers, and the third one is leaning against a pillar, trying—and failing—to look nonchalant.

I don't have to tell Anderson which men are of concern, he can read the situation as well as I can. But then two more men enter the foyer and the odds aren't as favorable; I have no idea where Rayment's man on the ground is either. I glance at Anderson. He's not going to panic, in fact he looks like he's enjoying himself. *Shit!* I really hope he isn't going to start anything.

When they see Anderson, four of the men start chanting.

"Bigger cages! Longer chains!"

"Eat the rich!"

"Power to the people!"

"A specter is haunting the world!"

Anderson rolls his eyes.

"Oh, for fuck's sake, could they be any less original?"

I'm amused: four men are yelling in his face, and he's irritated by their lack of originality. Does *anything* faze this guy? I note that a reporter camped out in the foyer has woken up and is snapping photos. I'll deal with him later.

Hotel security is moving at a sluggish pace, converging on the four chanting men. The parking valet is standing open-mouthed with his thumb up his ass instead of bringing the car around. Fucking idiot.

The fifth man, the size of a linebacker, has my antenna twitching. He's clearly the one in charge and he's got something concealed in his hand. It could be a weapon, and I'm definitely treating him as the number one threat.

But someone from hotel security barges between me and Anderson, and I see the fifth man make his move.

I shove the guard out of my way when the fifth man raises his hand.

"Sir!" I yell at the top of my voice as I hurdle the falling guard.

Anderson swivels, sees the danger, drops into a boxer's crouch and lays out the attacker with one punch. The man flails backwards, dropping his weapon. Anderson kicks it away, rolls the man onto his front and pulls his gun hand behind his back, using his foot to lever the man's arm into a brutal arm-lock, still keeping his own hands free. He flicks his eyes around, looking for more danger, but hotel security has contained the other four men.

From the corner of my eye, I see Rayment, weapon drawn, and two other pros exiting the auditorium.

Anderson lets one of the security guards pull the attacker from the floor. I retrieve the fallen weapon. Actually, no. It's not a weapon, but a can of red spray paint.

Rayment strolls on over to me.

"Alright, mate?"

"Yeah, thanks for the heads up, Rayment."

"Your quaffer?"

Fucking limeys. I never have any idea what they're talking about.

"Your guvnor? Eyebrows he sorted that gobshite. And the muppet. Fat knacker!"

I shake my head, and see that Rayment is smiling. I look at Anderson, wondering if I still have a job. I shouldn't have let hotel security get between us. He's glaring at the photographer who's just scored the pictures of a life time: reclusive billionaire Devon Anderson manhandling an anti-capitalist protestor in one of Manhattan's top hotels.

I walk towards the photographer, and he's snapping pictures the whole time, backing away from me.

"You can't touch me! I'm just doing my job, man!"

I ignore him. He's doing his job? *Yeah, well, I'm fucking doing mine!*

I pull the camera out of his hands and scroll through all the photos he's taken. The guy's pretty good: he's caught the whole thing, including the look of fierce enjoyment on Anderson's face as he floors the fucker. I delete every image, and just for good measure, take out the memory card, bend it between my fingers, then give it back to him, completely mangled. He knows he's just lost the best part of twenty grand by losing those pictures. From his reaction, his camera doesn't automatically upload to the Cloud. I'd bet my next pay check he'll have that facility from now on.

He starts screaming about the First Amendment, but I don't give a shit.

Anderson, on the other hand, still looks like he's enjoying himself.

"I'll get the car, sir," I say, throwing an evil look at the parking valet who is still opening and closing his mouth like a damned goldfish.

"Thank you, Trainer," Anderson says affably.

The hotel manager comes running up, his eyes wide with apprehension. It'll be his job if billionaire guest Devon Anderson makes a complaint.

"I'm so sorry, Mr. Anderson. We never ... I can't believe ... I'll be speaking to our security ... such a shock ... not at our hotel, never before ... my apologies, sir ... I..."

Anderson waves him off with an amused look on his face.

"A memorable fundraiser," he says dryly, then walks away, leaving the manager tugging at his tie, his face sweaty with fear.

The valet has finally arrived with the car. He drops the keys into my hand and dodges out of the way before I can say anything to him—or worse. Wisely, he doesn't wait for a tip.

Anderson slides into the back seat and I lock the doors as we slowly plow through a crowd of photographers who are furious to have missed the action.

As I drive, I catch Anderson's eye in the rear view mirror.

"Thank your friend for me, Trainer. Box seats at the next Cubs' game?"

"Thank you, sir," I mutter.

There's that same amused expression on his face, but he doesn't speak again.

I guess it makes a change from mergers and acquisitions.

Chapter Ten

BEWITCHED

Close protection, bodyguards, we're deeply misunderstood.

We're not unthinking, uncaring masses of muscle and testosterone, we have feelings, too.

I'm a guy totally in touch with my emotions: I fucking hate my ex-wife.

I've also developed a deep dislike of my new boss's BFF, Frederick   I-want-to-drink-your-blood-and-piss-on-your-grave Landon. He took great pleasure in filling me in on the boss's hobbies: Anderson is a Dom—and all those whips and canes in his meditation room get used on his submissives, a series of dudes who get off on getting the crap beaten out of them as a form of foreplay. Apparently Anderson has been without a submissive for a while, which, according to Landon, is the reason for the boss's crankiness.

I don't fully understand the hold he has over Anderson. I've got some thoughts though, but nothing concrete. The boss seems irritated when Landon's around, but he doesn't kick him out either. And I know for a fact that he's the boss's fucking dealer. Yeah, Landon supplies him with Anderson's drug of choice: men who fuck while they call him 'Sir'. Maybe women, too. The jury is still out on that. And like any junkie, he's on edge till he gets his next fix.

But there's more to it than that; there's their sick history. And it's not just conjecture on my part because I had the deep misfortune to overhear part of their conversation.

Landon: Senator Rodriguez will be coming to our next little gathering at the Farm. He'll make a fine sub. And his charmless wife. I thought you'd like a Hispanic for a change. Take you back to your roots.

Anderson: Very amusing, Frederick.

Landon: Although I recall that you used to have other tastes, Devon. When you were at school, I recall you being very fond of ... how did you put it? It was rather poetic, I seem to remember. Yes, you said to me, 'Your hair is like sunshine, Master'.

Anderson: I don't remember that.

Landon: Oh, but I do, Devon. I do.

I nearly hurled my Cheerios when I happened to overhear that.

It confirmed everything I'd thought but didn't want to know: Anderson and Landon have been fuck buddies, maybe for years. And under his family's nose. Maybe even while the boss was at school. But does he mean high school or when he was at college? I'm really hoping Landon meant college, but the shudders crawling up my spine sing a different song.

It stinks. And I can't help feeling that Landon can definitely add pedo to his list of attractions.

But by Anderson's admission, they're still friends. Maybe it's some sort of weird Stockholm Syndrome shit. Or grooming.

I don't know. I'm just happy that I'm not inside the boss's head. Life is shitty enough.

The conversation took place when they were in his home office looking at photographs of guys—fuck buddies into S&M. Apparently, you can pick them off a shelf like dental floss. High priced dental floss.

Finally, they choose a new one. Together.

Cozy.

When I'm with my buddies, I might look at car or truck websites, shoot the shit over whether American metal is better than Italian engineering (yes). We might even grade the women in the room, idly chatting about whether big tits automatically make a woman a nine (they don't). I can't ever recall asking them to find me a new fuck buddy on Craigslist. But that's what's happening with Anderson and Landon.

The new politician and his wife have been vetted, put on order, and will be at the Farm this weekend.

There is an interview process, but seeing as Landon has put his mark of approval on this one (probably 666), I'm betting the interview is just so Anderson can say it was his decision.

His name is Manuel Rodriguez. That's what it says on the security report that Mason sent over. He's forty-nine, Harvard MBA, senator for Arizona. Republican. He's signed his NDA, and the boss has an appointment to meet him at 8PM. The headshot shows a regular-looking guy with even features, cropped brown hair and a red tie.

The meeting appears to go well, because when the Senator comes out, his tie is gone and he's adjusting his shirt. So, not a couples thing after all? The Senator is a closet gay and his wife is the beard? The confusion is giving me whiplash.

So why the fuck does he want to be Anderson's fuck buddy? Why do any of them? Is it the money? Because the bastard is generous. Or is it the power? Maybe the gay guys think that they'll be Mr. and Mr. Loved-up one day? Or maybe ... shit, I don't know, maybe they just like the whole BDSM scene. Stranger things have happened—and most of them at the Farm.

I've worked for quite a few rich men since I got into personal protection. Anderson isn't the first one to use pay-for-play services, or the first time I've been asked to procure them. Some of the hookers I've known, professionally that is, have been well-educated, rational people who see it as a simple transaction based on market forces: they have something to sell and someone else is prepared to pay for it. They've been well dressed, well washed, and drive more expensive cars than I can ever hope to afford. I've seen the other side, too: dirty, unwashed, crackheads that I'd happily cross the street to avoid. You'd be amazed how many men get hard just thinking about that kind of trip. Reckless endangerment doesn't even begin to cover it. If a man behaves like that, I'm out of there.

And then there's Anderson. He's generous with gifts for services rendered—Rolexes, gold cufflinks, $1000 bottles of champagne—but it's a gray area whether or not it's prostitution: excuse me while I look for my law degree.

Or maybe I'm just letting the line blur because I need this job. Maybe, after all, I'm just like them and I have a price.

Christ, I hope not.

Perhaps it's a small distinction, but I have my limits.

The whole Dom/submissive thing is not something I get. I didn't even know there was a distinction between that and S&M until I started working for Anderson. Live and learn.

Not that we've spoken about it. I don't go up to my boss and say, "Hi, sir! How's it hanging? So about that male prostitute you're planning on banging: all the whips and chains, how's that work?"

No, I listen, I pay attention, and I do my homework.

It turns out that Anderson has been having these relationships ever since he moved out of his parents' house—maybe even before that, for all I know. He keeps files in a locked drawer in his desk of everyone who goes to the Farm. I've seen them.

Thank fuck he doesn't have a thing for Rachel. Beating the shit out of your boss for looking too hard at your woman is not a great career move. Or the woman who might be your woman. My woman.

I've worked for Anderson for three months and I've gotten

nowhere with Rachel. Probably because I'm reluctant to push it—we work together, after all. She's friendly, we talk, we laugh together … and that's it. I've checked my contract with Anderson again and there's nothing in there about relations with other employees, but I'm still not sure that he wouldn't fire my ass if something happened between me and Rachel. I don't care about that so much, but if I got Rachel fired, well, I'd feel fucking awful.

I don't know what her financial situation is except that she's a widow and stays with her sister during the weekends, so I'm guessing she doesn't own a house anywhere. In all probability, she needs this job as much as I do.

All reasons that I haven't asked her out.

But a few days later, I get the chance to find out more about the intriguing Mrs. Smith.

And it starts at lunchtime. The boss doesn't need me, so for once I decide to get out of the office and into what passes for fresh air in Manhattan. I'm thinking about heading to a nearby sports bar, not because I'll be drinking on the job, but just to have a burger and fries, watch a game and enjoy what passes for normal.

As I step into the elevator, the boss's P.A., Ryan, joins me.

"Wow, we're both getting a lunchbreak on the same day—the fates have aligned!" and he grins. "Don't worry, big guy, I'm not hitting on you. I've already got a hot date waiting for me."

I shrug.

"I'm saving myself for the right billionaire."

His jaw drops and then he starts laughing.

"Holy shit, I almost believed you! Although you definitely don't appear on my gaydar. So you and Anderson, huh? All those long meetings where you guard his body. I should have guessed."

"Yup, it's torture," I admit, although for different reasons than the one he's implying.

He's side-eyeing me, like there's more he wants to say. I don't think we've ever had this much alone time together before, and I'm usually not such a chatty guy.

"You know, I always figured you were anti-gay, being ex-military and all. Plus, you've got that whole strong, silent, man-in-black thing going on."

"I am," I deadpan. "I hate everyone equally. Especially gays."

He grins.

"Well, I'm meeting my boyfriend for lunch. Want to join us?"

"Only if I can glare at you both."

"Sounds fun."

As we weave through the lunchtime crowds, he catches me up on some minor changes to Anderson's schedule before the conversation turns personal again.

"So you live with Anderson?"

"I have a room in the staff wing," *next to his dungeon.*

"What's Rachel Smith like? I've talked to her a bunch of times but I've never met her. She seems really nice, friendly, but knows what she's doing. She's a widow, right?"

I glance at him, wondering why he's asking. He shrugs.

"Just curious. I read it in her personnel file. None of my business. I just find it curious that at work Anderson surrounds himself with gay people, well, me and Pam, present company excluded, but in his home life, two screaming heteros."

"Screaming hetero?"

"Well, *you* are. Rachel Smith sounds like a complete sweetheart. Even when Ike in transportation asked her on a date—she blew him off really nicely, at least that's what the rest of the guys in transportation said. Rachel never gossips, as you know."

What?! I'll kill the son of a bitch!

"But never mind, you can't help it," Ryan smiles. "I guess the boss is ... undecided. When I first met him, I assumed that he was gay, but I don't think so. If anything, I'd say he's asexual. I've never seen him show the slightest interest in anyone, male, female, bi or trans."

Ryan obviously knows nothing about the Farm, but that doesn't mean I think he's wrong either, especially about the boss being undecided. Most people who know what I know would probably define the boss as bi, but it's more like he doesn't care. Sex is a physical release, emotionless, cold. Almost as if it gives him no pleasure, like a duty that has to be performed. And then he beats the shit out of himself for punishment. I still haven't figured that part out. If he feels guilty for having sex, why not just stop? It's like some sort of compulsion with him.

"By the way, Tessa asked me if you were seeing anyone?"

My eyes slide to his, surprised as all hell. I've hardly ever spoken to her. Then again, she always looks like she's on the verge of tears. Besides, I thought she had a thing for Anderson?

"Not interested? Nothing? No?"

I shake my head.

"So you are seeing someone?"

He holds up his hands when he sees my annoyed expression.

"Don't shoot me! I was just asking on behalf of Tessa—and several interested parties on the twenty-ninth and thirtieth floors—all the ones who've given up on Mr. Anderson."

He sighs at my silence.

"You're no fun. Fine, I'll just tell them *it's complicated*."

We arrive at the small coffee shop and I'm introduced to Gene, Ryan's boyfriend, who's a banker and a Mets fan, but I don't hold that against him, and we shoot the shit for a while.

Watching them reminds me that two people can have a relationship that doesn't involve yelling at each other. It's normal. I can't believe how much I'm craving a slice of that.

For once, the boss doesn't have a meeting or a fundraiser, has already sweated blood with Basqiat, and is in his home office after dinner, working on all those multimillion dollar deals.

I've been up since 4.45AM because Anderson had a breakfast meeting and wanted to get a run in first. Right now, I'm happy to veg out on the sofa with a Lite beer in one hand and the remote control in the other.

I'm pleased when Rachel comes to join me, plopping down into an easy chair, a glass of white wine beside her.

She kicks off her shoes and curls her legs under her, contented like a cat as she lets out a long sigh.

"I'd hate to have a schedule like Mr. Anderson's," she says. "Being out most nights. I'm much more of a homebody."

"Depends on who you're home with," I say, thinking back to the uneasy truces that followed fights with Carla.

"Very true," she smiles. "Brian used to say, 'there's no place like home—but it depends on the home'."

"Brian?"

She studies her glass of wine.

"My late husband."

"You miss him."

It's a statement, not a question.

"I do."

Her reply is simple but heartfelt. And suddenly I'm in the crazy position of being jealous of a dead guy.

"Do you want to talk about it?"

I'm not usually this touchy-feely, but Rachel has me behaving in all sorts of ways that aren't normal for me.

She sighs again.

"He was a good man. You remind me of him."

Her comment makes me uncomfortable, so I go with humor, my fallback position.

"Every woman's dream?"

"Don't get all modest on me, Justin," she laughs. "No, he was a Fire Fighter and he had the same 'I'm in command' air about him, like nothing bad would ever happen when he was around."

Her lips turn down and her eyes gloss with tears.

I'm in unfamiliar territory and wondering whether to comfort her or to make a strategic retreat. Comforting crying women is not really within my skillset, but I'll give it a go...

"He sounds like a great guy. He must have been smart, too, if he married you."

She gives an unhappy hiccupping laugh.

"He used to say marrying me was the only smart thing he'd ever done."

We sit in silence for several minutes before she starts speaking again.

"He died trying to save a meth addict in a house fire. It was so stupid. The whole building was blazing and he was trying to get everyone out, but the house collapsed. Brian's men couldn't get to him in time. I hate that. I hate that he died alone."

"He wasn't alone, Rachel. I promise you that."

She gazes at me, her eyes wide.

"What do you mean?"

"Because I know that if I'd been in that situation, my last thoughts would have been of ... of someone I loved. And I wouldn't have been alone."

She smiles through her tears.

"Thank you, Justin."

On a Friday evening in early summer, I'm driving Anderson to an evening appointment at his office before we head to the Farm: two nights of fucking, whipping, and a load of dark kink.

Do I approve? I don't need to. But I have to say it sits awkwardly with me because I know what he wants to do with these men—or rather *to* these men—women, as well. If he just wanted to fuck them, I could understand that. After all, it's consensual. But I know he wants more than that. I've seen the shit he's got in his so-called meditation room: belts, canes, whips, chains, and stuff I don't even want to think about, plus a similar selection at the Farm. Why would a man want to hurt someone else like that? Why does Anderson want to hurt himself?

If he thinks sex is all evil and against whatever religious code he follows—which still remains to be seen—then why continue to do it? Why continue to punish himself?

He's a fucking control freak at work, but thanks to him a lot of people get to pay their mortgages every month. To people who work hard and deliver, he's generous to a fault. And I know he's sincere about his project at UVM. Plus, he's paying for Lilly to go to a great school next September; even her mother has had to admit it's shit hot.

The truth is, Anderson's a fuckup, but at least he knows it. I've noticed that he's cool and distant with everyone. The exception to that rule is Landon. Whatever their history is, I'd bet my last dollar that he's encouraged a dark part of the fucked-upness.

When the Senator arrives without his wife, he looks nervous and older than his photograph.

I take him to the boss's office and wait outside. I can't help wondering what sort of questions Anderson is going to ask. Some weird sort of fucking job description where the boss asks employees if they take it up the ass. Most bosses don't bother to ask. Although I guess that the Senator is more of a fuck buddy. Maybe Anderson will donate to the next campaign.

Forty minutes later, the Senator walks out looking pleased with himself, so I guess it's a done deal. Maybe he'll bring his wife tomorrow. Fuck knows.

Although it's only just occurred to me that maybe I've gotten it wrong—maybe the boss just likes to be beaten? Could be it's mutual.

A shiver runs through me. That is seriously fucked up.

But reading up on the internet tells me some dudes like that shit. I don't get it *at all*. There are even places, nightclubs in New York, where men and women pay people to beat them and fuck them. Maybe I'm in the wrong job. I suspect the boss used to go to places like that, but it would be way too risky for the mega famous, mega control freak that he is now. I guess that's one crisis averted. But it seems to me that his *special interests* are on borrowed time. One day the media will find out.

I'm relieved when everything at the Farm runs smoothly. Van Sant avoids me all weekend; I avoid the Senator's wife, who prefers dames anyway. After a weekend of looking the other way, I'm relieved to go home.

Anderson heads to his study when we get back to Wolf Point, and I head to the staff kitchen for my fix of Rachel.

She smiles when she sees me, and it's like suddenly seeing the blazing sun on a gray, Manhattan morning. I can't help grinning back.

"Hello, Justin. How was your weekend?"

"Boring. Yours?"

She laughs.

"Really? I find that hard to believe. Well, perhaps I can cheer you up with *linguini alla puttanesca*."

"Sounds good, Rachel. But everything you cook is damn fine."

She passes me a glass and a bottle of beer. "I don't think flattery is in your job description."

I sigh, thinking of some of the weird shit that *is* in my job description.

"What's wrong?"

I wish I could talk it over with Rachel, but I can't.

"Work stuff."

"Oh."

Her face falls.

"Landon," I say, and that's all the explanation she needs.

I can tell she feels the same way about it that I do. Then she sighs.

"I don't understand it. Mr. Anderson has such a good heart. I just don't understand where this ... this *darkness* comes from, why he's friends with that awful man."

I think I've got a better handle on the situation than Rachel, but it doesn't mean I really understand it.

"Rachel, can I ask you something?"

She looks up at me expectantly, her wide blue eyes curious.

"Of course, anything. You know that."

"Well, I was wondering, what did the boss say to you about his, um, meditation room when he interviewed you?"

For the briefest of moments, I think I see disappointment flicker across her face, but it's gone too fast for me to be sure.

"Well, when I came for the job, I signed my NDA, of course..." *Of course.* "And we had an ordinary sort of interview. He asked me about other places that I'd worked, why I left my last job and so on. I thought he was a pleasant young man, very serious, a little earnest. He explained that he lived here alone, but he was planning on hiring additional security for his personal protection ... but that was all. He had no family living with him: no wife or children. I knew the job required me to live in during the week and that he might need me occasionally at weekends, to be agreed in advance. I'd run the house: planning the menus, grocery shopping, cooking, organize the cleaning crew and any household maintenance. You know, the usual."

She pauses.

"I admit that I had reservations about working for such a young man. I wasn't sure if he would ... try anything. Especially as I would be living alone with him for several months to begin with. But then he said that he had a vacation home where he went on the weekends. I was relieved because I thought he meant he had a girlfriend. Or a boyfriend. I wasn't sure..."

She sighs.

"Oh dear, then he said, and I'll never forget this, 'My weekend guests don't mix with either my family or my business acquaintances.' I was surprised but not as shocked as you might think: one sees a lot of ... eccentricities as a housekeeper—as I'm sure you have."

I nod. *Too fucking true.*

"Then Mr. Anderson suggested that I look around so *I knew what I was getting myself into.* Those were his words. I was delighted: the place was modern, light and airy; both the staff kitchen and Mr. Anderson's kitchen were well equipped and just a dream to work in. And then ... and then I walked into his meditation room."

She shakes her head in disbelief at the memory.

"I felt like Alice falling down the rabbit hole. My immediate reaction was that I couldn't possibly work for him. And so I went back to his study and told him that I couldn't take the job. He didn't look surprised, he just asked if he could explain the situation in more detail. I nearly walked out but ... I suppose I was curious as to what he could possibly say. He told me that the meditation room was solely for his use. He also assured me that our relationship would be purely professional. But I had my doubts. I said I'd have to think about it, but really I had no intention of taking the job. We shook hands and I left."

"What made you change your mind?"

And now I'm so fucking curious.

"I met his mother. Mrs. Anderson happened to arrive just as I was leaving. He was so *sweet* with her. And she was so, well, loving and normal. Mr. Anderson introduced us, and she smiled and said it would reassure her to know that someone was looking after her boy. Mr. Anderson laughed and rolled his eyes at her. I went home and thought long and hard. In the end, I decided I'd give it a month's trial. And ... well, here I am."

She smiles. And I'm stunned: she is one brave woman.

"But I'm curious. What were your first impressions?"

She's put me on the spot. I go for honesty.

"I thought he was a twisted son of a bitch."

Rachel gasps then laughs.

"Well, quite!"

"And if there was anything illegal or if he was into kids or ... goats or anything, I was out of here."

I think I've shocked her, but then she starts giggling, and I can't help laughing, too.

"Goats?" she says, her eyes dancing with humor.

"Yeah!" I say, laughing, "No goats!"

"No goats!" she agrees.

Suddenly, I sense that we're not alone and look up. Anderson is standing at the door watching us. I wonder how much he's heard, but he doesn't seem annoyed.

"Oh! Good evening, Mr. Anderson," says Rachel. "I'm afraid Mr. Trainer isn't too keen on my recipe for curried goat!"

I nearly choke on my beer.

Anderson pulls a face.

"I can't say curried goat would be an item I'd like to see on your menu, Mrs. Smith."

"No, sir," she says, with a straight face. "No goats."

There's an awkward pause while I keep my eyes down, staring into my beer like it's the last water in the desert.

"The *linguini alla puttanesca* will be ready in five minutes, Mr. Anderson," she says, smiling at him gently.

"Thank you, Mrs. Smith, that sounds excellent. And I'd like to go through the week's menus later."

"Certainly, sir," she says.

He walks away, and I think how lonely it must be to hear the laughter of other people in your home but know that none of it is for you. The thought is sobering. I look up and Rachel is still smiling, distracting me from my thoughts.

"Well, Justin," she says, "can I ask you something?"

"Sure, Rachel, what is it?"

"Are you ever going to ask me out?"

Rachel takes my breath away.

She's funny and clever and has the most fantastic ass of any woman I've ever known. And believe me, I'm going to make the most of her lapse in judgment.

She doesn't have to ask me twice. The only thing that has been holding me back is my concern that she could lose her job. Most employers prefer to think of their employees as celibate, inanimate household objects. I don't know Anderson's view, but if Rachel doesn't care, well, I don't need a written invitation.

There she sits, looking right into me, seeing everything with those beautiful blue eyes, so warm and trusting. Her gaze is magnetic, pulling me in. My hand reaches across the table and I stroke her cheek. Her eyelids flutter and she leans into my hand, sighing softly.

The distance across the table is too far. I stand up and walk around, drawn to her. And I know that one of us could get burned. If it's me, that doesn't matter, but I can't, won't hurt someone as good and kind as Rachel.

She puts her soft, cool hands in mine and I pull her upwards.

She smiles, and I feel the breath leave my body. So beautiful. So fucking beautiful.

Gently, she wraps her arms around my neck and pulls my face towards her. Her lips touch mine, and desire pulses through me. I can't hold back any longer, God help me. I want her, every inch of her. Badly.

She pulls away from me, gasping for air, my vehemence taking her by surprise. Then she smiles, her fingers touching her lips.

"That was…"

"Yeah, it was."

We stare at each other across the empty air, then she looks away.

"I think I'd better serve dinner."

Did I go too far? Should I apologize? She doesn't seem mad, but you can never tell with women.

She takes Anderson's food into the dining room and I slouch in my seat, brooding. I acted like a horny teenager. I've probably scared her off.

When she walks back in, there's still a flash of red staining her cheekbones, but she holds her head high.

"Rachel, I'm…"

"Please don't say you're sorry for kissing me."

"Fuck, no! I mean … shit! I'm sorry if I took it too far."

"It was a very nice kiss," she smiles, the flush deepening.

"Nice? I must be losing my touch."

"Do you kiss many women?" she asks.

It sounds lighthearted but I sense a note of anxiety beneath the words.

"Not many. Bad divorce," and I shrug.

Her smile is sympathetic, but she doesn't speak again, simply placing my food in front of me.

For once, the silence is really awkward, and I'm cursing myself for causing that.

"Rachel...?"

"Yes?"

"Do you still want to go on a date? With me?"

She smiles slowly and nods.

"Yes, very much."

Chapter Eleven

THE BIRTHDAY PARTY

A week later and I'm so full of frustration that I'm damn near choking on it. I haven't had a single chance to take Rachel out. Every evening, Anderson has been busy: three fundraisers, two late meetings with overseas suppliers, one opera, and one dinner with Landon where I had to wait in the car outside a French restaurant. Boring as hell.

I suppose it's understandable that he's out every night when he has nothing to come home to—no *one* to come home to.

I decide I can't wait any longer to spend some quality time with Rachel, so I'll improvise. If I can't take her out on a date, I'll bring the date to her.

On the rare occasions when Anderson stays at home, our normal routine is to eat together and then watch a movie. I treasure those evenings.

Tonight will be even more special.

After we've all eaten dinner and Anderson has closed his office door, Rachel starts cleaning up in the kitchen. That's when I get the flowers that I had to sneak into my bedroom, along with a not very chilled bottle of champagne that I stuck in my sink with cold water, and the expensive French chocolates.

I lay everything on our dining table, get two wine glasses out of a cabinet and pop the champagne cork.

Rachel walks in from the kitchen, wiping her hands on a paper towel.

"Justin, I thought I heard ... oh! Oh, flowers? And chocolates? Champagne? What's the occasion?"

"Our first date. The slave driver hasn't been very cooperative, so I thought if we can't go out on a date, I'd bring the date to us. Is it okay?"

She's so quiet, I'm worried that she doesn't like it. Maybe she thinks I'm cheap, not taking her to dinner.

"Justin ... it's perfect! Thank you!"

And she kisses me sweetly, the lightest brush of her lips on mine. After that, I know it's going to be okay. In fact, I'm pretty certain it's going to be the best damn date I've ever had.

We talk and laugh, drink champagne, and I watch as Rachel makes her way through the French chocolates, licking her lips and saying, "Just one more and then I'll stop."

She doesn't, and I really kinda like that.

I like it even more when she snuggles against me on the sofa and we watch some movie. I can't even tell you what it's called because I'm more interested in stroking her hair and kissing her neck.

Snuggling is fun. Who knew?

It's been a great evening and I'd love to take it further, but I'm happy to go at Rachel's pace.

She surprises the hell out of me when she stands, yawning, then without speaking, takes my hand and leads me into her bedroom. *I'm not going to say no.*

I've never been in her room before, and although it's decorated the same way as mine, it has a completely different feel. I see family photographs crowded onto her dresser, including a younger Rachel with a blond guy who I assume is Brian. They look happy.

There are lots of throw pillows, books and magazines. It's homey. My room is just a better class of barracks.

I follow Rachel to the bed, waiting as she stands in front of it.

She pauses, and for the first time I see uncertainty in her eyes, so I go for my fallback position of humor.

"I like what you've done with the place. Breakfast at yours or mine?"

I take a step closer and her eyes widen as she laughs breathlessly.

"That is such a cheesy line!"

"Yeah. Is it working?"

"I think it might just be your lucky day, Justin."

"Nah, it's my lucky night. My lucky day was when I met you."

Her smile drops but I'm not sure why.

"You're sweeping me off my feet," she says seriously.

"I'll make it a soft landing."

"Will you?"

And I know what she's asking and what she wants. I can't promise forever because a guy like me doesn't even know what the word means. I could be fired tomorrow or given another assignment overseas for God knows how long.

There's a thousand reasons why I can't think about forever, not forgetting the ex-wife who ripped my heart out and tried to shove it up my ass as a farewell gift. I've been burned and buried, flayed, fucked and fucked over, and that makes a man gun-shy.

And yet ... there's something about Rachel's softness and kindness that soothes the hurt and pain. I've seen her goodness and willingness to accept another human being's frailties and flaws. She trusts me, although she probably shouldn't.

So when those beautiful blue eyes of hers beg me not to hurt her, there's only one answer I can give.

"This isn't a casual thing for me, Rachel. You know that, right?"

"I ... thank you. It ... it's been a while."

"For me, too."

"Really?"

"Yeah."

I'm not blowing smoke, it's true.

I never cheated on Carla, but we were apart more than we were together while I was deployed. She never followed me when I was based in San Diego either. I guess that should have told me something. Since I stopped being a bootneck, I've worked in Qatar and Saudi, both places where the punishment for unmarried adultery is a hundred lashes, or stoning, if you're married. And in Qatar, adultery is punishable by death when a Muslim woman and a non-Muslim man are involved.

You could call that a deterrent. And maybe part of me thought that Carla and I still had a chance, that saying 'I do' meant something to me. Yeah, I never said I was smart.

There were a couple of hookups between jobs, well, more than a few if I'm honest, but nothing with any real connection, you know? Not like between me and Mrs. Smith.

Whatever this is, whatever it becomes, I want it badly.

She laughs a little, and it sounds like there's relief in her voice.

"I think I can remember what to do," she teases gently, driving me wild as she runs a finger down the buttons of my shirt. "What happens if I undo this one?"

She slides her fingers under the cotton and against my skin. Her touch is cool and soft, and she's already making me lose my mind. My dick is like an over-eager puppy, straining at my pants 'cause he doesn't want to be left out of the fun times.

She undoes another button, and my heartrate sky-rockets.

My hands find their way to her hips, gripping tightly, because if I don't hang onto something, I'll be ripping her clothes off like a fucking caveman.

Slowly, watching me every second, she undoes each button, then slides the shirt from my shoulders.

It drops to the floor and she glances down, frowning. I know what she's thinking because the woman is a neat freak.

"If you pick that up and fold it, I'll be tempted to pick *you* up and fold *you* over your bed right now."

My voice is a low growl, making her eyebrows arch.

There's a small smile on her face, happy that she's driving me crazy.

And the only reason I don't take her now, is because she's a woman who deserves to have it all: which means me taking it slow and giving her every ounce of pleasure first.

She runs her hands over my bare skin, tugging gently at my chest hair, twisting her fingers into it.

Her smile turns impish, and she leans forward, running her tongue over my nipples.

It's more than flesh and blood can bear, but I hold myself rigid, letting her explore me.

"You're so hard, Justin," she whispers as her hands continue to roam. "So strong. Your stomach is like granite."

"That's not all that's like granite," I say wryly, watching a heated flush creep up her neck.

Tentatively, she reaches down and strokes her hand over the bulge in my pants.

"That is ... rather alarming!" she says, as her eyes open wide.

I laugh silently, watching her eyes as my muscles contract and loosen.

Her hand flattens against my stomach and I don't feel like laughing anymore.

I study her skin, paler than mine, her fingers long, the nails cut short.

And I can't stand not to touch her as she explores my body. My hands close over hers, and then I lean down, pressing soft kisses along her collarbone and up her neck, kissing her ear, biting the lobe gently, breathing in her warm scent.

My hands run over the smooth fabric of her skirt, cupping her generous ass and massaging lightly.

She moans, a soft, feminine sigh of pleasure that has my balls tightening.

And she copies me, running her fingers lightly over my ass and digging her fingers in.

"C'mere."

I sit on the bed, holding out my arms to her and she comes to me immediately, hiking up her skirt so she can straddle my hips.

As she leans down to kiss my chest, I run my hands appreciatively across the smoothness of her stockinged thighs, frowning when my callused palms snag on the delicate silk.

"Don't worry about that, Justin. I have plenty of thigh-highs—they're cooler than pantyhose when I'm cooking and ..."

"No, I think I'd like to fuck you while you're wearing them ... and nothing else."

Bright red heat floods over her skin, but her eyes are glowing.

"That sounds..."

She doesn't finish the sentence because I'm reaching up to massage those full, soft, luscious breasts, still trapped beneath a couple of layers—too many layers—of fabric.

I lean up, undoing the buttons of her blouse one at a time.

Wanton is a good look on her I decide, pulling off her sexy-as-fuck white bra.

As I start to suck on her left tit, she lets out a moan and her head falls back while I massage the other with my free hand.

I stand up suddenly, making her gasp, and place her on the bed carefully, hovering over her.

She slides her leg up my thigh, rubbing and squirming against me. She's not even anywhere near my dick, but I have to take a breath as electricity shoots from my balls to my spine, warning me that I'm about to lose it.

"Rachel, honey, if you do that, I'm not going to last a second," I spit out between gritted teeth.

At first she looks surprised, then a wicked smile spreads across her full lips.

And she does it again. And again. And again and again, until my blood is pounding and I think I'm about to have a heart attack. I can't think, I can't breathe, and I can't fucking move or I'll be finished.

"Rachel!" I say again, and this time I'm fucking begging.

"Do you have a condom?"

The barbarian in me doesn't give a damn. I want to jizz in her, on her; I want to mark her as mine so no other fucker even breathes in her direction.

She has to ask me three more times, before I grunt and point in the direction of the kitchen.

"What? You keep condoms in my kitchen?"

She sounds amused and enraged.

"Jacket," I croak. "Wallet."

"Oh!"

She slides away from me, the most excruciating deprivation. I grab my balls and tug on them hard. *Not yet, you fuckers!*

Rachel walks back into the bedroom, her tits bouncing, her eyes glittering with lust, her lips wet. She's got my jacket in her hand and she throws it at me.

I fumble around until I pull out my wallet. I snatch the lone condom, hoping to hell the expiration date hasn't passed, not that I bother to check. As I pull it out, credit cards go flying and Rachel giggles.

But when I yank down my zipper to release the beast, she sure as shit ain't laughing anymore.

I sheathe myself quickly then look up to meet Rachel's eyes. She looks excited but nervous, which is exactly how I'm feeling.

I kiss her deeply, urgently, and as she claws at my back, I know that she's feeling the same.

I pull up her skirt so it's rucked around her waist, and ease those sweet, plain white panties down her satin thighs. I can smell her arousal, and my fingers tell me that she's more than ready.

I thrust in steadily, wanting to be sure. But with no warning, she shudders and comes on my hand. *Fuck, that's so hot.*

Moaning and calling my name, pawing at my back, I lower her to the bed. I can't wait another second, and I slide inside, pushing all the way in with one determined thrust.

She gasps, and her legs lift, locking her ankles behind my back.

My last chance of controlling this has just gone up in smoke, and my body responds, doing what it's been longing to do for too many weeks. Sweat breaks out across my skin, and my heart kicks up another gear.

And I'm right, I don't take long, but it's one helluva ride while it lasts.

My body goes rigid and her short nails dig into my ass, my eyes squeeze shut and my dick swells and pulses inside her.

I have just enough presence of mind not to crush her as I reluctantly slip out of her and collapse onto the bed.

I tug her into my arms, holding her until our bodies cool, and the whole time, I'm smiling.

We don't speak, but after I've disposed of the condom, we face each other in her bed, eyes open, hearts exposed, and it feels so damn good.

Now, I don't want you to think I'm a romantic guy, because I'm not. I'm a double-hard bastard with skin like a rhino.

But this woman ... this woman.

Once isn't enough.

And lucky me, I have an unopened box of condoms in my wall safe, along with spare ammo for my Smith & Wesson.

Her smile kills me, and I'm ready for more. Much, much more.

And we've got a whole night to play...

A thousand images collide in my memory: her skin, her scent, her softness, her warmth, the tenderness of her touch, her passion scorching through me. Over and over again, our bodies joining, the loneliness erased in sweat and kisses and heat. Fucking fireworks! Nothing cool, calm and collected about a passionate woman taking what she wants.

We've slept maybe an hour when the alarm on my phone goes off.

"Fuck! Fucking alarm!"

I sit up dazed and slightly disoriented. Then I see Rachel

smiling up at me, her blonde hair all mussed like cotton candy, a bright halo around her.

"Good morning! You're very eloquent, Justin!"

She's laughing, teasing me, and I'm so fucking happy, I've got this ridiculous schoolboy grin plastered across my face.

I swoop back down to kiss her, and for the briefest of moments the connection is there again.

Then she puts her hand against my chest and pushes gently.

"Up!"

"I am up."

She laughs.

"Not that part of you! You have work. Go! Time for Mr. Anderson's morning run!"

I groan. After last night's workout with Rachel, the last thing I need is a six mile sprint with the boss.

She pushes me again.

"I'll have breakfast waiting for you when you get back."

"God, you're a fantastic woman. Where have you been all my life?"

"Justin, you've already had me. Flattery won't get you any further."

I shrug.

"Sure about that?"

She laughs again, then reaches to the floor and throws my clothes at me.

"Go! Don't forget your pants!"

"The words every man wants to hear."

But now I hustle, because she's right: I'm running behind time. I scoop up the rest of my clothes and do a nude sprint across our living room, taking a chance that Anderson isn't going to come looking for me just yet. I pull on my sweats and running shoes, and get ready to head out.

But I take a second to stop by Rachel's bedroom, and she looks up, surprised.

"You still owe me a date, Mrs. Smith."

Her eyes sparkle as she smiles at me.

"I'll look forward to it, Justin."

Anderson is waiting in the foyer. He looks pissed. Guess I must be a second late. I think he's going to chew my ass out, but then he raises his eyebrows and looks like he's hiding a smile. *What's his problem?*

But when I get in the elevator, I catch a glimpse of myself in the mirrored walls. *I look like hell.* I'm unshaven, I have bed head, and I haven't had time to shower. I'd better not stand too close to the boss. Basically I look like shit. I may as well hang a sign around my neck: 'Well fucked'. I wonder if he's going to say something.

But nope, no comments, no reaction at all. That changes when we get outside. Instead of the usual medium-fast pace, *the bastard speeds up.* He fucking motors around one of our longer circuits, and when I catch a glimpse of his face, I can see that he's smirking at me. *He knows.* I don't usually have trouble keeping up with a client on a run. I'm used to fat fuckers who wheeze their way around a half-mile track. *Anderson's killing me.* And he's enjoying it. Twisted fucker.

By the time we get back to Wolf Point, my legs feel like lead, and my eyeballs are about ready to pop out of my head and I'm drenched in sweat. But he still hasn't said anything about Rachel. I get the feeling that he's already made his point.

Rachel is in the kitchen. She looks damn fine in her neat uniform of white shirt and black skirt, her hair shiny and smooth.

I can't help myself. I walk up and wrap my arms around her waist while she's cooking and nuzzle her neck.

"Hi honey, I'm home," I say softly.

She laughs.

"Well, go shower and I'll get you some breakfast. Now! Or I'll end up burning this."

God, I love her ordering me around.

By the time I climb out of the shower, the kitchen is empty. She must be serving Anderson. Suddenly, I'm anxious that he'll say something to Rachel when I'm not there to defend her. *If he starts on her, I'll fucking kill him.*

I'm halfway along the corridor when Rachel returns. She stares at the expression on my face.

"What's wrong, Justin? You look..."

"Did Anderson say anything to you?"

"About what?" she seems genuinely puzzled, but I'm relieved.

"I just ... I got the impression this morning that *he knows*."

She blushes.

"Oh! How?"

"I guess I looked rougher than usual this morning," I remind her.

She smiles.

"Yes, you weren't your usual debonair self."

"Debonair? I don't think anyone has ever called me that before."

"Really? I think you look very handsome in your suit. But this morning..." she laughs, "not quite as suave as usual."

"Suave and debonair? I could get used to these compliments, Mrs. Smith."

"You might have to, Mr. Trainer." Then she frowns. "Mr. Anderson didn't say anything to me: he seemed exactly the same as usual. Oh, he did ask me to tell you that he's going to Scarsdale tonight for supper with his parents."

I groan.

"You don't like the Andersons?"

"Yeah, they're fine. It's just ... Abigail."

She laughs.

"Justin! Are you telling me that an ex-Marine with your experience in close protection can't handle one nineteen year-old girl?"

"Yeah, that's about the size of it."

"You want me to come and protect you?"

"Would you, Mrs. Smith?"

"Why certainly, Mr. Trainer. If you're scared."

"Fucking terrified."

Chapter Twelve

CH-CH-CHANGES

The day drags. There's nothing urgent at Anderson HQ, so I head to the CCTV room and doze with my eyes open, my head propped up on my hand. The rest of the security team leaves me alone. Most are ex-services and they know the look of someone who's been awake all night. They just assume it's to do with Anderson, certainly not the delectable Rachel. And they aren't going to know.

By 6PM, most of the employees have left, just a few ass-kissers who want to impress the boss with their work ethic. They'd have to work 24/7 to put in longer hours than him. And there are a few females hovering in reception, hoping that he'll notice them. *Dream on, ladies, it ain't gonna happen.* Not now that he's got his next fuck on order. Although I'm still curious about the female that I saw him with at the Farm, and how those husband and wife pairings work out. Although not curious enough to ask. Or watch.

The thought sours my mood. Rachel will be away this weekend. She hasn't even gone yet and I miss her. He hasn't mentioned that we're going to the Farm, so maybe he'll be working at Wolf Point and I'll be able to take a day to see Lilly. Just depends on whether Anderson is planning on leaving the building.

But first, I've got to get through an evening at the Andersons', or more specifically, spend the evening avoiding Abigail Anderson's attentions. I ponder the idea of camouflage, but figure the boss might ask questions.

He's quiet on the drive over to Scarsdale. Fine by me, although a little conversation would help me stay awake.

The Andersons' mansion is beautiful and serene, and again I wonder how someone so fucked up could have come out of a place like this. Maybe there are some memories that no number of happy years can entirely erase. I should know: one tour of Iraq, two in Afghan.

Mrs. Anderson is waiting, her face lighting up when I open the boss's door and he steps out of the car.

"Devon, darling!" she says, kissing him on the cheek. "Happy birthday!"

"Mother," he smiles briefly.

His birthday? He didn't say anything. But then again, why would he? Although some people I've worked for expect the help to give them a fucking parade every time something happens in their insular little worlds. Not Anderson.

"Trainer, you can park the car around the side. There'll be a meal for you in the kitchen ... or you may prefer to sleep in the car?"

His face is impassive but I can tell he's amused, referring, no doubt, to the pile of shit who escorted him on his run this morning. *Bastard.*

"Sir."

I hurry back to the car just as Abigail Anderson gallops into view. I catch sight of her disappointed face in the car's side mirrors. I have a feeling I'll be seeing more of her later.

Security at the Anderson mansion obviously isn't a priority. There are multiple entry points, not least from the golf course that borders their land. If the boss is going to spend time here, there'll need to be changes. In fact, I'm going to recommend that Mason speaks to him about upgrading security for his whole family. If someone wanted to make a quick buck, his family would be a softer target than Anderson himself, living in his Wolf Point fortress.

After checking out the perimeter, I wander into the kitchen. The cook introduces herself as Nora. She's a friendly woman in her fifties and has produced a fine meal of poached salmon. Objectively, I'd say not quite up to Rachel's standards, but pretty good.

I'm thinking about heading back to the car for a nap when Abigail Anderson crashes into the kitchen. Nora is serving in the dining room, and Miss Anderson's eyes light up when she sees that she's caught me alone.

"Hi, Trainer! Devon said you'd be sleeping in the car, but here you are. Are you waiting for me?"

I need to nip this in the bud ... before my nerve fails.

"Miss Anderson, you're going to get me fired and I like being employed—and having all my limbs attached."

"Oh! Don't worry about Devon! You're so cute when you're serious! What's your first name? Devon won't tell me. Have you got a girlfriend? Oh, you're the strong, silent type, aren't you? I think you and Devon must get along famously."

Suddenly she turns bright red and her eyes widen.

"Oh! I don't mean like *that*! Not that there's anything wrong with *that*. Wow, I'd never have guessed! I mean I did, guess, that is, but wow!"

What did I miss? Now she thinks I'm the boss's butt-buddy? How'd she go from flirting with me to that?

Thankfully, Nora returns before I manage to connect my brain to the parts that speak. Nora casts a stern and disapproving eye at me but smiles warmly at Miss Anderson. *Fucking typical—some women always think men are the bad guys!*

I make my excuses and leave while Abigail pouts. She's going to give some guy a stroke one day—and it might be me.

I manage to get an hour's shut-eye in the Rover with the seat tilted back before the boss leaves. His father is with him, and I can see from the way he's eyeing me that Miss Anderson has apprised him of her latest theory. *For fuck's sake! Now I'm the boss's beard?* But at least it'll keep Miss Anderson off my ass. Oh crap, unfortunate expression, given the circumstances.

I just want to get the hell out of here.

We drive back to Wolf Point in silence. I wonder whether I should wish the boss happy birthday, but I'm so pissed off with his family I can't summon the enthusiasm. I think back to how I spent my thirtieth birthday: shit-faced with the rest of my Unit. Anderson doesn't seem to have any friends. In fact, despite his vast wealth, he's not a happy guy, just miserable in luxury. The thought reminds me that the Senator will be oiling his asshole this weekend.

I drive into the garage, and Anderson is out the car door and into the elevator before I even have the car in park. I do a quick recon, but there's nothing out of place.

It's after midnight, so I assume that Rachel has already gone to bed. She's left a light on for me in the staff kitchen—with a glass of milk and a plate of cookies. God, this woman!

Under the cookies, there's a note. She's written one word: 'Tired?'

Hell, no!

Friday night, and Rachel has left for the weekend. The staff quarters are so empty without her. Shit, I miss her smile.

She's gone to stay with her sister, as usual. She enjoys spending time with her nieces. I wish I could see Lilly, but we're leaving for the Farm.

Mason's team have been all over it. They found evidence that recording devices have recently been removed, leaving some hastily patched up holes where cabling and cameras were situated.

Despite this, Van Sant still has a job and is still the manager at the Farm. I have no idea why, and if Anderson is playing the long game, I wish I knew what it was. Because right now I don't know what the game is, I'm unsure who are the players, and no one's told me the rules.

Landon is there, too, saggy ass on display, withered dick sticking out like a cocktail sausage. Van Sant avoids me.

It's all guys tonight, no women anywhere, but with ages varying from twenties to seventies. I don't recognize any of the faces but I saw the cars they arrived in—all costing more than a year's salary for a Marine.

At least I have help with security this time—one of Mason's guys does the door checks, a quick sweep of the metal detector and for any weapons, cell phones or covert recording devices. Two other men patrol the perimeter, making sure that no one is sneaking in. I've pulled the oh-so-lucky duty of being the man on the inside.

I keep my eyes open for anything of concern—and learn that glitter lube comes in multi-packs.

I've learned not to be affected by seeing what goes on here, six or seven men fucking and being fucked in a pile of sweating, heaving bodies, but even I have to look away when one guy proceeds to defecate on another guy—literally squats down and shits on his chest.

By dawn, the orgy has wound down and a new team takes over outside. Anderson won't have anyone but me inside, so I take a quick shower to wake me up, then do another sweep of the main house before napping in one of the chairs downstairs.

By mid-morning, the guests start leaving, dressed in their weekend casual of golfing t-shirts and loafers.

When they've all gone, Anderson appears with Landon, and I drive the two of them back to the city. At least Landon sleeps the whole way, his mouth hanging open. Anderson works on his laptop.

Saturday evening, the Senator arrives and once I've escorted him to Anderson, I stay resolutely out of sight.

I wander into the CCTV room, now my office and work until my eyeballs desiccate.

Despite my tiredness, I don't sleep well. About 2AM, the meditation room door slams and I dream uneasily for a few more hours.

When I wake, just before my alarm, there's no uncertainty—I know exactly where I am. The bed feels very empty. Not that I've slept in it much the last few nights, so I'm aware of Rachel's absence all the more. It's not a good idea to feel like this. After Carla, I told myself I wouldn't make myself vulnerable again. I think Rachel's different, but how well do I really know her? Christ, this place makes me nuts; I can't think clearly.

I arrive in the foyer at the same time as Anderson. I know he can't have slept more than two or three hours, but he doesn't show it, except maybe around the eyes. He'd have made a helluva Marine —if he wasn't so fucking crazy.

When we get back from our daily run, Anderson gives me the rest of the day off. I guess that means the Senator is staying. So I try and arrange some time with Lilly, but apparently my Princess has another play date with one of her friends from school, and fathers are surplus to requirements. I offer to pick up Lilly at the end of the afternoon, but that's not convenient either. Next time I should *give more notice*. Carla knows that's next to impossible with my job. Not that she cares. If I didn't push so hard, I wouldn't have any kind of relationship with my daughter.

Instead, I head downtown and find Lilly a postcard of Central Park and a dog making a funny face in the shiny surface of the lake.

I sit on a bench and write small so I can tell her how much I miss her and all the fun stuff we'll do next time I take her out.

I wonder what her mom says about me when I'm not there.

When I did my first tour in Iraq, two guys in my platoon got Dear John letters. Un-fucking-believable. And do you know what one cunt wrote? *Things could maybe have worked out if we'd spent more time together*. What the fuck did she think he was doing? Sitting in the fucking freezing mud of an Afghan winter just for the hell of it? We passed the letter around so we could all make our feelings known about the ho he'd had a lucky escape from.

The point is, you have to fight for what you want, but you've got to have weapons and you've got to have opportunity. I don't know what the boss wants to fight for. He's got every physical comfort money can buy; he's rich and successful—and he acts like he's had his heart and soul surgically removed.

But then I think back to his fucking awful meditation room and I know that despair is at the root of it all.

No amount of money can chase away the horror.

I text Carla and ask if I can take Lilly out next Saturday. The boss is going to the Farm by helo with one of Mason's men, and I'm following on later with the car, so I'm free for most of the day.

I fume helplessly while it takes her three hours to text back a single word: *Fine*.

Chapter Thirteen

THE PARENT TRAP

It's the next weekend and Rachel left for her sister's last night. As the Senator was visiting and I had nothing else to do, I hit the gym, got in a couple of hours lifting weights, doing crunches and squats. Running every day with Anderson, I don't usually bother with a cardio workout, as well. Benefits of having a health freak boss. Make that just freak.

Saturday morning, we leave the Senator alone at Wolf Point, a situation that I really don't fucking approve of and Anderson really doesn't fucking care.

We run the usual six miles and then I'm off duty for the next ten hours while they ... you know what? I don't even care what they do to each other. All I'm told is that Anderson is flying to the Farm late tonight and I'm to meet him there with the Rover. Mason has a guy on standby in case shit happens.

I shower quickly and reach the outskirts of Naugatuck, CT, by 10AM.

It's a strange feeling parking in the driveway of the house I bought with Carla over ten years ago. It's a one-story, ranch style home, kind of ugly, but set on an acre of property. The land is what sold it to me, all that space. Even back then, I knew that when I came out of the Marines one day I wouldn't want to be cooped up. Which makes it ironic that I'm living in the middle of a city with heat bouncing off the concrete buildings and steam rising from the ground.

It feels a little cooler here, and I stare at the tall trees fringing the boundary. I was going to build Lilly a treehouse. I never did.

At least Carla keeps the place nice. The grass has been cut recently and everything looks tidy. She told me the neighbor's kids help out.

The guilt never goes away. I pay to keep the wheels rolling, but I'm not here. Not that I'd want to spend a second longer than I have to with Carla, but I miss my baby girl. Not so much a baby anymore.

Taking a deep breath, I climb out of the Rover and knock on the front door.

"Daddy!"

Lilly throws open the door so it bounces on its hinges, and launches herself at me.

I pick her up, squeezing her tightly until she giggles and squirms.

"You're not prickles today, Daddy," she says, running a finger across my shaved cheek.

"Nope, not for my Princess. I'm dressed to impress."

"Am I Princess Buttercup today?"

"Every day."

She snuggles into my neck, and I close my eyes, enjoying the best feeling in the world. Complete unconditional acceptance: you get that from kids and dogs. And it doesn't last long with kids so I'm going to enjoy every second of it.

"Put me down, I need to go to the bathroom. You squeeze too hard."

I said it didn't last long.

She runs inside and I follow more slowly, then skulk in the hallway. It's not my home anymore and I don't assume I've got rights to go wherever.

I study the photographs on the wall. Our wedding picture has long gone, but at least Carla has left up one of me with Lilly. It must kill her to pass that every day—a smile crosses my face as I look at it.

"Justin."

I turn around and see her standing on the stairs, arms folded as her eyes ice over.

"Carla."

"Where are you taking her today?"

"I thought we'd go to Bridgeport, check out the zoo."

She pauses, her lips twisting.

"Don't let her have more than one slushy—it gives her a headache. And don't take her to the snakes again—she had nightmares about them for a week."

"Fine."

"And don't let her have too much candy or sugary drinks…"

"Jeez, Carla!"

"You're not the one who has to put up with her getting hyper from a sugar rush at bed time!"

"Okay, okay! One slushy, no snakes, not too much candy. Got it."

She scowls, then hands me a huge bag full of Christ knows what.

"I think she's grown out of needing a diaper bag, Carla."

"Sunscreen, bottled water, hat, Band-aids if her sandals rub—they're new, and her cell phone. Don't let her have it because she keeps losing it."

"You bought her a cell phone? You didn't tell me."

"Don't growl at me, Justin! It's new. She's only had it a week, so she's still getting used to it."

"She's had a number I could call her on for the last week and you didn't think to tell me?"

"You call her on the landline!"

"And it didn't occur to you that I might like to text her during the day?"

"Don't be ridiculous—she won't be allowed to have it turned on at school."

"Yeah? Well, it's summer vacation right now."

I ignore the implication that me calling my daughter will be a nuisance, and I take the bag from her, pulling out Lilly's cell phone to program my number. Carla watches, her face blank.

I'm tempted to hack into the phone account and make my ringtone Green Day's *American Idiot*. Carla hates that song. Can't imagine why.

I wonder if she's going to say something else, but she forces her face into a smile when Lilly runs into the room.

"Have fun, sweetie. Remember to put on sunscreen later, because Daddy might forget to do it."

I narrow my eyes at her but she's not even looking at me. Over the last couple of years it seems to have become ingrained in Carla that I'm totally incapable of taking care of my own daughter. I have no idea why—I've never given her any cause for concern.

We walk out to the car together, Lilly talking away, happy and excited; her mother silent with a face like she's trodden in dog shit.

I lift Lilly into the booster seat that I already put in place, and tighten the lap belt and shoulder restraint. I've got that shit down.

I wink at her as I close the door, but when I start to walk around to the driver's side, Carla stops me.

"Justin, wait."

"What now? I'm on the clock here, Carla."

"Don't be obnoxious. I want to know if you're carrying."

She looks at the expression on my face.

"Oh God, of course you are. I've told you before: I don't want Lilly surrounded by guns!"

I try not to let her push my buttons, but it's hard.

"It's my job."

"For God's sake, Justin! You're not working now!"

"This isn't up for debate."

I climb in the car and drive away before she can say another word.

I glance at the rearview mirror and see Lilly's solemn expression.

"Are you and Mommy fighting?"

"What? No, honey. Just ... disagreeing. We're fine."

Her lips turn down and my heart cracks a little more.

"I thought we'd go to the zoo. Would you like that?"

She nods, still staring out the window.

"Mommy likes the zoo. I wish she was coming with us."

I clench my teeth together because it hurts so bad.

"We'll have fun. Promise!"

I sound super fake.

After Carla and I separated, I bought a book about being a long-distance dad. The opening line said something like,

'You're already a good dad. Now you can be a great one because you bought this book'.

I didn't read any further.

I want to be a good father, but it's like tiptoeing through an IED field: you never know when you'll make the biggest mistake of your life. I want to keep my baby safe, but the world's a scary as shit place and I won't always be there for her, no matter how much I want to be.

And yes, I am armed, but right now my piece is locked in the Rover's glove compartment. The car has state of the art security, so I'm not worried exactly. Just slightly uneasy.

I don't like crowds. Too many opportunities for things to go wrong. A day at the zoo shouldn't bring out my anxiety, but it does. I've used every behavioral cognitive shit the shrinks taught me to redirect my thoughts away from everything that could go wrong and concentrate on my daughter.

It's all going well until she drops her blueberry-flavored slushy in the wallaby enclosure of the petting zoo, and two baby wallabies end up with blue tongues. That shit is too funny, but Princess Lilly cries like her little heart is breaking. So I buy her another slushy, a strawberry one this time. I just know that's gonna get back to her mom and she'll think I did it on purpose.

We walk around, laughing at the antics of the sea otters, cringe at the New Guinea singing dog exhibit (I cringe, Lilly loves it), and spend some time feeding lettuce to the otherworldly Galapagos tortoises.

Lilly's hands are sticky and most of that ends up over my t-shirt and khaki shorts, but I don't care.

We eat our lunch at a picnic table, and I give Lilly her hat and put sunscreen on her face, arms and legs. I love doing this daddy shit.

"Mom says you're going to see Granny Woods next week." I try to sound like it's the best thing I ever heard of. "Sounds like fun."

"It's okay. She likes going shopping and she lets me paint my nails different colors."

A memory stabs through me. The first time I met Carla she had her fingernails painted ten different colors. I was nineteen and thought that was pretty cool.

Long time ago.

"My friend Mandy is going camping with her mom and dad. Can we go camping?"

"As it happens your old man is a pro at camping. I'll try to get a few days off and..."

"Can Mommy come, too?"

Her dark eyes stare up at me, accusing, pleading.

"I don't think so, Princess. Mommy hates camping."

Which is true, but a half-truth all the same.

Lilly sighs and looks at her half-eaten slice of pizza.

"Okay."

Her voice is soaked in disappointment and quiet acceptance. I hate it. Guilt overwhelms me again.

Just when I think I'm winning.

By four o'clock, she's exhausted and I know our day is ending. Plus it's going to take me three hours to get to the Farm from here. The traffic out to the Hamptons on a weekend is a real bitch ... especially in the summer. Guess that's why the boss took the helo today.

Lilly falls asleep in her booster seat, cheeks pink from the sun, rosebud mouth slightly open. Dreams of the innocent. I never sleep that well.

And at that moment, I wish it was Rachel that we were going home to.

The thought shocks me.

I think I'm in trouble.

I drive into the Farm thirty minutes before the first guests are scheduled to arrive. In the weeks since I've been here, Mason has upgraded all the security, including the perimeter, installing motion sensors and infrared CCTV.

As I change into dark slacks, white shirt and a black tie, I glance out of the window and see Van Sant staring up at my room. He can't see me, but the look on his face is angry.

Whatever his game is, my presence is a serious irritant.

The guests start to arrive and it's my job to watch discreetly, a shadow that most of them ignore.

I don't recognize any of them, certainly no one who was here last time, and the boss seems to be keeping the Senator to himself at Wolf Point. I do know a couple of the names from the guest list: two other politicians and their respective wives—one Democrat, one Republican. I've no idea which way Anderson votes—probably with whichever sides gives him the best tax breaks. Most of the others look like they're in business, and I notice that Anderson appears to stay away from anyone in the world of showbiz. Maybe he doesn't trust them to be discreet.

I'm creeped out when Landon arrives. He makes a point of ignoring me, but looks over his shoulder at me as he pats Anderson on his ass and gives it a light squeeze. Because Landon is staring at me, he misses seeing the annoyance on the boss's face, but I don't.

I really don't get their relationship. Why the fuck doesn't the boss get rid of him and Van Sant?

Four hours later, I nearly gag when I see Landon, his saggy butt and wizened dick on display for all to see. He gets handsy with a young guy who could be Anderson's twin brother, and the thought makes me shudder. There's definitely something unresolved between them.

But what? Is it really what I'm starting to believe?

I hope to hell I'm wrong.

I'm never wrong.

Chapter Fourteen

FRIENDS WITH BENEFITS

Rachel and I have spent every week night sharing a bed for the last three weeks, but we still haven't been on an official date. She only gets time off during the week when the boss is out, which means I'm working. And although I don't do much on the weekends, she's at her sister's, and I'm still needed on those long-ass morning runs that the boss likes, as well as any driving duty, or I'm at the freaking Farm.

The delay is frustrating. Rachel is not the kind of woman you fuck and forget, and right now she must be thinking that I've got a sweet deal going, a friends with benefits kind of gig.

I want to take her on a date, do things right for once. But it's not proving easy. I could ask the boss for time off, but I definitely don't want to owe him another favor. Working for someone and living in their space, it's a tricky balancing act. It's actually a lot easier when there's more hired help, but with just the two of us ... yeah, not so simple.

But then one morning, the boss tells me that he's meeting Mason that evening, and I'm not needed.

Excellent. Time to put my well thought out date plan into action.

. . .

Rachel

Justin texts me in the middle of the day, every day. I look forward to his messages, although very few are ones that I could share. To say they're suggestive would be like saying Polar Bears like cold weather.

One thing I've learned about the saturnine Mr. Trainer, he's a very sexual man.

Lucky me.

And I really do mean that. His body is incredible, like an athlete, or one of those boyband singers on the posters that my niece Kimmi plasters across her bedroom. But more than that, he's not a selfish lover; he's tender and sweet ... and has a lot of stamina. I've dropped five pounds in the last three weeks just from our ... workouts.

Even my sister Allison noticed that I'd lost weight. She's been on a diet for twenty-five years, so on my last visit, she badgered me to know my 'secret'. I didn't tell her, of course.

She's very protective of me, especially since Brian died, but she can be rather judgmental, too. I just gave her some vague reply about using the gym at Wolf Point. Technically, it's not a lie.

I'm not sure what this is with Justin, why a man like him would want someone ... well, I may as well say it, so much older than him. He's 32 and I'll be 41 on my next birthday. But for now, it's wonderful. I know it will end one day because these things always do. In my experience, nothing is forever. I'll enjoy it while I can.

But today, Justin's text is completely different.

> McTwisted has given us the evening off.
> I'm taking you out for dinner. Dress sexy.
> Clothing optional when we get home.

We're going out? On a real date?

For some reason, I'm shocked. I just assumed that Justin

enjoyed having me in the bedroom. No matter how sweet he is, I never thought that he'd want to *date* me.

His short text has me re-evaluating everything, and to be honest, it's sent me into a tizzy. He's a gorgeous, sexy, hot, ex-Marine, and I'm a middle-aged housewife from Quakertown, PA. I've already taken him into my bed, so why on earth does he feel the need to take me out for dinner?

A small voice in the back of my head whispers, *Because he wants more*.

I dismiss it instantly. Dreams like that only end in heartbreak.

Even so, I dress carefully, choosing my favorite cocktail dress in a modest, knee-length Navy blue.

It used to be rather tight on me, but now it fits beautifully, even giving me a nice bust-line.

I wonder what sort of place he'll take me. For all I know, we'll have beer and burgers in a sports bar.

And I realize with a pang that I hardly know anything about the man I take into my bed.

Except he's sweet and kind and funny and a generous lover.

And he carries a gun to work. I hate guns. Always have. I guess you can't be brought up in a place named Quakertown and be okay with weapons.

After losing Brian so suddenly, I couldn't risk it again. I don't think love is on the cards for me again. I love Brian with all my heart.

But there's something about Justin—and it scares me.

If I was smart, I would guard my heart against the intriguing Mr. Trainer.

Although I think it might be too late.

I make great lasagna, but I guess I'm not so smart after all.

At 7:30PM, I'm fixing my lip gloss and trying not to get too excited or too nervous. I'm failing at both.

I know Justin is home because I heard the shower running in his room. And I cannot tell you how tempted I was to go and join him. There's something about thinking of him in the shower, the heat and steam, the cool marble tile. I'm sure shower sex must be an accident waiting to happen, but I always feel safe in Justin's arms.

Oh God, I'm turning into such a cliché!

There's a light tap on my bedroom door, but Justin doesn't open it and walk inside; he's always very respectful of my space when I'm dressing and waits for me to open the door. I appreciate that.

He looks wonderful. That strong jaw has been shaved for the second time today, and his dark brown hair is still wet and looks black. He's wearing a crisp blue button down shirt that must be new because I know for sure that I've never ironed it. He's also wearing black dress pants, and his shoes are so shiny, I can see the reflection of my pumps in them.

Across one arm, he's draped a suit jacket, but in the other, he's holding a bunch of yellow and pink roses, tied with a ribbon.

"Oh! Oh, Justin! They're beautiful! Thank you so much!"

He looks a little amused.

"It's a date, Rachel. I'm not taking you to McDonalds."

Thank goodness for that.

"Oh, but roses!"

I doubt that Justin knows the language of flowers, what the colors mean, but I do. Yellow roses mean friendship, joy, and the promise of a new beginning; pink roses mean admiration, gladness, and gentleness.

I'd love to think the colors were significant, but Justin is a man's man, so he probably just thought I'd like the combination of pink and yellow. I do.

I take them from him, feeling the soft brush of his fingers, and breathe in the intoxicating scent. It's wonderful. They're wonderful. He's wonderful.

And I'm really looking forward to tonight.

After I've put the flowers in a vase, we head to the elevator. Justin is staring at my mouth in a way that makes me uncertain whether or not we'll make it any further than the underground garage.

I can't help licking my lips, because after years of being a widow and alone, his presence, his sexual aura, is overpowering. And even though it's a warm evening, goosebumps break out on my skin and I shiver.

He traps me against the wall of the elevator and growls against my neck.

"You look so fucking hot, and those red lips would look so good wrapped around my cock."

And I should also mention that he has a very dirty mouth and he doesn't care when or where he uses it.

"Justin!" I gasp, even though no one can hear us or see us.

"I really want to smudge your lip gloss," he says, his breath hot on my flushed skin.

Then he stands up straight and backs away from me.

"Later, Mrs. Smith."

"Indeed Mr. Trainer," I reply.

His voice is steady, unlike mine, but I can't help noticing the bulge in his pants.

A frisson of pride pulses through me. *I did that to him. Yay, me!*

He opens the door of the SUV and helps me inside, and I really do need the help, because it's quite high up and this dress is very tight.

He slides the satin up to my thighs.

"That'll make it easier," he grins.

I glance up at the security camera and he laughs.

"I'll watch the reruns later, baby."

We drive for twenty minutes through the evening traffic. Justin is a picture of calm competence at the wheel. It's very sexy.

"Where is Mr. Anderson tonight?"

Justin frowns.

"Can we have one night where we don't talk about him?"

His tone is abrupt, maybe even annoyed.

"Of course. I'm sorry."

He glances at me, his expression contrite.

"He has a meeting with Mason to discuss security at one of the overseas factories. I wasn't needed."

"Thank you."

I smile at him, because he took the time to tell me what I wanted to know even though he really doesn't want to talk about Mr. Anderson. I'm sure that he'd hate me saying it, but Justin is sensitive.

He finally parks outside a small Thai restaurant that I remember reading about as one of the Village's up and coming trendy eateries, and I'm touched and how thoughtful he's being. Excited, too. And it'll be so nice to eat someone else's cooking for a change. My mouth waters at the aromas as Justin opens the door for me.

He takes my hand in his, warm and strong, and walks up to the hostess.

My mouth drops open a little at his very public display of affection, maybe even possession. It's unexpected and rather thrilling.

"Reservation for two, under the name of Trainer."

"Yes, of course, Mr. Trainer, Mrs. Trainer. This way, please."

I stumble, shocked by the words, and inside I feel an ugly stab of guilt. It's ridiculous, I know. I've been a widow for more than five years. Brian wouldn't want me to be alone, but being called 'Mrs. Trainer', I feel as if I'm cheating on my husband.

Justin grips my hand more tightly, his eyes questioning.

I shake my head and paste on a smile. That's what we widows do, I think.

I regain some equilibrium when the server brings us the menus, and my stomach rumbles in anticipation of all the wonderful dishes on the menu.

I choose Pad Kaprow Gai Kai Jea, which is spicy basil chicken with Thai omelet, and Justin opts for the grilled prawns with tamarind sauce.

He also orders a glass of rosé wine for me, but sticks to sparkling water for himself.

And then there's silence.

For a scary moment, I wonder if we only have sex and Mr.

Anderson to talk about, but then he starts asking me about myself and my family, where I grew up, funniest high school story, and so on. The conversation is easy and fun. Even though he doesn't like talking about himself, the exception being his daughter Lilly.

I was surprised when I found out he had a daughter, but even though he doesn't see her that often, he obviously dotes on her, and I know he calls her at six o'clock most evenings if he's not working.

"It sounds like she's got you wrapped around her little finger, Justin," I laugh, as he recounts the time he took her shopping, totally forgetting that he was wearing a tiara she'd put on his head.

"Yeah, she does," he smiles. "Got hit on by a lot of women that day." Then he frowns, "a couple of dudes, too."

I splutter into my wine, picturing the scene in my head.

"I bet you looked adorable!" I laugh.

"You know it, babe," he grins at me. "I can't wait for you to meet Lilly. She'll love you."

He says it so calmly, so easily, and goes back to eating his food, but my fork falls to my plate.

He wants me to meet his daughter?

I'm shocked—in a really good way.

Suddenly, our moment, whatever it was, is interrupted by raised voices.

Four businessmen seated in the corner have been getting rowdier throughout the evening, but now one of them is yelling at the poor server, a young girl who's probably still in college.

Justin's gaze hardens.

"Can't hold his fucking liquor," he mutters, leaning back in his seat and taking a long drink of water.

I can't hear what the girl is saying, but it seems as if she's apologizing for something.

I feel sorry for her: being a server is a miserable job when you get belligerent customers.

The bullying tone gets even louder.

"Listen, you dumb bitch! My order still isn't fucking right!" He grabs the menu and waves it in her face. "How many fucking times do I have to tell you before your dumb brain comprehends that I don't want *this* shit or *that* shit. I've told you..."

He rants on, his friends grinning as his face turns purple. All the other diners are embarrassed, and the hostess rushes over. Unfortunately, the argument just seems to escalate, and the man's language is appalling. Justin regularly swears like curse words are on sale, but never in public like this, never once in all those times he's driven me to the store or grocery shopping.

By now, the server is in tears, and that's when I realize Justin is no longer sitting opposite me, but striding across the room.

He says something too quiet for me to hear, but the angry man yells at him, and his friends start shouting, too. My heart is in my mouth, wondering if I should call the police. It's four against one.

And suddenly, I'm not watching my passionate lover—I'm watching a steely-eyed soldier whose hard expression is terrifying. He hauls the angry man up by his tie, cutting off his oxygen with astonishing speed. He looks lean and dangerous, and I'm afraid he'll hurt the angry man.

He says something, his voice low and rough. The angry man's head bobbles like it's on a spring, but I think he's nodding.

Then Justin drops him, and the man's butt thumps into his seat. He looks up at Justin, his eyes full of fear, and with shaking hands, pulls out his wallet, dropping some bills on the table. The other men do the same, their eyes darting between Justin and their friend.

Justin crosses his arms over his chest as the no-longer-angry man stands on trembling legs.

The businessmen leave, scuttling past Justin in silence.

In the restaurant, I think everyone is holding their breath, and the hostess follows him with her eyes wide.

Justin slides back into his seat and winks at me.

"I fucking hate foul language," he says.

Chapter Fifteen

IN THE LINE OF FIRE

Trainer

Anderson is swearing so badly, even *my* ears are burning. Ryan has taken cover behind his desk and Howard ... yeah, he's the same as ever, rambling on about the possibility of putting a terra-farming operation on the moon.

On the other hand, maybe that's not entirely unrelated to the boss's tantrum.

I have no idea how that Howard dude has lasted so long working for Anderson. I know that MENSA says he's a genius, but I'd say the guy has a few screws loose. Even so, there isn't anything he doesn't know about IT, computers, or hacking. Although, come to think about it, he knows a lot about everything, even terra-farming. I'd guess that knowing about women could be the exception to the rule. Possibly humans in general.

The swearing in the boss's office has reached a new velocity. I'll give it another five minutes then either call the boss's therapist for an urgent consultation ... or maybe a veterinarian for a rabies shot.

Pam strides out of the elevator, clearly having been summoned by Ryan. She listens for a moment, a small smile of amusement on her face, and she glances at Anderson's P.A.

"Really? The President wants to meet him?"

Ryan nods and whispers, "Mr. Anderson isn't very happy about it."

"Yes, I can hear that." She glances at me. "I'll talk to him. Trainer, with me."

"I've made a tactical withdrawal," I state, refusing to move.

"Well, now you're making a strategic ambush, followed by a little divide and conquer. You've got my six, big guy."

She marches into the room, and reluctantly I follow her.

"Devon, you're a thirty year-old billionaire entrepreneur. Of course the President wants to meet you: you're an icon of everything he stands for—America is open for business."

Anderson snaps and snarls some more, but he knows she's right.

"It's a fucking waste of everyone's time," he growls.

"It's a good PR opportunity," Pam bats back, unaffected by the boss's mood. "God knows, you don't let us do enough of that."

It's true. The boss is to PR what vampires are to a vacation in the Florida Keys.

But by the time we've left his office, Pam has confirmed the meeting and I've spoken to one of the security grunts a.k.a. Secret Service who I'll be liaising with about the visit.

Genital warts would be more fun than the upcoming *Anderson Vs President* stand-off. I like to be in charge of the boss's security, but the Commander-in-Chief's dogs of war have made it quite clear what my role is: unwanted, like shit on their shoes.

Which is why, two days later, I'm getting ready to leave with an expression on my face like a Texas cowboy at a vegan buffet.

Rachel watches as I pack for the trip to D.C.

"Take the blue tie, it matches your eyes."

Pissed as I am, I smile at her in amusement.

"Babe, no one is going to be looking at me."

"Justin, any woman with a pulse will be looking at you."

"Jealous?"

"Of course."

Her words make me smile, but I don't want to think she's got anything to worry about. I glance up again, but I don't think she's joking.

"Rachel, I'm many kinds of jerk, but I'm not a cheater."

Her eyes soften.

"I never said you were. But..."

"No, baby. No buts, unless it's yours pressed against my cock when I wake up in the morning. I'll be away for one night, two tops, and then I'll be back warming your bed..."

"And stealing the duvet and taking up all the room."

"Yeah, you love it."

She doesn't answer, but hands me the blue silk tie.

I put it in the suitcase.

There's only one word to describe the drive to Teterboro Airport: gruesome. Traffic was backed up everywhere, and it took longer than the flight to D.C. on Anderson's Learjet 60. One of the smaller private jets. Yeah.

Anderson spent most of the time in the cockpit getting a free lesson from the pilot. Or maybe they call it multitasking. I'm guessing that piloting his own jet will be the next thing on his bucket list. The man's going to be disappointed when he gets to thirty-five and finds that he's done everything he wants to do. Maybe he'll write a novel. His autobiography would be a bestseller. Or banned.

Maybe *I'll* write a bestseller. I mentioned this to Rachel once as a joke. But as usual, the joke was on me.

"I'm sure you could, Justin, if you put your mind to it. You'd have to change all the names, all the places, and well, most of the facts—after all, who'd believe the truth anyway?"

Her eyes lit up.

"Or maybe a movie! Jason Stratham could play you, except he's too short. Oh, I can hear the voiceover now: *I'm the silent bodyguard at the back of the room. I'm the eyes watching you. I'm the ears listening to you…"*

"I thought I was a foul-mouthed grunt?"

"That, too. But what about me, Justin? I'm in this story, as well!"

Her blue eyes were going for outraged, but I saw the humor behind them.

"Babe, if my book was about you, it would be called 'Cooking for the Billionaire'. But it's not. It's all about me."

"Men! It's always about them! As if the sun revolves around you."

I love it when my woman gives me grief. Makes me horny.

I pick up a town car from Dulles and put in the address for the hotel Ryan booked—the Four Seasons in Georgetown.

I'll say one thing for Anderson: the guy isn't stingy when it comes to hotel rooms. Ryan reserved the Royal Suite for Anderson which is three times bigger than the house I grew up in. Four thousand square feet, ten-seater dining room, bullet resistant glass. And a ninety gallon bathtub. I shit you not.

Oh, and a private gym with elliptical, treadmill, air-bike and free weights. A steal at only $18,500 per night.

My Premier Deluxe room on the same floor pales in comparison. Yeah, kidding: it's a friggin' palace in its own right.

You'd be amazed how many employers put their security team in shitty rooms and bitch about the cost. Not Anderson.

I check out his room first as part of my job. I'm impressed, but he doesn't even glance up at 'the galaxy of Swarovski crystals' in the ceiling at the suite's entrance. Nope, he finds a desk, plugs in his laptop and goes to work.

He mumbles something about room service, and I'm given the next two hours off.

In theory.

In actuality, I'm meeting with the Prez's Secret Service so I know exactly which hand to use to wipe my ass in the morning. They call it 'managing expectations of the guest and entourage'.

I met the old President once. Got a medal pinned on me and all of that shit. I don't know about this other guy but I definitely don't want his hairdresser. I heard that when they tried to make a wax figure of him, they couldn't get the hair right. So they ended up using yak hair—the same stuff they used for Chewbacca.

After a quick shower so I smell nice for the G-men, I trek on over to the private meeting room. Even though they're expecting me, and even though my ID checks out, they still do a body search and confiscate my Smith & Wesson. I'm *not* happy about that, but not surprised either.

"Nice weapon," says the least douchey of them. "All the wannabes use them."

Nope, I was mistaken: he's the full douche-canoe.

I watch eagle-eyed as he takes out the clip and places everything out of reach at the end of the long table.

I'm happy they don't do a full-body cavity search, although I can't help thinking that the boss might enjoy one. Different strokes for different subs, I mean, folks.

Then they sweep the room for bugs but don't find any. But just in case, they set up a Bluetooth blocker and WiFi-jamming equipment—well, the Secret Service equivalent. Their radios use DES encryption keys, and at least one of them has a military grade radio I recognize that uses Type 1 encryption algorithms. I have no fucking clue what that means, except that this stuff works and I want a set for the Farm. These boys sure do love their toys. Although Howard has them beat in this department; not that I'll be sharing that morsel of information with the guys in polyester. I wonder if they're interested in terra-farming on the moon.

They go through all the normal protocols and there's nothing unexpected, which makes everyone a lot happier. It's the unknown that can sucker-punch you.

They're professional, only slightly condescending on their power trip. After all, I've got the job they'll want once they retire from the Secret Service. Having fewer resources, powers and all the luxuries of a 100 man team makes a better operator—respect where respect is due. Plus, they've read up on who I am and what I've done. I don't know jack-shit about them, but we all have that ex-military look. It's easy to spot in someone else when you've been there.

So their obvious lack of respect pisses me off. But it's the old private Vs working-for-the-government Washington two-step.

Really, the meeting is just confirming what I've already been told by email and in a personal phone call: they'll send a car for me and the boss, code word for the driver so we know it's legit, don't bring any laptops or flash drives, don't bring food or drink, no large bags or suitcases, no restrooms available (unless you're invited to dinner, I guess), cell phones will be checked along with my weapon at the White House, Anderson will meet privately with the President for thirty minutes. Same protocol on the way back.

"You know, Trainer, there's no need for you as CPO to accompany Anderson."

I shrug.

"If he says he doesn't want me there, I'll stand down, but until I hear it from him, I guess you'll be making me coffee tomorrow morning."

They exchange looks, but I really don't care.

The rest of the meeting is what I expected. Right up until the goons are leaving. The youngest one, who looks like he's got something to prove, turns to me with a smirk on his face.

"What's it like working for Anderson? Not too much spare pussy, heh?"

"Wow, you know what a pussy is? Was that before or after you learned to jerk off?"

"You're a funny guy. You crack me up."

"You're cracked? Gee, maybe a shrink could help."

The younger guy doesn't seem to think I'm funny—either that or he's constipated.

"Or maybe you and Anderson are butt buddies?"

"Jealous, G-man? Did you Botox those lips or just suck a lot of cock?"

His face turns purple and I think his next trick might be an aneurysm. The other G-men are laughing their brass asses off.

"Did you just call me a cocksucker?"

His tone is so indignant that it makes me burst out laughing. Okay, not really, but I may have raised an eyebrow.

"Guess you weren't recruited for your brains."

"See how funny you think you are when I get you fired! See how you like that, funny guy!"

He has no idea how fucking amusing that is. Or how shit their deep research is. The Prez should be worried.

I shake my head and sigh.

"You have no idea."

It's not the response he wanted, so he walks off with his panties in a bunch.

What is this? Amateur half hour? No wonder the country is going to Hell in a handbasket.

By the time I'm back in my room, I have a cozy twenty-five minutes to write a postcard for Lilly and get something to eat before I drive the boss to a public debate on genetically modified farming. The boss isn't interested in being media-friendly, but Pam encouraged him to go, and since this really is something he's passionate about, they worked with the schedule. She also pointed out that the Agriculture Division at UVM needs all the help they can get. The boss agreed—eventually.

It's a complete contrast to the meeting I just had. The public talk is at the International Food Policy Research Institute. Security is minimal, and it's gigs like this that worry me the most. The security team is made up of students, supervised by an ex-cop who's ready to retire. He knows what he's doing, but his guys haven't had extensive training. They do quick searches of purses and bags as the audience enters, but it's not a ticketed event, so there's no way of knowing who's attending. Sure, there are metal detectors, but otherwise, the place is wide open.

I've learned that genetically modified agriculture is a touchy subject and it would be easy for some crazed fanatic to enter the building. I keep *very* close tabs on Anderson, minimizing his contact with the great unwashed.

There are three chairs on the stage at the front of the hall: one for the boss; one for the Chairwoman, some college type; and one for the opposing speaker, a hippy chick with blue hair and tits that reach her knees. She really shouldn't have burned her bra.

She's been staring at the boss since he shook hands with her.

Yeah, he's a good-looking bastard, although he barely knows she exists. But his old fashioned manners and natural reserve are rubbing her the wrong way, and I see the light of battle in her eyes.

The Chairwoman invites Moonbeam Herbaceous or whatever the fuck her name is to speak first. She rambles on and keeps looking at her notes, but states her points against genetically modified agriculture eventually: environmental risk; we don't know enough about the long-term effects, a.k.a. "remember when cigarettes were supposed to be good for you?"; big business is bad for small farmers; and finishes up with a rather trite, 'nature knows best' argument. Yeah? Is that why whitefly and lack of rain decimated crops in India in 2015, and 2,500 farmers committed suicide?

All facts I've learned since working for Anderson. I attend a lot of meetings and just 'cause I blend with the wallpaper, it doesn't mean that I'm nodding off. I listen. I lurk. And guess what? I learn stuff.

The boss stands and eyeballs his audience, connecting with every person in the room before he opens his mouth. The anticipation is killing them. They don't know what to expect from Mr. GQ in his shiny shoes and Armani suit. Half of them want to hate him, but they can't.

"I know what it is to live without hope."

I'm more than a little surprised by his opening words. I hadn't expected anything so personal. Nor had anyone else in the room.

The flower child has her mouth open and is watching with rapt attention.

"There are seven billion people in the world today. By 2050, it will be nine billion. Food production needs to double, but the amount of farmland is shrinking year after year. Genetically modified crops are the *only* way to meet that need.

"My company, DMA Solutions, ensures that we work *with* farmers in both developed and developing countries.

"Stronger crops mean fewer pesticides, not more. Introducing genetically modified soybean and corn into the U.S. has reduced the use of pesticides by ten million gallons in the last decade. Not only can we make food healthier, we can improve the taste as well. For example, increasing the antioxidants in tomatoes that we know help prevent cancer and heart disease."

Anderson winds up his speech and sits down.

The environmentalist chick is speechless. For some reason it didn't occur to her that the billionaire businessman might actually know his ass from a hole in the ground.

The next morning, we're pounding the streets of Georgetown, and following the Chesapeake and Ohio Canal Towpath. The air is crisp and fresh, and Fall is right around the corner.

A few people are out rowing, and I wonder if the boss feels nostalgic. Nah, he doesn't seem the type. If he was, then it would be his private college kissing his ass for research money, not the Agri Division at UVM.

Or maybe he just doesn't like being predictable.

He never talks while we run. I used to think he was pretending that I wasn't there, but that's not it; it's his time to let his mind roam free, his thinking, planning and plotting time, his *other* meditation. I get that. All those post-exercise, happy endorphins. Must be why he's such a relaxed, easy-going guy.

We're back at the Four Seasons before most people have

enjoyed their first piss of the day, then looking all spiffy in our snazzy suits, we head off to meet the Wizard.

Anderson is scowling the whole way, irritated that the President of the United States is taking up so much of his precious time.

And you know what, I kind of dig that about Anderson.

Once we arrive at 1600 Pennsylvania Avenue, he puts on his game face.

The security guys I met yesterday aren't making any jokes today, but if looks could kill, my ego might be slightly bruised. Nah, probably not.

Even as guests of the Prez, we still have to go through metal detectors like everyone else, and weapon and ammunition is checked in with the Whitehouse security. I don't take it personally: even Capitol Police are required to check their weapons when visiting the WH.

Anderson strides into the White House radiating latent power and carefully controlled energy. He's in CEO mode. I've seen it before: he can turn it on and off like a damn light switch. I guess it's what us lesser mortals call charisma.

Anderson shakes hands and almost smiles for the Prez's official photographer. It's over quickly.

I'm not allowed into the meeting, so I can't tell you what Anderson and the President discussed.

Instead, I'm invited for a cozy coffee with the G-men. Aw.

In reality, they escort me to a shabby break room, point me to a coffee machine and either ignore me, or give me blank stares while I search without luck for a donut.

Anderson doesn't seem to enjoy his meeting any more than I have.

All I do know is that once we're back in the hotel, he mutters 'waste of fucking time' in a stream of foul language that is almost impressive, and orders his jet to be ready as soon as we can get to the airport.

It's anticlimactic, and I didn't even get to check out the yak hair rug. At least the Prez tweeted the photo of him and Anderson.

I'm surprised when the boss tells me that his therapist will be flying back with us. Apparently he was in D.C. for some symposium, and he's hitching a ride in style.

I've never spoken to the chief headshrinker, although I've escorted Anderson to his office every week since I started working for him. I do know that the sessions can be hard, because sometimes Anderson comes out looking like he wants to shoot someone, and sometimes more quiet and thoughtful than usual. Occasionally, he's calmer. I never know what I'll get, and I'll bet the doc doesn't either.

I escort him on board, intrigued to see how he interacts with the boss.

I'm disappointed that he looks normal. I was hoping for a hang-out hippie with a soul-patch, love beads and maybe a tat with pictures from the Kama Sutra. It would have been fun fucking with him. But this dude is wearing a three-piece suit and I'm already bored.

"Good morning, Devon. How was your meeting with our esteemed President?"

"A PR exercise. He wasn't interested in hearing about the strides made at UVM. So I told him about our solar powered comms technology and cell phones, and I think he confused me with Evan Spiegel."

"The likeness is striking," the therapist says with a straight face.

"I don't wear Chucks."

Holy shit! I think the boss just made a joke!

The therapist glances up at me, one eyebrow raised.

"I look forward to seeing more photographs on Twitter," he says.

The boss grunts and opens his laptop. Conversation over.

When it looks like the shrink might start talking to me, I move to the back of the jet, plug in my earbuds and open a book.

I've got nothing against him, and he seems like a decent guy, but I'm not letting any shrink dick around with my brain ever again. There are some things that I don't think about for a reason. Call me repressed, but talking about my fucking *feelings* isn't going to help me, isn't going to stop me remembering what I've done on half-a-dozen different deployments. You can't un-see Hell.

I had a shrink ask me once where I felt safest. I think he wanted me to talk about going hiking in the hills, or swimming with dolphins, talking to turtles, I don't know; but he wasn't happy when I said, 'Behind a set of gun sites with a weapon in my hand.'

You can't fix shit. You just learn to move on.

The best therapy is in Rachel's bed, and I can't wait to get back to it.

When I spoke to Rachel earlier, she mentioned that she'd got me a gift. I made the mistake of reading out her horoscope in the newspaper last week because it said Venus was in Uranus and romance was in the air or some shit. Then she asked what my star sign was and I admitted that it's Scorpio—you know, passionate, assertive, determined, the jealous type.

So we're celebrating my birthday when I get home. Thirty-three. That's fucking middle-aged.

At least I wasn't born on Halloween, whatever my ex-wife says.

We're in the car and I'm heading for Manhattan when the boss throws one of his curveballs.

"Trainer, I'm going to the Farm."

"Now, sir?"

He scowls, hating to repeat himself.

Gritting my teeth, I head away from Wolf Point.

I'm growing to seriously dislike these visits. Even with the new security Mason installed, it's a scandal waiting to happen. Hell, with the number of guests he has up there, it's a small miracle that Perez Hilton isn't camped out in the front yard.

Unfortunately, Van Sant shows his ugly face the moment we arrive. He's kissing the boss's ass like a pro. How the fuck can

Anderson stand it? He doesn't normally surround himself with yes men, so why here? Why now?

Or is Anderson is playing the long game?

Thirty-two long and miserable hours later, I finally walk into our living room at Wolf Point.

Rachel is stretched out on the sofa, deeply asleep. Something inside my chest, something buried deep—it tells me that this is *my* end-game. Everything I've been through is to earn the right to a moment of peace with this woman.

She wakes slowly, her eyelids fluttering as I sit silently on the sofa, stroking her soft hair.

"Oh, Justin! You're home! I was waiting up and…"

My lips settle across hers as I drink in her words. When I finally pull away, her skin is flushed and she's smiling.

"You look tired," she says gently, brushing her finger under the dark shadows that ring my eyes.

"Been a long week. Missed you, babe."

"I missed you, too. Do you want your gift now?"

"Best gift is you," I mumble, my eyes drifting closed as she leans against me, her soft warmth soothing.

"Tomorrow then," she says sweetly.

I shake myself awake and sit up straight.

"No, I don't want to wait any longer. It's been a shit birthday, but seeing you makes it better."

My hands reach for her but she slides out of reach and digs around inside her purse. It's huge—whole constellations could exist inside there—but I do enjoy seeing her ass stuck up in the air as she peers inside.

She returns to the sofa with two packages: one flat, one a box, both small and both giftwrapped.

"Two gifts?!"

"Well, there is a third, but you'll have to wait till later," she winks at me.

I'm tempted to go for gift number three now, but she's gone to all this effort. I pull the wrapping off the small box and find a pair of monogrammed gold cufflinks.

"Someone who looks as handsome as you do in a suit should have their own engraved cufflinks," she smiles.

They're 18 carat gold and must have cost her a packet. I can't believe she's done this for me. I try to find the words, but I can't find the right ones.

"Aw, I love them, baby. I'll wear them tomorrow."

Then I open the second package and find a gift card for the Museum of Natural History. I'm a little puzzled when I see it's for *A Night at the Museum*, a sleepover for kids and parents—and there are two tickets.

"I ... well, you said you wanted to take Lilly camping but she doesn't like sleeping outdoors, so ... I thought this would be a fun thing to do for you both..."

Her words trail off when I don't speak, but honestly, I don't think I can. I'm so fucking touched that she'd do something so thoughtful for me.

"If you don't think Lilly would like it, I'm sure I could exchange..."

I rest my forehead against hers, breathing deeply, breathing in the scent of Rachel.

"I love it. I fucking love it. Thank you."

And when I kiss her, I can feel her smile.

Chapter Sixteen
TALKING TURKEY

Halloween is over and I'm a thirty-three year old CP officer working for a twisted bastard and wondering what the next decade will be like.

After stunning me with her gifts, Rachel threw me a birthday party for two, which ended up with her losing her underwear and me eating the cake she made for me off of her tits, so I score that as a win all around.

But now it's the holidays, and that puts me in a shitty mood.

The boss is going to his parents for Thanksgiving which will be interesting. I'd hoped to get some time off and go see Lilly, but my Princess is going away to see the coven leader, a.k.a. my ex-monster-in-law, and I'm not wanted.

Rachel will be going to her sister's as usual, so I think I'll catch up with some of my Marine buddies. I know a couple of them will be in NYC. Drinking beer, watching football, eating greasy burgers, it all sounds good to me. A little slice of normalcy. Fuck knows I could do with it.

At least, that's what I tell myself.

I'm laying on the sofa with my head in Rachel's lap, half asleep after a long-ass day that started before dawn, and she's watching some chick flick. Her hands are stroking my short hair, and it's so relaxing, I'm almost in a coma.

When her phone rings, I want to throw it across the room.

Rachel huffs out a sigh of annoyance.

"It's my sister."

I try not to look too pissed, but I guess I failed because Rachel gives me an exasperated look.

It's not that I don't like her sister, I've never even met her, but she does seem to have an uncanny knack of interrupting the few free hours we have. And when I say 'interrupting', I mean cock-blocking.

Rachel takes the call and they chat away about crap like knitting yogurt or whatever.

"Okay, Allison, I'll let you know. Thanks for asking us."

My ears prick up at that last word.

Rachel is frowning slightly as she looks at me. I force myself into a sitting position and rub my eyes, yawning.

"What's up, baby?"

"Allison has invited us to spend Thanksgiving with her, Bill and the girls."

Now it's my turn to frown.

" 'Us' as in you and me?"

Rachel smiles tentatively.

"Well, yes. That's what it usually means. What do you think? Would you like to?"

I realize this is one of those 'next step' moments you come across in relationships; that moment when it's a case of move things forward ... or not. I can't say the idea of spending time with Rachel's sister thrills me.

Rachel hasn't said anything—it's probably what she doesn't say —but I get the distinct impression that Allison doesn't approve of me. Normally, I wouldn't give a shit, but Rachel is special, really special, and I don't want to risk losing her.

I admit defeat: whatever happens, it's a lose-lose situation.

"Sure, baby, why wouldn't I?"

She raises her eyebrows in a way that tells me she's not buying my brand of bullshit. That woman can read me like a book: either that or she saw me shudder with horror at the whole Thanksgiving-ritual-slaughter-holiday—and I'm not just talking turkey.

"Well, I thought you might want to see Lilly."

Yeah, I really would like to see my daughter.

"She'll be with her mother and grandmother in Salem."

"Oh, I'm sorry, Justin. I know you miss her."

I don't like talking about that because it makes me want to break something. Only kidding. But I wouldn't mind smashing the shit out of that ugly wedding china her family gave us.

I realize that Rachel is still looking at me.

"It's cool. I'll see Lilly after they're back."

Unless my ex- changes her mind, which is pretty damn likely since the personality implant didn't work.

"What about Mr. Anderson? Will he give you the time off?"

"Yeah. He told me today that he's planning to spend time with his parents in Scarsdale."

"Really? For the whole weekend?"

I seriously doubt that. The guy is chained to his laptop, and I strongly suspect he won't want to spend more than one night at his folks' place.

"Probably not, but he said he didn't need me. I think he's just planning on working..."

Rachel shakes her head and sighs.

"Such a shame."

I know what she's referring to, but even though he's a fucked-up bastard, he's got more than most thirty year olds could ever dream of. *Yeah, I know, and a lot less, too.*

"So, do you feel ready to meet my family?" She pauses and looks away. "You don't have to, Justin. I'd understand."

"Of course I want to, Rachel. It'll be great. Don't worry."

Famous last words.

Which is why, on the day before Thanksgiving, we're heading west along the Brooklyn Queens Expressway to Quakertown. Yep, that's a real place. I also learn that both Rachel and her sister were brought up as Quakers but have moved away from the faith. Growing up, they didn't celebrate Thanksgiving, but Rachel says they do now for the sake of Allison's kids.

"Who's going to be at this shindig, baby?"

"Well, Allison, of course. Her husband, Bill; their two girls Megan, who's fourteen, and Kimmi, who's eleven. I expect they'll invite the neighbors, Douglas and Virginia; oh, and Bill's mom, Celia."

No Uncle Fester?

When we arrive, there's snow crunching under the Rover's wheels and the air is freezing. The sister's house is one of those suburban ranch houses that you see everywhere in small towns: a patch of grass in front and a larger yard at the back.

I pull up onto the small driveway, and Rachel reaches over and squeezes my thigh.

"Ready?"

"Sure, baby. Follow you anywhere."

She smiles and gives me a reassuring kiss on the cheek. But I catch her chin, and turn it into a full-out, knock 'em down and drag 'em out kiss on the lips. I can neither confirm nor deny the presence of tongues.

Her skin flushes and she smacks me lightly on the arm before climbing out of the car.

She's just about to knock on the door when it flies open and a girl comes running out.

"Aunty Rachel!"

I guess this is Kimmi. She's got light brown hair, braces and a cute little round face. I can see a family resemblance. She's so happy to see Rachel, it makes the absence of Lilly feel worse.

"Mom says you have a *boyfriend*, Aunty Rachel! She said you'd *never* get a boyfriend, but you did, didn't you? Maybe *I'll* get a boyfriend next."

Rachel laughs, but I can tell that it's slightly strained. What the hell is this? Why wouldn't someone as gorgeous as Rachel have a man in her life? I'm pissed off before I've made it through the front door.

"Kimmi, this is my friend Justin. Justin, this is Kimmi."

"Hi," she says, shyly.

"Hi, Kimmi. Nice to meet you."

I hold out my hand and we shake formally, then she blushes and giggles. It kinda reminds me of my Princess, and I can't help smiling back.

I look up and see a woman who must be Rachel's sister. I catch her as she's running her eyes up and down me.

I stand impassively while Rachel and Allison hug. Then I'm introduced and she shakes my hand, a chilly expression at odds with the way she was checking out my package a minute ago.

It's weird seeing some of Rachel's lovely features on this stranger's face, but she's got none of Rachel's appealing softness.

For some reason, she's decided that she doesn't like me.

This should be a fun weekend. I just know we're not going to get along. I feel like I should have a map that says, *Here be dragons*.

Kimmi shows us to our room. Well, she shows me; Rachel used to live here and knows the way.

"This is my room and you're not allowed in here," Kimmi states. "Well, I don't mind, but Megan can't come in unless I say so. Do you want to see my room?"

"Uh, sure."

I'm expecting it to be an explosion of pink like Lilly's room, but I can't see the color of the walls because they're covered with posters of *Rock Boys*. It brings back memories and a shudder runs down my spine.

"Do you like *Rock Boys*, Justin?" asks Kimmi.

"I have both their albums."

Rachel coughs, although I think she may have been laughing, but Kimmi squeals happily.

"Oh em gee! They're a-may-zing, aren't they? *Strolling with Rocks* is like THE BEST SONG EV-ER!"

"I preferred *Beach Baby Blues*."

Kimmi nods her head seriously.

"That's my second favorite song ever." She smiles happily. "Gareth is so cute!"

I don't tell her that I know all of those guys since I was in charge of their security detail when they toured SE Asia and Europe. And yes, I still have both their albums, signed. I'm blessed.

"Your room is down the hall," Kimmi continues. "Mom wanted to give you separate rooms, but Grandma Greene is staying so there's no space. Mom said she didn't want you guys doing it in here. What did she think you were going to be doing?"

"The crossword," says Rachel, quickly. "She doesn't want us getting newsprint on the sheets."

"Oh, okay," says Kimmi, wandering off. "I thought she was talking about sex."

Rachel's mouth drops open and she turns to stare at me, blushing again in a really cute way.

"Your sister got a problem with you *doing it*, baby?" I ask, raising my eyebrows.

"I ... I don't know what to say. I'm so sorry, Justin."

"S'okay, baby. I like breaking the rules."

I look around the room that has been Rachel's part-time home for last five years when she was between jobs. There are family photographs in frames on the dresser and on the walls; recipe books on the bookshelves; and her clothes in the closet with a stack of brown boxes, still taped up.

"I don't know how you managed to break the rules in the Marines," she says.

"Didn't get caught, mostly." I pull her into my arms and kiss her softly. "Wanna break some rules now?"

"Tell me first how you know so much about *Rock Boys*? I thought you were just teasing her, but you know all the songs!"

I shrug.

"Toured with them."

"Wow! She'll be so impressed!"

I cringe at the possible interrogation.

"Better not tell Kimmi. I don't want to have to lie about the sex, drugs and rock 'n' roll."

"Oh! Really? Okay, I won't!"

She kisses me back passionately, showing me that wild side that I really fucking like. She's got one hand on my ass and the other up the inside of my t-shirt, and things are getting *really* interesting when there's a polite cough.

I pull back and see a paunchy guy in his late forties smiling at us.

"Uh, hi! Sorry to, um, interrupt. I'm Bill. A pleasure to meet you, Justin. Hey, Rachey. How you doin', honey?"

We shake hands and he gives Rachel a hug.

There aren't many men I'd allow to touch my woman, but he gets a pass ... just ... because he's family, but mostly because Rachel says he's a good guy.

I know from what she's told me that Bill has some sort of job in computers. I could have done a check from Mason's database, but that felt like spying on Rachel's family. I may have peeked: an unpaid parking fine. *Living on the wild side, Bill.*

"Welcome to the mad house, Justin. I hope you have got a strong stomach."

Yep, gotta lot of practice working for Devon king-of-crazy Anderson.

"Thanks, Bill. Appreciate you inviting us. Oh, hey, brought you this."

I hand him a bottle of Tequila Gold and his face lights up like a freakin' Christmas tree.

"Oh, man! Thanks!"

"And I've brought some pies and cakes, too, Bill," adds Rachel.

"Rachel, you are a saint ... and some of your special stuffing?"

"Of course, Bill. I couldn't let you down, could I?"

"Justin, this woman is a saint."

He gives Rachel another hug.

"Kinda noticed that, Bill."

He winks at me.

"So, did you meet Megan yet? I think she's in the den watching

TV. Either that or sulking in her room," he mutters under his breath.

Yeah, this is going to be a fun family get-together.

"I'll go get the luggage, baby."

While I'm out at the car, Bill comes to help me. Rachel has packed enough food for several platoons of hungry grunts.

"Um, Justin, don't take this the wrong way..."

Oh, fucking what now?

"But would you mind not mentioning the tequila to Allison? Just between you and me, buddy?"

His look is borderline desperate, so I nod, keeping my expression immobile. I'm usually such an open book.

"Sure, no problem, Bill."

"I'll keep it my play room."

I nearly choke.

"I make model airplanes and submarines. I keep them in the garage. Allison calls it my 'play room'—her little joke."

Thank fuck for that. I don't think I could take seeing any play rooms, meditation rooms, or punishment rooms like the boss has at the Farm—especially not in rural Pennsylvania. They might have antlers on the walls. I'm already scarred for life. And I *really* don't want to imagine Allison in bondage gear. *Aw hell! Too late.* My stomach heaves and I nearly lose my lunch.

Bill helps me carry Rachel's boxes of food into the kitchen. When I see what Allison is making for our dinner, I regret not bringing any MREs with me. Yeah, they're vacuum-packed military rations that have a ten year shelf life, but they look a helluva lot better than the brain-colored sludge that Allison's cooking. She calls it 'risotto'; I call it risky on my stomach.

It's not until we're all sitting around the dining table that I finally meet Bill's mom, Celia, who's been taking a nap; and the oldest daughter, Megan.

Celia: It's not easy for a widow, you know. If I had to

rely on my kids to look after me, I'd be on the streets.

Bill: Now, mother...

Allison: [*snarling*] You're not on the streets, Celia. You're in our very comfortable guest room.

Megan: So, you're, like, a driver?

Me: Yes.

Rachel: Well, Justin is also...

Megan: And you were a soldier?

Me: A Marine.

Megan: Isn't that the same thing?

Me: Fu— um, no.

Celia: I know I'm just a burden to you. I can eat dinner in my room.

Bill: Aw, mom...

Megan: And you're, like, a bodyguard?

Me: Yes.

Allison: If you'd prefer to eat in your room, Celia...

Celia: Well, I...

Kimmi: Aunty Rachel, if Justin is your boyfriend, are you going to, like, sleep with him?

[*Cue: echoing silence and tumbleweed as all eyes turn to Rachel.*]

Allison: Kimmi!

Bill: Kimmi!

Kimmi: Mom, you said that Aunty Rachel ought to know better at her age than having a boy-toy, so I was just wondering if...

Megan: Oh wow! You are in *so* much trouble!

Allison: Kimmi! I didn't...

Rachel is staring at her plate, mortified. And I am so fucking angry with that bitch of a sister of hers. I reach over and take Rachel's hand.

"If anyone's got a problem with me seeing Rachel, I'd rather they said it to my face," and I turn to stare at Allison. "Not that it will make any difference whatsoever."

"That told her," mutters Celia in a stage-whisper.

The rest of the meal passes with tense indigestion, although whether that's from the fucking awful food or the arctic atmosphere, I couldn't say. Rachel is quiet, and I know that she's still upset. Bill tries hard to keep the conversation going, and I really appreciate that.

"It must be interesting working for Devon Anderson: he's making quite a name for himself. What's he like?"

"Interesting," I offer.

"Mr. Anderson is really very sweet," says Rachel.

"I believe his company is developing a new operating system, is that right?"

"We don't get involved in the business side of things," replies Rachel.

See why I love that woman? She's smart, she's loyal, she's kind and so fucking sexy. Did I mention sexy?

When we finally get to be alone in our room, I pull Rachel into a hug.

"You okay, baby?"

"I'm fine. Allison didn't mean it like that—she just worries about me. Are you, okay? My family can be rather full-on."

"Like water off a duck's back, Rachel. Marines are trained to survive in hostile environments."

She laughs softly.

"What other training did they give you?"

"Stealth, concealment ... in fact, I'd really like to be concealed in you, baby."

"Oh, really? Well, we'll have to see what we can do about that, although the stealth will come in handy, too: these walls are very thin."

I fucking love a challenge. But to clarify...

"I'm not allowed to make you scream?"

Her blush is sexy.

"Uh, well, no. I guess not."

"That's just mean."

Her gaze snaps to mine and she's trying not to smile.

"I'm only mean to you because I like you."

"That's messed up."

"Would you rather be ignored?"

"Are those my only two options?"

She starts to laugh, but we manage to keep the noise down.

Shortly after dawn, I'm woken by a loud scream and I automatically reach for my gun—which isn't there. It's locked in a steel box in the trunk of my car.

"What the fuck?"

Rachel lays a hand on my chest, looking scared.

"I'll go see what it is."

I pull on my jeans commando, moving quietly towards the kitchen, keeping an eye open for anything I can use as a weapon. But by the time I get there, I realize that Bill is the one who needs a weapon, and it's Allison who's doing the screaming.

"I can't believe you, Bill! I ask you to do *one* thing! One solitary, *single* thing—and you even manage to screw that up! All you had to do was take the turkey out of the freezer. But, no! That was too difficult for you!"

"I'm sorry, honey, I just…"

"Oh, shut up, Bill! If only you were half the man your mother is!"

Ouch.

As I'm not needed, I'm just about to go back to Rachel when Allison turns and sees me. She can't help herself from staring. She starts with my bare chest, her eyes bugging as she moves to my abs then lower. Okay, so I'm not so sartorially elegant as usual, but *come on! Have some fucking class, lady!*

"Heard screaming. But I guess you're okay in here."

"I wouldn't say that," Bill mutters.

The guy really looks like he wants backup, but I've had enough domestic ear-batterings to last me a life time. I give Bill a look that tells him he's on his own.

"Okay?" shrieks Allison. "Okay?! No we are *not* 'okay'; we are so far from being okay that we're living in a world where Marge Simpson has won the hair-style of the year award!"

"I forgot to defrost the turkey," says Bill, glumly.

"How can we have a Thanksgiving meal without the turkey?" Allison screeches.

By this time Rachel is padding into the kitchen wearing just her robe. Knowing that she's naked under the soft material distracts me from the matters arising to my own personal uprising.

"Allison, there's lots of food. I'm sure we'll manage."

"But the turkey," moans Allison. "It's a 22-pounder. We'll never get around to eating all of that if we don't have it today!"

"Well, look, it's early. If we put it in the oven now..."

"What about the giblets?"

Bill is looking pretty fucking nervous—guess he's worried his giblets will be on the menu if this doesn't work out.

"Do you know if they were wrapped in paper or plastic?"

"Paper. I always buy organic."

Rachel is calm, as always. Well, unless I've had my hands on her, in which case, all bets are off.

"When the turkey is cooked enough, we'll use tongs to get them out," she says, squeezing Allison's talons, um, hands.

I back out of the kitchen and Bill follows me. When talk turns to giblets, it's time for a man to be invisible.

I take a quick shower, and for a second I think about not shaving. But Rachel isn't into stubble because her skin gets burned really easily and she says it's like having a neon sign advertising what we've been up to. Ah, what the hell, I'll shave before bed tonight.

I pull my jeans back on and a sweater. Rachel hasn't returned, so I assume Camp David is still going on in the kitchen.

Allison's discordant tones echo through the house. As I pass Celia's room, she sticks her head out of the door and I nearly have a heart attack. She's not wearing her wig and she hasn't got her teeth in. And the appalling thought crosses my mind, *Bet she gives one helluva blow job.*

Fuck! I've been working for Anderson too long: my mind has been twisted. I've got to get another freakin' job.

With the image replaying like a horror-movie in my mind, I practically run into the kitchen.

Rachel gives me a strange look. I must look pretty fucking freaked.

"Justin, we have a problem—with the turkey."

"Yeah, heard the war-cry, baby."

Rachel hides a smile as Allison throws me a look that could freeze underwear.

"A different problem, Justin. The turkey is too big for the oven."

Bill looks like he wishes he could be beamed aboard an alien spaceship where anal probes are used randomly.

"You could chop its legs off, baby."

"Excuse me?"

I turn to Bill.

"You got an axe? Good for chopping wood?"

"Why, yes, I do, Justin. What are you going to do?"

"I'm going to chop its legs off, Bill. Wanna help?"

"Don't make me laugh!" snarls Allison. "Bill with an axe? He needs both his left feet!"

Jeez, with a wife like that, I'm surprised Bill hasn't committed homicide or suicide. Maybe he can't choose.

I throw a look at Rachel who shrugs and glances sympathetically at Bill.

I pick up the turkey, which is looking kinda sorry for itself, and carry it into the backyard. Bill follows, mumbling wearily.

He shows me the axe next to a pile of logs by the porch and I pick it up. The blade is a little blunt but it should do the job.

I swing the axe at one of the logs and it makes a satisfying thud as the blade bites into the wood. The sound makes Bill jump.

"Thought it might be an idea to get some of the rust off it first, Bill."

"Oh, right. Yes. Whatever you say, Justin."

After a few blows, I decide to take on the turkey.

I look at the turkey, where the head would have been: the headless turkey looks at me.

You lookin' at me? Hey, turkey! You lookin' at me? Then who the hell else are you lookin' at? You lookin' at me? Well I'm the only one here. Who the fuck do you think you're lookin' at? Oh yeah? Eat this, turkey-head!

And I aim the axe at its right leg. The axe catches at an angle and slides off.

"Fuck!"

"Still got all your toes, Justin?" asks Bill, quietly.

Fucker!

I wrestle the turkey back into position and show it who's boss. This time the axe lands in the middle of its chest and there's an odd splintering sound.

I hit it again, and its left leg is partially severed. I hit it again and again and again.

THWACK! BIFF! KER-CHANG! BOING! PING! KER-POW! THUD!

That fucking turkey is fucking laughing at me! You'll be laughing on the other side of your giblets, mother-fucker!

I can feel the sweat starting to run down my back as I axe that bird into the next life. It's one helluva Thanksgiving turkey massacre.

Finally, I get the legs off and Bill carries them into the kitchen like trophies from a war.

There are chunks of frozen turkey spewed across the garden like some macabre splatter gun.

I drag the battered carcass inside, feeling a sense of achievement as well as pity for a vanquished foe.

The turkey fought well, but I am The Victor. *Eat that, turkey-brains.*

Rachel looks appalled at the mangled meat and Allison swallows like she's about to vomit. Or cry. Or both.

"Got the legs off, baby."

"So I see, Justin."

I shrug and wander off to the den. Kimmi's watching 'Chicken Run':

"So laying eggs all your life and then getting plucked, stuffed and roasted is good enough for you, is it?"

"It's a livin'."

I can relate to that. Kinda reminds me of working for Anderson.

"Hey, Justin."

"Hey, Kimmi. Happy Thanksgiving."

"Thanks." She pauses. "Everyone's shouting."

"I noticed."

"Is the turkey dead?"

"It was frozen, Kimmi."

"So it's dead?"

"Yeah, very dead."

"Did you shoot it?"

"Excuse me?"

"Mom says you carry a gun. That's pretty cool."

"No, I didn't shoot the turkey."

"So, how did you kill it?"

"Well, it was already stone cold dead, but I hit it with an axe."

"Cool."

"Frozen."

"You're funny."

"I know."

Celia shuffles into the room.

"Happy Thanksgiving, Granny!"

"You, too, Kimmi-kins!"

"Justin killed the turkey with an axe."

"Really?"

She turns to stare at me.

Shoulda seen it, lady: poultry in motion.

"Yeah, must have lost my head." *And then kissed my ass goodbye.*

Bill comes in to rescue me.

"So, Justin, how about seeing my play room?"

I can't help wincing. Must be Freudian.

"Sure, Bill."

I spend the rest of Thanksgiving morning sitting in Bill's garage as we freeze our asses off while drinking Tequila Gold and inspecting his models. I just wish the submarines didn't remind me of Anderson's set of anal plugs. There are some images a man can live without.

The doorbell rings and Bill staggers off to answer it. I take another quick hit of tequila and head to the Russian front where Rachel is doing her best to bully Allison's cooking into something edible. But nobody ever won on the Russian front. They say Napoleon's army ate their own officers on the retreat. Probably weren't as chewy as Allison's turkey-giblet burgers.

Rachel uses a long roasting fork to poke the turkey in the oven, and I feel a certain sympathy for the poor, tortured beast. Hasn't it suffered enough?

"Hey, baby. Need a hand?"

"You've been drinking!" she scolds.

Fuck, I love it when she tells me off. Makes me horny.

"Seemed like a good idea at the time, baby. I was in Bill's *play room.*"

"I'm so sorry, Justin," she whispers. "This isn't how I imagined spending Thanksgiving."

"I've known worse, baby. And I got to wake up with you."

She runs her hand down my cheek and kisses me gently.

I start to give her kiss the attention it deserves, when Queen Cock-blocker sails into the kitchen.

"For goodness sake, you two! There's a time and a place for that sort of thing!"

"An empty kitchen seemed like the perfect place to me," replies Rachel, coolly.

I shove my hands in my pockets and leave the room whistling the chorus to my new favorite song:

"Me and Mrs. Jones

We got a thing goin' on..."

Bill introduces me to the neighbors, Douglas and Virginia, as "Rachel's partner".

And it makes me think. 'Partner'? Is that what I want from Rachel? No, she's much more than that to me. A few months ago I would have had a different reaction: *get married again? Woah! Halloween is over!* I promised myself I'd never go there, not after Carla ripped my guts out and wore them for garter straps. But Rachel's not like that and she's sure not like her sister.

So, 'partner'? No. I want more. Me and Mrs. Smith are going to have a conversation about that.

But not today.

We all take our places at the dining table and the sacrificial beast is wheeled in. *Jeez, it looks so ... flat*. Kinda deflated and humiliated.

And the image of hacking its legs off, chunk by icy chunk, surges to my mind. My stomach lurches in sympathy.

"Turkey, Justin?" asks Allison, looking for all the world as if she'd like to do something violently unpleasant with my giblets. *Maybe I should introduce her to Anderson.*

"No, thanks, Allison. I'm vegetarian."

Rachel looks at me, and I shrug.

Chapter Seventeen

TRAINER VERSUS TRAINER

Landon creeps me out. I may have mentioned that before.

The more I see of him, the more I don't like him. He's always watching: watching the boss, watching me, just *watching*. Whenever I turn a corner, there he is, all glassy-eyed like some pornographic Stepford-bot.

I caught him in the CCTV room one of the first weekends he was here, and I wasn't fucking happy about it. When I questioned him, he sneeringly said that thinking was beyond my pay grade and that he was looking for the boss. I didn't believe him then and I don't trust him now.

The boss doesn't care. He seems to think that Landon is trustworthy, part of the inner circle. But I'm not so sure. I think he's one accordion short of a polka band.

To the point where I had to initiate a conversation with the boss.

And it went something like this:

Me: Sir. [*Pin your ears back, dickwad.*]
Anderson: What is it, Trainer?

Me: I have some concerns about Mr. Landon. [*He ain't got all his dogs barking.*]

Anderson: Such as?

Me: I found him in my off— the CCTV room without authorization. [*Creepoid factor infinity.*]

Anderson: I've given him authorization to go anywhere except my bedroom or office.

Me: Does that include the staff wing, sir? [*You bastard.*]

Anderson: No. Has he been in there?

Me: Not that I'm aware of. [*Probably.*]

Anderson: Then what's the problem?

Me: As your head of security, I must insist that the CCTV room is off limits to everyone—including all of your guests. [*So shove that up your ass, asshole.*]

Anderson: You insist?

Me: Yes, sir. [*Raising your eyebrows and flaring your nostrils means jack-shit.*]

Anderson: Fine, I'll tell him.

Me: I want to install fingerprint locks on the CCTV room and your office, sir. [*And it should have been done before you let him in, asswad.*]

Anderson: No. This is my home. I'm not having locks on the inside.

Me: Your *guest* has access to areas that contain sensitive information. When we're not here, I can't stop him looking at...

Anderson: He won't.

Me: [*Hobble the bastard.*]

Anderson: Besides, Freddi— Mr. Landon is a family friend. As for the Senator, you can trust him implicitly.

Me: [*You fucking idiot.*] We'll have to agree to disagree. Sir.

Anderson: Noted.

I haven't seen Landon in my office since, but I make sure that I keep all my files locked away and I've changed the passwords on my desktop, laptop, phone and personal wall safe. I insisted that Anderson do the same.

Why hire fucking security if you're going to leave your life wide open to some Scary Mary? And trust Landon over my instincts?

There is something seriously fucked up here, and I think I might set up a little covert op of my own.

What a fucked up way to live.

So I bug the landline that guests use, and then suggest to Mason that it would be totally illegal to also record Landon's calls on his cell phone. Very illegal. Completely illegal. So he shouldn't do it. At all. So far: zilch. But I can feel it in my gut—he's up to something. I can be patient.

Rachel

I've had another lovely weekend at Allison's. I made gingerbread with the girls, and Allison and I went Christmas shopping. It was good to get away from everything and just have some girl time. But I've missed Justin. More than I should. I'm falling too fast and it's not safe. Caring about someone ... loving someone ... it's dangerous.

Over the last few months, coming back to Wolf Point feels like coming home. After Brian died, I couldn't bear to keep the house, so Allison and Bill took me into their home. I've been there ever since in between jobs, but now everything has changed and...

"Good evening, Mrs. Smith. How nice to see you again. Baked any cookies lately?"

My spine stiffens as Frederick Landon's sly voice hisses in my ear. I didn't hear him walking up behind me. I've only just locked my car in the underground garage—I certainly didn't expect to see *him* this evening.

Justin will be mad at me: he's always telling me that I should be more aware of my surroundings.

I meet Mr. Landon's icy gaze and ignore the implied insult. I won't let him know how much he bothers me.

"Good evening, Mr. Landon."

We stand in chilly silence as the elevator seems to take forever.

"You don't know what you're missing out on," he says suddenly.

"Excuse me?"

"Devon. You should give that stallion a ride sometime. Or maybe you prefer fucking the hired help."

He laughs softly as my mouth drops open.

The elevator doors close, and I'm left with a very uneasy feeling.

If I tell Justin, he'll be furious and do something that could get him fired. So I say nothing.

Trainer

I fucking hate Christmas. It reminds me of everything I've lost: a family, a home, my daughter.

I've had to fight like hell to be able to see Lilly for even one afternoon over the holidays. The ex- blocks me every step of the way: it's never *convenient*. Yes, I got some visitation rights in the divorce decree, but the nature of my work makes it very hard to stick to a schedule, and Carla knows that. Her lawyer used my service history against me, making me look like some crazed monster who could snap at any moment, even bringing up medical records where the Corps doctor mentioned PTSD. How the fuck he got access to those, I'll never know. But it all weighed against me during mediation.

I'm pacing up and down the living room, my cell phone clamped in my hand, trying to resist the impulse to hurl it against the wall. I can see Lilly on December 23 for three hours, and that's the last and final offer.

I've never seen my daughter at Christmas, never sat with her to watch snow fall on Christmas Eve while we look for reindeer in the sky, never been there to see her wake up, never seen that magical moment when she realizes that Santa has visited in the night.

Carla has all the power, and she loves to use it.

"Justin! Justin, sit down, darling, please."

Rachel's voice breaks into my furious thoughts.

"Wearing a hole in the carpet won't help. Come and sit with me."

She reaches up to me, holding out her hand. And I want to go to her, but I can't taint something so fucking perfect with all the rage that I have inside. I won't do that to her.

Instead, I turn on my heel.

"I'm going to the gym."

As I leave the room, I see the hurt on her face. It's the opposite of what I want, but I'm too wired to explain. I wouldn't find the words.

I throw on old sweats and running shoes, then take the stairs because waiting for the elevator takes too damn long.

I jump onto the treadmill, pounding out every frustration, every furious thought, every bitter word that I want to spit out. I set a fast pace and soon sweat is pouring from my body. I keep going, keep running, trying to find some peace or ... I don't know ... make some sense of the shitty hand life has dealt me.

Then Rachel's face floats in front of my eyes and I wonder how long I can keep her. She's come to mean a lot to me, more than I could have hoped for. And that thought alone gives me the clarity I need.

I have savings now. Anderson pays me well and housing is covered. I can afford to take Lilly's mom back to Court. It's time.

I dial back the speed of my run, surprised to find that I've been damn near sprinting for the best part of an hour. I'm going to feel it tomorrow. I slow to a walk, coming back to my surroundings.

I'd really zoned out on that run in a way I never do when I'm outside, because then I'm constantly scanning passing cars, other pedestrians, the skyline, behind me, using windows and shiny objects to amplify peripheral vision.

So the treadmill is a quiet place. The only other thing that shuts off my brain is being balls deep inside Rachel.

I glance over and I'm surprised as hell to see Anderson by the weights, lifting some serious poundage. How long has he been here? I get my thoughts in order, put on my game face and stroll over to spot him. He doesn't acknowledge me, but he's aware I'm there.

After another few lifts, he sits up and runs a towel over his face. Then he reaches into the pocket of his sweatpants and passes me a business card.

"My lawyer. Call her."

I frown, wondering what the hell this is about.

"Sir?"

"See your daughter at Christmas, Trainer." He pauses, looking away. "Family is important."

He stands up and exits the room, leaving me stunned and speechless.

I run my finger over the thick paper and fancy embossed print. Any lawyer Anderson uses won't be one I can afford. But he's right. I can't take this on without professional help.

Deciding that the least I can do is get a referral for a good family lawyer, I make the call to Anderson's tame shark.

"My name is Justin Trainer and I..."

The woman answering the phone interrupts me.

"Ms. Addams is expecting your call."

"Excuse me?"

She pauses, talking slowly as if English might not be my first language.

"Mr. Anderson's assistant emailed to say that you'd be calling. May I put you through?"

"Yeah, thanks."

A moment later, the line clicks and I hear another woman's voice—this one with the nasal tones of a New Jersey native.

"Mr. Trainer, I'm Moira Addams and I'll be your lead attorney when we take your wife back to court. My assistant will liaise with Mr. Anderson's P.A. to schedule an initial meeting. I can assure you that you'll be seeing your daughter on Christmas Eve. Any questions?"

My jaw is dangling and I wonder if I've slipped into an alternate reality. Then reason catches up with me.

"Ms. Addams, I was calling to ask for the name of attorney that I can afford. No offence, but if Ander— Mr. Anderson retains your services, you're out of my price bracket."

There's an impatient huffing at the other end.

"Mr. Anderson has asked that all bills pertaining to my services be settled directly by him. I thought this was understood? My office will be in touch."

She hangs up, and I'm left irritated and grateful at a ratio of about 50:50. I don't like it. I don't want to be in Anderson's debt again, but I *do* want to see my daughter on Christmas Eve. This woman says she'll make it happen. Guess I'll suck it up ... and then figure out a way to pay the bastard back.

I head to the elevator, and stand dripping with sweat and stinking like a dead skunk, wondering what the hell just happened. I wish the boss would stop being so goddamn nice—it's freaking me the fuck out.

Rachel's standing in the staff kitchen when I walk in. I know that the smart thing to do would be to apologize, but there's something raw and painful inside me. Why didn't I meet her first? Why isn't this amazing woman the mother of my child?

She turns around and the expression on her face slays me.

"I'm sorry."

My voice cracks on the words.

She doesn't hesitate and she doesn't make me say it again. She walks toward me and wraps me in her arms.

"I know," she whispers.

I kiss her hard, claiming her, because I'm a little lost right now, and the words won't come, so I tell her with my body.

We make it as far as the shower when I pull her into the steam with me and fuck the anger out of my body, filling it with the calm she gives me.

Hearing her call my name when she comes soothes me in ways I don't understand. I just know that I don't want it to stop.

Sated and wrapped in thick bath towels, I carry her into the bedroom and take her again, warming us both in an old fashioned way.

Breathless and flushed, she sprawls across my chest as I stroke the silk of her hair, feeling like the world is a better place because of this woman.

"Justin..."

I hear the hesitancy in her voice, and my hand stills on the back of her head.

"Yeah?"

She lifts her eyes to mine, holding my gaze as her lips tremble.

"I know this is terrible timing..."

"Whatever it is, just say it." *Just don't say it's over.*

She takes a deep breath.

"Why me, Justin? Is it because I'm ... convenient?"

Hot, red anger flares through me, colored with darker shades of sadness.

"What the fuck have I done that would make you think that?" I ask roughly.

Her eyes are glossy with tears.

"Because you're amazing and gorgeous and loyal and only thirty-three. And I'm ordinary and boring and forty-one. My thighs high five each other when I walk."

I'm having a hard time understanding the turn in conversation; I was expecting her to kick me to the curb, but she's telling me that she's insecure? This wonderful, caring woman thinks she's just *convenient?* But even though I'm just a dumb grunt, I know that now isn't the time to be angry with her.

"Rachel, no, baby! I had a hard-on for you the first time I met you. You're a goddess in the bedroom and a demon in the kitchen. Could be the other way around." I take a deep breath. "But I ... um ... you know, the love thing ... because you're so fucking sweet, you're kind, you're so smart, and you have a way of seeing the good in people."

Her smile looks tortured.

"The 'love thing'?"

"Ah, sheesh, don't make me say it!"

Slowly the pain recedes from her face and her sweet pink lips curve into a small smile.

"Maybe I need to hear it, Justin."

I suck in a lungful of sex-scented air. *Time to grow a pair of big, round, hairy cojones.*

"Fine. I fucking love you."

Her lips quiver, torn between tears and smiling. I'm relieved when she chooses to smile.

"Eloquent as ever. I love you, too, by the way."

I pull her into my arms, holding her close.

"Rachel, I don't have smooth moves. I can't sweet talk you. I don't do that shit. But I'd take a bullet for you, baby. Every fuckin' day of my life, I'd take a bullet for you. So don't ever doubt what you mean to me. And don't ask me to say it again."

Her reply is a whisper.

"Thank you, Justin. I won't."

Moira Addams, Attorney at Law, is one scary beast from the Black Lagoon. Her eyes are colder than a Polar Bear's dick, and she's got a handshake like a Russian Spetsnaz sergeant. I'm happy she's on my side.

Her offices are a block from DMA Tower, and her conference room projects a picture of authority. It's also stripped down; nothing sweet or feminine here. The furniture is industrial and uncomfortable. I can't help thinking she'd be right at home in Anderson's meditation room. Except she's not his type, and definitely not into dudes.

She's thin and angular; nothing soft about Ms. Addams. I'm not surprised that her nickname is Morticia.

She's also a bigger shark than Carla's hotshot lawyer, making him squirm like a tadpole, and that's just over the phone. I can't wait for them to meet in person. I think she might actually bring thumbscrews. I'm betting odds she has a dungeon in her office basement. It's where she puts the clients who don't pay on time. I can't help shuddering, relieved that she's on Anderson's payroll; especially when I find out that she bills at $1200 an hour.

Kids, if you're reading this, stay in school and be a pointy-toothed lawyer.

And if you *are* a kid reading this, you're so fucking grounded.

The interview goes like this:

Morticia: Well, Mr. Trainer. I have spoken to your ex-wife's lawyer, Frank Fordham. Frankly, she should have come to me.

Dumb Grunt: Um... [*Thank Christ she's on my side. I think.*]

Morticia: We'll cut him off at the knees. [*And I mean that literally.*]

Dumb Grunt: Ah... [*I bet you use a dry cleaning service to get the blood stains out of your suits.*]

Morticia: I've filed the paperwork to modify the custody order, and I'm confident the judge will rule in our favor. [*Or I'll make her life a living hell.*]

Dumb Grunt: That sounds...

Morticia: I'll send Anderson my bill.

Dumb Grunt: Thank y—

Morticia: And next time tie a knot in it so you don't knock up a woman who hates your guts.

Dumb Grunt:...

Morticia:Merry Christmas.

I can see why she and Anderson get along.

Rachel is waiting for me at home.

"How did your meeting with the lawyer go?"

"Pretty good, I think. She's going to get it fast-tracked—I didn't ask how—and she says I'll be seeing Lilly on Christmas Eve."

Rachel's face softens and I can see the tension drain away. *She was worried for me.* My whole body warms with that thought. I haven't had anyone care about me like that in a long, long time.

She rests her head against my chest and I hold her. For once, it's not sexual. I'll always want her, but the peace in this moment is something that I crave. Usually, I try not to be inside my head too much because I don't like the thoughts and memories rattling around in there, but right now, I can imagine a lifetime of holding this woman in my arms. That should worry me, but it doesn't.

Eventually, she loosens her arms, kissing my cheek as she slides away from me.

"Dinner in twenty minutes."

I watch her moving around the kitchen, calm and competent. I like watching her, and I don't mean that in a creepy way. I just like the way she moves, the way she seems to be doing three things at once, but nothing is rushed.

Feeling better for being home, I loosen my tie, kick off my shoes and put my feet up on the coffee table. I should go shower, but you know what? I can't be bothered.

I'm checking emails on my phone and watching the game on TV when Rachel returns from serving Anderson dinner. Other than cleaning up after him later, which never takes her long, we're pretty much off the clock now. I look forward to these quiet moments.

"Since the Bears are playing, I thought you'd enjoy a TV dinner," she smiles.

"That sounds great, babe. Wait, you know that the Bears are playing?"

She laughs, shaking her head at me.

"I didn't think it was a secret."

"No, but ... I'm just surprised. I didn't know you liked football."

"I don't mind it. When Allison and I were little, we used to watch it with our dad. We'd pile onto the sofa with milk and cookies and he'd explain all the plays to us. He probably wished he had boys, so he was making the best of it. He loved having Bill and Brian over to watch with—finally got the sons he wanted."

It sounds like the Waltons to me. I don't have any memories like that.

"Dad would have loved you, too," she says softly.

"Yeah?"

Neither of Carla's parents liked me much. They wanted a college-educated guy for her. I can't blame them. I want that for Lilly—not for a couple of decades—but a guy who has a nice, safe office job. A guy who'll come home every night and have clean fingernails. More than I ever gave her mom.

Rachel frowns, watching me carefully, then walks across and leans down to kiss me.

"I mean it, Justin. Dad would have adored you. Almost as much I do."

She slips away as I try to make the kiss deeper.

"Dinner's ready."

She returns from the kitchen with two lap trays of ... purple food?

"Moussaka," she laughs as I poke at the eggplant with my fork. "I'm working on a new recipe. Just try it."

It's good. Of course it's good.

"Not bad," I say, grinning at her so she knows I'm not serious.

She doesn't rise to the bait, just smiles at me and I smile back.

I kinda like smiling these days. Who knew?

After a few minutes of watching the game, Rachel crinkles her eyes.

"Those aren't the Bears playing."

"You only just noticed?"

She huffs softly.

"So who are we watching?"

"Vandals versus Fighting Illini."

"Oh, College football? I know the Illini, but who are the others?"

"University of Idaho."

"Because you're from there?"

I feel a tug in my belly. I don't like talking about where I grew up. It wasn't much of a home.

"Yeah," I reply shortly, but because I see the disappointment on Rachel's face, I keep talking. "Bonners Ferry. Real small town, only thirty miles from Canada." The school mascot was a badger. Don't know why I was reminded of that. "Most of the kids either went into the services or lumber. No way I was going into lumber like my old man."

There's a short silence.

"You've never mentioned your father before."

I push my plate away, appetite gone. That happens on the rare occasions I think about the asshole, or the rarer times I talk about him.

"He wasn't a good father, definitely not a good husband. The only good thing about him was that he used to be away a lot. He headed up crews who went deep into the forests for logging: bigger, older trees. It was better when he was away. One day he went away and never came back. Heard he was shacked up with a waitress from the next town over."

"And ... and your mom?"

I shrug, wishing I'd never started this.

"We're not in touch."

Rachel has stopped eating, too. She's staring at me like I'm a broken toy. I don't like it. I don't like that feeling. I became a Marine so I wouldn't have to feel like that anymore.

There were a lot of guys like me in the Marines—men and women looking to trade up on the families they'd been given. It's no surprise that there are more foster kids in the armed forces than in any other profession.

Rachel is still watching me with a worried expression.

"When was the last time you talked to your mom?"

I run my hands over my hair and take a deep breath, pushing away my growing irritation. I'm not annoyed with Rachel but with myself. After all this time, after everything I've achieved, it still gets to me.

"I asked her to fly over for Lilly's Christening. She said she didn't have the money, so I sent her a check for the airfare. She cashed the check but never showed and I never heard from her again. I'm done making excuses for her."

I don't remember my mom ever coming to any of my football games, and she never came to a parent-teacher meeting. As long as I attended school and wasn't getting a failing grade, she fed me, put clothes on my back and she never hit me, but she never showed much interest in me either. It's hard to admit that. Makes me feel weak and worthless.

Rachel takes my tray from my lap, wrapping her arms around my neck and leaning into me.

"You're a wonderful man, Justin. Hard working, loyal, a loving father. It's her loss."

I want to believe her so badly.

Chapter Eighteen

MY GIRL 2

"You asshole!"

Oh, hark! The sweetly lilting tones of the ex-wife.

"Nice to hear from you, Carla."

"You absolute fucking asshole!"

"Merry Christmas."

"Fuck you, you fucking asshole!"

"You lose points for repetition."

I know exactly why she's calling and I'm going to enjoy every second of this.

I can hear her breathing hard, and mentally I'm imagining smoke coming out of her nostrils and fire out of her ass. Sometimes it's really hard to remember that we ever loved each other enough to create a baby, a little girl as special as Lilly.

And she's the only reason I'm hanging onto the frayed threads of my temper when I take the call at work one evening.

"Do you really want to screw up Christmas for Lilly? Are you that much of an..."

"Asshole?

"Aaaaaagh!"

She screams so loudly, I have to hold the phone a foot away

from my ear. She's set off the fucking tinnitus again, and that pisses me off.

Most guys and gals who've served in the military get fucked up hearing. Being around weapons discharging and explosions will do that to you. Half the artillery guys you'll meet are stone deaf. Robin Williams totally nailed that scene in *Good Morning, Vietnam*.

When the yelling dies down, I wonder whether to hang up or see if Armageddon has been averted. If not, *Arm-a-geddin-out-of-here*.

"Justin..."

"Wow, you remembered my name."

"Don't be an even bigger asshole than you already are."

"Did you call just to yell at me, because I thought it might be fun to go try and cure my constipation instead. Seems like it's already working though."

"You're vile!"

"Bye, Carla."

"Justin, wait!"

"You have ten seconds before I hang up."

"You're screwing up Lilly's Christmas."

I clench my jaw and spit out words between gritted teeth.

"I just want to see my daughter."

"We've already made plans and if you go ahead with this bullshit visitation order, you'll be responsible for ruining your daughter's Christmas."

"I repeat: I just want to see my daughter on Christmas Eve. You get her for the rest of the holidays."

"I already told you! We've made plans!"

"Jesus, Carla! She's six years old! She doesn't make plans."

"No, I mean we already..."

Her words trail off as she realizes that she's made a mistake.

"So who have you made plans with, Carla?"

"My mother," she snaps back.

She's lying. I know she's lying. She's seeing some limp-wristed asswipe and has made plans with him that involve Lilly.

No.

Fucking.

Way.

"I'll be at the house at 9:30AM. Don't make me come looking for you, Carla."

"Is that a threat?"

"It's a fucking promise."

"Congratulations on ruining your daughter's Christmas, Justin."

She hangs up.

Talking with my ex-wife is less fun than an enema with much the same result. Shit happens.

When I wake up on Christmas Eve, Rachel is in my arms, her soft golden hair spread across my chest, and one hand cradled over my hip. I'm hard, but I try to ignore it, instead enjoying the peaceful puffs of her quiet breaths washing over my skin.

It's pretty fuckin' perfect, until I glance at my watch and see that it's time to let the Chief Head Case off the leash.

With extreme reluctance, I slide out of bed and tug on sweats and sneakers. And my Smith & Wesson. I don't take a shit without that.

That sounded bad. Maybe I should say I don't leave home without my weapon. Either of 'em.

Anderson arrives at the penthouse lobby the same time I do and we nod at each other.

"Sir."

"Trainer."

And that's all the communication until we arrive back forty-five minutes later, sweating like hogs on a Texas ranch.

I shower quickly while Rachel works in the kitchen, preparing food for the beast from 20,000 fathoms. After that, she's heading out for some last minute shopping, then driving over to her sister's later. I was invited but I figured they'd already put up with me for

Thanksgiving and I didn't want to wear out my welcome, especially since Allison still thinks I'm vegetarian.

I pull on jeans and a long-sleeved gray tee, then strap on the Smith & Wesson again. Carla hates me wearing a gun around Lilly. It's not my favorite thing to do either, but the time you need a weapon and don't have it, is the time you're severely fucked and don't even get a thank you in the morning.

"I don't often see you in jeans, Justin."

"Missing the suit?"

"Not necessarily. You look very handsome in either."

"You know it, babe."

"A little humility, Justin?"

"Nope, life is too short. Now give me those gorgeous lips."

She shakes her head, backing away from me.

"I just fixed my makeup and now I have to serve Mr. Anderson's breakfast. Behave yourself!"

"Where's the fun in that?" I call after her.

I'm only half-teasing, but she's too professional to let me get away with that crap.

A few minutes later, I'm saying goodbye to her. It's only for two days, but I hate it all the same. I'm aware it's pussy behavior, but when you meet someone who treats you well and makes you feel like you're a decent human being after all, when just being in the same room as them makes the fucking sun shine, you don't want to let them out of your sight. Even more so at Christmas.

But I'm not going to be a possessive asshole with Rachel. I want her to be happy more than I want it for myself. Wow, I must be growing as a person.

Good to know.

"I'll miss you, Justin."

"Your sister won't."

"Oh, I don't know. I seem to remember she rather liked looking at you, especially your cute little tush."

I cringe.

"Babe, please! 'Cute' and 'tush' are not words that belong in a sentence about me. And jeez, Allison? Really?"

I do *not* need that image in my head.

She laughs, then makes the world a better place by kissing me on the mouth, her lips warm and sweet-tasting against mine.

"I've left your present under the tree."

Yeah, we have a Christmas tree in the staff quarters. I came home one evening and found this gimpy little three-foot high silver tinsel tree, all decorated with lights and ornaments.

I saw a small square box under the tree this morning and the tag had my name on it. Rachel caught me shaking it, so I couldn't continue my investigation, but I think I can guess.

I don't say anything about her gift because I tucked it in her purse when she wasn't looking. Stealthy. I know she's angling to find out if I got her something. I did. When Anderson was shopping for his sister, I saw a sapphire pendant that matches the color of Rachel's eyes. It has tiny diamonds around it in a halo and was set in white gold. Cost me $800 bucks. It's a lot of money, and I don't doubt for a second that Rachel is worth it, putting up with my grouchy ass.

Anderson saw me buy it but didn't say a word. I like that in a client. Because some of the assholes I've worked for would have a problem with the hired help shopping in the same store. Not exclusive enough for them. Some rich bastards have the stores come to them.

Rachel sighs and rests her head against my chest, and there's nowhere else in the world I'd rather be.

"Enjoy your day with Lilly."

"I intend to."

"Have you decided where you're taking her yet?"

"Got a few things planned."

"Of course you do. The man with the plan."

"Not always. You weren't planned and neither was Lilly, but you're the two best things I've ever done."

She blushes and gives me a sweet smile.

"You are so getting thanked for that when I get back," she whispers.

Yeah, I still got game.

In the underground garage, I reluctantly help my woman into her compact, then take the Rover and follow her out into the city traffic.

A quick wave, and she's gone.

When I park in the driveway of Carla's house, Lilly comes racing out of the door, climbing me like a jungle gym.

"Daddy! Daddy! This is the best Christmas present *ev-er!*"

I hug her tightly, breathing in her special little girl scent that is part sugar, part spice and all Lilly.

"You're my best present ever, too," I say, letting her down gently and tickling her to make her giggle.

She pats my cheek with her hand.

"No prickles, Daddy?"

"Not today, Buttercup."

I glance up and see Carla watching us, her expression frozen between disapproval of me and love for Lilly.

I know she loves our daughter.

I also know that she loathes me.

"Carla."

"Justin."

"Merry Christmas."

"Have Lilly home by 6PM."

"Seven. That's what we agreed."

"It's past her bedtime."

Lilly breaks into the Axis talks.

"Pleeeeease, Mommy! Pleeeease!"

Carla's lips twitch.

"Six-thirty."

I nod, but I'm planning on being late. I'm not missing out on a single second of Lilly-time.

I strap her into the booster-seat and head back to the city. I'm kind of regretting letting Lilly choose the music we listen to, but at least now I know all the lyrics to every song from *Frozen*. That could come in handy if I ever need to torture someone for information.

First stop is the Botanical Garden Holiday Train Show. Kids are screaming with excitement, and the noise knifes through my skull like an ice pick. I look as tortured as every other adult here, and even Santa has a glazed look on his face, but at least he's planned ahead and is wearing earplugs. Lilly loves it and that's all that matters.

Next stop is Macy's, and Lilly's eyes widen. The windows are decked out as a snow scene with reindeer snoozing in a stable, and one with a red nose is munching on hay. The animatronics are amazing, but the awe on Lilly's face is even better.

She turns to me, cupping her hands as she whispers.

"Daddy! It's Santa's reindeer."

"I know, Princess."

"They're sleeping."

"Yep, so you have to be real quiet."

"I wrote a really long Christmas list," she whispers back, cupping her hand over her mouth again, eyeing the reindeer.

I already know that. Her mom showed it to me, expecting me to fork out for everything. I got most of the shit on the list. Thank God for online shopping.

"They have to deliver all my presents, and presents for other children, don't they?"

Lilly puts her tiny fists on her hips, looking a scary amount like her mother.

"They shouldn't be sleeping! Those naughty reindeers should be at work!"

I can't help laughing.

"It's okay, Buttercup. They're magic reindeer. They got time to sleep, chow down, then they'll be going to work."

She doesn't look convinced.

We go inside the store and she soon forgets about the naughty reindeer. I spend an indecent amount of money on everything that she wants. I know it's the typical behavior of every absent parent, but I can't find it in me to care, not when it makes my daughter smile like this.

Last stop of the day is the ice rink at Bryant Park winter village. I'm exhausted. We've done a ton of stuff on a really busy holiday, but Princess Lilly is still going strong.

I breathe out slowly, enjoying the cool crisp air and the feeling of space after the crazy busy stores. I love this place, plus it's got one of the best views of downtown at night. The Christmas lights are something else.

Lilly is excited because she's never been skating. Something else for me to feel guilty about. Life of a parent, I guess.

The assistant has to help me strap on those tiny little ice skates. It makes me sad, because none of the mothers around me are having any trouble stuffing tiny feet into skates. I just haven't had any practice.

Finally, we're ready to head onto the ice.

I skated a lot growing up. There are a ton of ponds and lakes that used to ice over every winter and we all had skates.

At first, Lilly looks like that Disney rabbit Thumper, chubby little legs going every which way, refusing to let go of my hand. But soon she gets the hang of standing up and I pull her around the rink, going faster and faster until she shrieks with excitement.

I'm with my daughter on Christmas Eve and it's fuckin' amazing. It's as special as I'd ever dreamed, and when snow starts to drift down, my heart hurts, but in a good way, as I watch Lilly try to catch the snowflakes, smiling when they land on her long lashes or in her hair.

Her cheeks are pink from the cold and her eyes are sparkling with happiness. It's the best damn feeling. I want to show her the world and protect her from it, or die trying.

But when I'm outside, I never entirely shut off and I'm aware of my surroundings. I'm keeping an eye on the crowd around the rink as well as the other skaters. So that's why I notice her.

Rachel stares at me in surprise, then smiles hugely and gives a small wave. She's holding a cup of coffee, surrounded by shopping bags.

I hadn't planned this, but I'm not going to let the opportunity pass either. I want her to meet Lilly. I know it's early in our relationship and all that shit, but when something is right, you gotta go with it.

"Hey, Princess, do you want to come and meet my friend? She's sitting right over there."

Lilly looks uncertain, staring up at me with big brown eyes.

"Okay, I guess. Which one is she?"

"The pretty lady with the red coat."

"Is she your girlfriend?"

Yeah, shoulda seen that question coming.

"Her name is Rachel."

We skate over and I pick up Lilly in my arms.

Rachel looks surprised and worried at the same time, which kills me, but she pastes on a smile.

"Hello, Justin! This must be the beautiful Princess Lilly. I've heard a lot about you, Your Highness."

Lilly giggles and pushes her face into my coat, peeking out at Rachel, then giggling again.

"Hey, Rachel! This is a nice surprise."

"Is it okay?" she asks in a low voice.

But then Lilly turns to look at her.

"Are you Daddy's girlfriend?"

Rachel's mouth drops open, unsure what to say.

"Yep, she sure is," I answer for her.

"Okay," says Lilly. "Can we have hot chocolate?"

"You can have anything you want, Buttercup."

Rachel offers to get in line for the drinks while I take Lilly so we can change back into our shoes. And no, it's not any easier trying to push her baby feet into snow boots than it was into ice skates.

The assistant gives me a pitying look before she steps in to help for a second time.

When we're ready, Rachel is standing with our drinks looking anxious again.

"I'd better get going," she says, glancing at Lilly.

"Stay and finish your drink, bab— Rachel."

For a moment we sit in silence, Lilly spooning cream and marshmallows into her mouth, smearing a milky-chocolatey mustache onto her face. I do the same and she giggles.

"You're so silly, Daddy!"

Then Rachel starts laughing, and it's the most amazing feeling. I try to think of the word. *Golden.* Yeah, that's it. Christmas Eve with my two best girls is golden.

Chapter Nineteen

FATAL ATTRACTION

It's a new year, but not much has changed at Wolf Point.

Carla isn't happy that Lilly met Rachel, but I pointed out that she'd been having boyfriends at the house since before we were divorced. That shut her up for all of three seconds, so I walked away, leaving her storming behind me and threatening all kinds of shit.

I shrug it off, knowing that my lawyer has bigger balls than hers.

Anderson is working eighteen hour days on some deal with a Japanese tech company. He's wound up tighter than a two dollar watch, especially when Pam finds a flaw in the contract. One of the lawyers is about to get his ass kicked. I'm sure somewhere in the Universe that's evening up the score.

Instead, we go to the Farm where there are some newbies to break in. I wonder about that. Does he have a waiting list, or is there some sort of website where they all get together and discuss their favorite kinks? Satisfaction guaranteed or your money back (free butt plug included).

Van Sant is obsequious, ass-kissing like his life depends on it, which it probably does. Landon is there, too, watching the action. The boss fucks a lot of different guys and a couple of women. I'm guessing that part since he left the room with them clothed and returned naked as a jaybird—but none of it seems to satisfy him. He doesn't sleep much either, haunting the Farm as much as he does Wolf Point when we're there.

Landon is everywhere Anderson is, jacking off to the boss's sex games. I never see Landon engage with anyone else—just the one time with the guy who looked like Anderson's younger twin brother.

Naturally, the boss is in a foul mood and taking it out on everyone at work. Not at Wolf Point, because I won't stand for that shit and I think he knows it. But I do take the opportunity to share my professional concerns with Rachel, who's doing her domestic goddess thing in the kitchen.

"He needs to get the crap beat out of him."

"Justin!"

She pretends to be shocked, but I just raise an eyebrow and kick back on a kitchen chair.

"Preferably by a guy who doesn't have a one-way ticket on the Disoriented Express."

"That's not nice, Justin."

I roll my eyes at Rachel, but I can't help smiling.

"His only friend is a creepy fucking psycho who doesn't have his boots laced all the way up."

She sighs, and I reach up to pull her onto my lap so I can nuzzle her neck.

"Justin! I'm trying to cook here! My hands are all floury!"

She laughs and swats my hands away.

"I like you floury. It's ... homey."

"Homey! Hmm, I'm not sure I like being 'homey'. And it's not what you said last night!"

"True. Last night you were hot, but right now you're *floury*, it's homey. I like it. And I still say the boss needs to get laid by a professional, not the S&M wannabes who come to the Farm."

It's true: they all think they're hardcore until the boss gets his whips out. Even that Republican Senator couldn't take it in the end.

Rachel shakes her head but I don't think she's disagreeing with me.

"I'm just saying, he'd be a much happier guy if he was well fucked."

Rachel pushes herself up, leaving white handprints on my shoulders.

"Well, I think you're wrong: sex by itself doesn't make people happy."

"Oh, I don't know. I'm sure there's a reason I'm such a happy guy."

"I'm serious! The *meditation* doesn't make him happy, does it? It's a distraction or a punishment—that's all. You said the same about the men he meets at the Farm."

"Maybe, but I don't think he's going to change, Rachel. I've known him for a while now and you've know him the best part of a year—it's just the same shit, different day."

Rachel frowns. She doesn't like me swearing. I try and keep it to a minimum when she's within earshot, but old habits die hard.

I did try to tell her once that some eggheads did a study proving people who refrain from swearing are more likely to be devious and dishonest. And if you don't believe me, enjoy a happy half-hour reading *Social Psychological and Personality Science*, January issue. Science fuckin' rocks!

I tried to give up swearing for a while just to prove I could.

Well, Rachel bet me fifty bucks and a blowjob that I couldn't go a day without swearing. I don't care about the fifty bucks.

Game on.

I managed most of the day. The morning.

Part of the morning.

Unfortunately, she overheard me having a telephone conversation with Dennis the Dickwad door security after he'd let paps get into the lobby of DMA Tower twice in one day.

"Listen, you fu— fungus! They'll say anything to get in. A woman wearing a skirt and high heels is not there to check the plumbing, you twatwaffle!"

And I slam the phone down to find Rachel glaring at me.

"That's a swearword, Justin."

"No, it's not."

"Yes, it is."

"No, it's not."

She takes a deep breath.

"Twatwaffle is a swearword, Justin."

God, I love it when she talks dirty.

"Can I say douchenozzle?"

"No."

"Dick?"

"No, no, no."

"Oh. Do I still get my blow job."

"Maybe."

Good times, but then I remember we're supposed to be having a conversation about the boss's subs and fuck buddies.

"He won't be happy until he changes," she sighs. "I wish he'd realize that."

"Maybe you should be his therapist. Is Dr. Smith on call?"

"Very funny, Justin, you should be a comedian. Oh ... I forgot, you are."

She swats me with a towel. I'm not taking that from any woman, so I pin her against the sink and give her a damn good kissing so she knows her place. But, as always, she's the one with the power and I'm helpless in her hands, my body pushing against her, wanting, needing her.

Eventually she pulls away from me.

"You are a bad influence, Justin Trainer!" she snorts, her rapid breathing matching mine.

"You know it! And while I'm influencing you, have you thought any more about my offer?"

There's a long pause, but she doesn't reply.

"Good God, woman! Are you rolling your eyes at me again?"

"Yes!"

"Is that 'yes' you're rolling your eyes, or 'yes' you've thought about my offer, or..." and I can hardly dare ask, "...or are you saying 'yes' you'll marry me?"

She sighs, and that tells me the answer is still 'no'.

I asked her on New Year's Eve. At first, she thought I wasn't serious. But I was then and I am now.

I did a lot of thinking over Christmas. I had a lot of time to myself. Anderson was with his family and drove himself, so I was at the house with one of Rachel's microwave meals, a bottle of craft beer, and a box of Reese's Pieces—my present from Lilly. She chose it herself. They're her favorite.

So there I was, watching a recorded boxing match, feet up on the coffee table, beer in one hand. It ought to be perfect, but there's an aching emptiness inside me. And because I'm a smart guy, it doesn't take me long to figure out I'm missing Rachel.

I call her up and hear the smile in her voice as she answers.

"Hey, baby. Merry Christmas. You having a good time."

"Merry Christmas, Justin. Well, it's lovely but..."

"Missing me?" I ask hopefully.

"Terribly. Horribly! And I only saw you yesterday."

"I'm addicting."

"Yes, you are. So I'm coming home tonight. Allison thinks I'm nuts—Bill says hi and thanks for the tequila."

She whispers the last part, but all I hear is 'coming home'.

"Rachel, honey, that's awesome, best Christmas present ever. Even better than the awesome watch you got me, but are you sure? It's your family..."

"I've never been more sure, although I won't be back till late."

"I'll wait up for you, baby."

"And I'm wearing your pendant. It's stunning. You shouldn't have spent so much on me."

"Yeah, I should. Just drive safely and get that beautiful ass home."

And she did. It was perfect. And that's what got me thinking. I know I said I'd never marry again on pain of death, but the thought of living without Rachel is worse. I don't know when it crept up on me exactly, but I liked her from the moment I met her. Liked her and respected her, thought she was pretty damn hot, too, and somewhere down the line, that changed to love. Quicker than I'd admit to, quicker than I realized, but I never said I was the sharpest pencil in the box.

So once the idea had excited my lonely brain cell, I was determined to execute my plan: bottle of chilled champagne, crystal champagne flutes, my best suit, wearing the wristwatch that she gave me...

Except the boss needed to be driven to some fundraiser New Year's Eve party. Fuming and bad tempered, I asked Rachel to marry me when we were in bed that night.

She turned me down without giving me a better reason than, "it's too soon." Gotta say, that burned like a bitch. But I'm a Marine, and Marines don't give up: *Improvise, Adapt, Overcome. Oohrah.*

This is the second time I'm asking, and we're only in mid-January.

"Justin, we've been through this. I can't talk about it now."

"Why not?"

"You want to marry me, but I know nothing about you."

"The fuck?"

"It's true. You've only once talked about your childhood; you never talk about the Marines. I only met Lilly by accident."

Snappy comebacks evade me. Is that what she thinks? That this is easy for me?

But then her tone softens.

"And because I'm busy and because you have to get your floury ass down to the garage to drive Mr. Anderson to work!"

"Floury ass?"

She smirks at me.

"It is now ... I've told you before not to interrupt me while I'm cooking!"

I wish she'd say 'yes', but I'm not worried. We live together, so she can't get that far away from me. I'll just have to wear her down with a touch of the ole Trainer charm. My cock reminds me that I like wearing Rachel down. I have to rearrange myself before I make my way to the garage and have the Range Rover ready for the short commute to DMA Tower.

The boss's foul mood hasn't improved. He snarls at me when the music is too loud; he barks when his phone rings for the third time; and Howard gets a tongue lashing along with one of his newer execs from a company he just bought. I don't take it personally: he can't help it, and there's a big difference between him being a miserable bastard and a bad boss.

Besides, he's one of the most straight-up guys I've ever worked for—no pun intended. For the first few months, I kept expecting to come across a sketchy business deal, a politician in his pocket—maybe one from the Farm, the palms that he'd greased to be as successful as he is—but that just ain't his way. He's clever and he knows how to get to and stay in with the right people, but they've learned that if they want to do business with him, it's his way or the highway. The only exception to this is when he plays golf to gain access to the word on the fairways—the informal information a smart guy can always pick up and use to his advantage. At least, that's the gist of it: it's kinda hard to figure out in between all the swearing.

It's obvious that golf offers him no physical or intellectual challenge, and if it weren't for the intel he gathers, I think he'd have wrapped his clubs around the nearest stop sign long ago.

This lunchtime, he's got a weights and reps session, followed by boxing, which is really his thing. I hope that Basqiat's session will burn off the boss's bad mood. Sometimes it works. Part of me, a bigger part than I'll admit to Rachel, wishes he'd hurry up and find himself a fuck-buddy or someone from the Farm so the rest of us don't have to walk on fucking eggshells the whole time.

I drop him at the entrance to DMA Tower and park the Rover in the underground garage. Anderson's execs circle like sharks for the chance of a parking permit in DMA Tower, but only a few ever get the chance of that perk. With another man, I'd say he enjoyed seeing them fight amongst themselves, but that sort of bitch-slapping is anathema to Anderson. All he cares is that everyone works, and works hard.

When I get to my own office, next to the CCTV room, I pick up the week's schedule from Ryan. Oh, fuck. This won't please Anderson: first thing this afternoon he's got interviews with three recent graduates from UVM, all hoping for an internship.

HR normally deals with this sort of thing, but the agriculture program at UVM is his pet project.

I flick through the details. One's a real babe, a blonde bombshell type; the second is a jock, a guy who was on the college baseball team and in the top 2% academically, but not Anderson's type since intel suggests he's straight; and the third is a girl from the Bronx. That's makes her very different from the other two who are Harvard and Yale graduates. So how did she get on the short list? The passport photo on her application shows dark eyes that are too big for her thin face. I bet she can't cook up a storm like a certain Mrs. Smith whose name I'm working on changing to Trainer. Yep, I'll wear her down—she doesn't stand a chance.

The blonde arrives first, looking confident in a dark red skirt suit and matching lipstick. Mason's background check tells me that she's the daughter of a broadcasting mogul, someone that Anderson would very much like to have owing him favors. I rank her chances highly until she tries flirting with the boss during the interview.

I cringe, watching her crash and burn as the boss pulls her résumé apart sentence by sentence, then sends her packing.

The guy is next. He's cool and impressive, doesn't crumble under Anderson's pressure. I think he may have aced this test.

The final candidate is running late. Anderson hates that, but when she finally shows up, she's a mess. She's got holes in the knees of her pantyhose and cuts that are still bleeding. She mutters something about slipping in the ice by the subway steps.

I check her out on the CCTV while I run a quick profile check, accessing the private data from UVM. Ah, so that's her in—Anderson funds a ton of agri-bio research there.

If she wasn't so sweaty and disheveled, she'd be quite pretty: slim, with long black hair. Nothing in her college file gives serious cause for concern. She's not a member of any radical groups as far as I can tell, and she hasn't protested the Agriculture Division's GM crop research. She's a good student, with a 3.9 GPA and SAT scores in the high 1500s, but less qualified than the other two. And Barbie definitely didn't make the cut.

I watch her twitching in Reception. The poor kid is nervous as fuck. She reminds me of Bambi's mom before she got shot. There's something vulnerable and almost endearing about her. I hope the boss doesn't give her too hard of a time: she looks like she'd break in two if he tosses so much as a harsh word in her direction. I'd bet money this girl doesn't stand a chance.

I let Reception know they can send up Ms. Alvarez.

She looks lost and pathetic with her grazed knees and blotchy face. She tries to answer the boss's questions but she's flustered. Jeez, the music for *Terminator* should be playing.

Anderson frowns and I can tell that he's decided to wrap this up.

"Why do you want to intern in my Agriculture Division, Ms. Alvarez?"

Anderson is bored, glancing at his Rolex.

"I believe that the future of farming is in the wider distribution of genetically modified crops as well as core assets, such as soils, are protected and improved and um..."

She stumbles to a halt, her words drying as she licks her lips nervously.

"Other agri companies are doing that," he says impatiently. "I'll ask you again: why do you want to work *here*, Ms. Alvarez?"

"Because you're also working with renewable energy and have the first anaerobic digestion plant."

That catches his attention, but not for long and he glances at Pam who is only slightly less formidable. *Time's up.*

"Ms. Alvarez, I found your résumé interesting. You say you have a good sense of humor."

I wonder where Pam is going with this as the girl's cheeks turn fire-hydrant red.

"Um, yes?"

"But only on Tuesdays. That's what it says on your résumé. Why might that be?"

Anderson leans forward, slightly interested at last.

"Um, well..."

The silence is painful and the girl is blushing so hard I can feel the heat from here.

"Idostandupcomedy."

"Excuse me?"

Her head jerks up and she meets Pam's confused frown.

"I do standup comedy. At a club. On Tuesdays."

Pam's mouth quirks up like she's trying not to laugh.

"You enjoy doing standup comedy? As a hobby?"

The girl wrings her hands.

"Actually, I hate it."

Pam rubs her forehead, like she's trying to erase a headache.

"Let me get this right: you do standup comedy at a club on Tuesdays, but you hate doing it? Do I understand you correctly?"

The girl nods.

"Might I ask the reason for this curious use of your time?"

The girl blows out a long breath.

"I'm tired of being scared all the time. I have three younger brothers so I've always had to be the sensible one. You know, *don't climb the tree in case you fall*, or *don't eat candy before dinner or you'll get sick*. No sense of adventure and then after ... well, I decided I was done being scared of everything. I hate speaking in front of crowds and, um, my brother says I can't tell a joke to save my life, so I do standup comedy every Tuesday—face your fears. It's not so bad. Skydiving is on the list. Maybe ziplining—there's this Treetop Adventure thing at the Bronx zoo ... I'm, um, afraid of heights."

Pam's mouth is hanging open and the boss looks ... I have no idea what that look on his face means.

At that moment, Ryan knocks on the door, interrupting us, and the girl stops talking instantly, her eyes worried.

"What is it?" Anderson snaps.

"Something that requires your immediate attention, sir," says Ryan, clearly on edge.

This is unusual. Ryan is the calmest dude I know, and tolerates all Anderson's bullshit, letting it wash over him like water off a duck's back.

Anderson raises his eyebrows the smallest amount, then turns to the UVM student.

"My apologies, Miss ... Alvarez. Thank you for your time. My office will be touch."

She's dismissed, blinking and confused, but I see a flash of annoyance, too. There's definitely more to her than meets the eye.

Once she's gone, Anderson turns to Ryan.

"Well?"

"I received an email to my personal account," Ryan begins, looking uncharacteristically nervous. "It suggests ... it shows ... ah ... film footage of ... of..."

And now I know where that sentence is going. Anderson has been found out.

And this time, it's blackmail.

Chapter Twenty

THE GLASS WEB

Anderson rises slowly, his face rigid, and follows Ryan to his computer.

The footage is grainy, but clearly shows two men fucking while a woman masturbates as she watches. The camera is positioned capturing a side view, a profile, and the boss's face is unmistakable. The guy being fucked is the husband of the woman—rich socialites from the Hampton Sex-party Set. He's a top divorce lawyer. Oh, the irony.

Ryan is side-eyeing the boss with interest, and I can almost see the tickertape of comments underlining his expression. *Sorry, Ryan. Your theory of 'asexual' just dove out the window.* He changes his mind and the shutters come down when the boss starts whipping himself as he fucks the other guy in the ass.

I can't say gay porn has ever been on my must-watch movie list, although I definitely need to get out more. But it appears to show three, consenting adults. Wouldn't go so far as to call it sane.

Ryan looks appalled and Pam just seems sad, her face full of pity.

Anderson is harder to read, his dark eyes clouded with secrets.

"Get Howard up here," he says, his voice cold, hard, impassive.

Ryan jumps as if 1500 volts just hit him in the butt—not that I've ever seen that happen, not even on Netflix—and dials Howard's number.

Pam is focused on business.

"How much? What's the blackmailer asking for?"

"Ma'am, Sir, I think we should ... consider the options in your office," and I raise my eyes to the CCTV cameras in the outer office.

Yeah, I'll make sure that any record of this conversation is erased from the tapes, but I need time to do that, and right now any of the security grunts could be, *should* be, watching.

Anderson nods abruptly and we all file into his office, waiting for Howard to slouch through the door.

The atmosphere thickens and Ryan surreptitiously tugs at his necktie, sweat beading on his forehead and upper lip.

Anderson stares out the window, looking down on the ant-like people below.

I wonder what he's thinking? He's built his business from the bootstraps up. A scandal like this could see it all go away. How much is he prepared to pay to make it stop?

"So what does the blackmailer want?"

My question is directed at Ryan, but everyone turns to hear the answer.

He licks his lips.

"Two hundred and fifty million or the tape is released."

Pam swears, her words hot enough to burn my ears. Not since I was a Marine have I heard such fucking atrocious language, but Anderson doesn't even blink.

A minute later, Howard ambles through the door, his eyes popping when he sees us all assembled in Anderson's office looking like Wyatt Earp just found himself in the OK Corral.

"Woah, heavy duty vibes!"

I step forward.

"Howard, we need you to focus. We have a serious security

breach. We need you to track the origins of a piece of film that's been emailed. Can you do it?"

His eyes flick from Anderson to mine and he nods slowly.

"Sure."

"How long will it take you to track him ... or her ... down?"

He scratches an armpit.

"Depends, Mr. T. Could be using a proxy server, or a virtual network. Probably the Onion Router..."

"I think I speak for most of us when I say, *what?*"

"Yeah, like a network of virtual tunnels, like simultaneously using hundreds of different proxies that are randomized periodically."

"Whatever. You can find him?"

"Yeah, sure."

He gives a huge grin, then his smile falls and he addresses the boss.

"Boss, dude, you can count on me."

Anderson nods curtly and Howard wanders off, his hands shoved in his jeans, forehead creased in thought.

The boss still hasn't spoken, but I can tell that his mind is spinning a million miles an hour.

Pam touches his arm briefly. It's the most emotion I've ever seen from her.

"Devon, we need to talk strategy. If this gets out..."

"It won't."

"Don't be short-sighted. Your private life is of interest to a lot of people. You've been this mysterious, private genius for the last ten years. People are curious. Two hundred and fifty million says there's *a lot* of interest. The fact that you like ... kinky sex makes the story even more scandalous, more marketable. You know this."

I can hear what she's not saying: *What the fuck were you thinking?!*

"Howard will find him."

"And then what?"

Anderson glances at me.

"Trainer will shut him down."

My expression tightens but I don't say anything.

Would I take someone out of the equation just to preserve the boss's secret? It ought to be a black and white question, but it's not.

The boss is fucked up, but the only person he hurts is himself. He does a lot of good, and a lot of people get to pay their mortgages because of the wages he pays them. He's invested heavily in technology to help developing countries: solar-powered laptops and smartphones, agrichems and genetically modified foods to help grow more food that will survive in harsh environments.

He's not a saint, definitely a sinner, at least in his own mind, but he's not a bad guy.

I ask myself again, would I kill for him?

I try to imagine a guy like Howard sitting at a laptop somewhere thinking he's going to make a cool $250 mil. Nope, I couldn't put my Smith & Wesson to his head and pull the trigger. If that makes me a pussy, so be it.

And then I imagine a manipulative, sadistic guy like Landon. If it was him, could I do it?

Yeah, I reckon I could.

But that leaves a lot of gray area in between.

I wait till Pam and Ryan leave the room.

"You want Mason's team to pick up Van Sant?"

"If he's behind this, I doubt he's still at the Farm."

"Mason has had men following him for weeks."

He raises his eyebrows.

"I don't remember authorizing that."

"No, your head of security did."

The smallest of smiles tugs at his lips, but it's soon gone. And I can't work out why he's not freaking the fuck out like everyone else. It's almost as if he *expected* this.

"Something I should know, sir?"

"Nothing at all, Trainer."

He goes back to his desk.

"Sir, why risk it? The Farm?"

His lips flatten and I think he won't answer.

"'Who is the happier man, he who has braved the storm of life and lived or he who has stayed securely on shore and merely existed?' Hunter S. Thompson."

The fuck?!

"Hunter S. Thompson? You're quoting *the* Hunter S. Thompson? The asshole who said, 'I hate to advocate drugs, alcohol, violence, or insanity to anyone, but they've always worked for me.' *That* Hunter S. Thompson?"

And before you ask, I haven't read his shitty brand of journalism, but I caught the movie with Johnny Depp.

Anderson answers in a clipped tone.

"Yes, that's the one."

I pause, anger filling my voice.

"You *wanted* to get caught? Because that's gonna fuck up a lot of people's lives."

His eyes flash as I push the boundaries of employer/employee, but now I'm seriously pissed off.

His shoulders lower a fraction and he looks away.

"Those parties have always been part of a certain select membership of the Hampton elite. I learned that very early in life. You'll probably find it hard to believe, but they were much less regulated than they are now."

"Prostitutes? Drugs?"

He nods, and I take a deep breath.

"Children?"

He pauses, studying his manicured fingernails. "Teenagers."

And you were one of them.

"But they were underage."

"Yes. I thought, when I bought the Farm, that if I hosted the parties I could stop ... that. It probably still goes on," he admits slowly, "but I've made sure that my gatherings are the best, the most outrageous, with the most desirable guests, but it's consenting adults only. It's for people who require a certain adventure, should I say, within safe boundaries."

"And you knew the filming was going on?"

"Yes."

"Did you arrange the filming?"

"Yes. It was how I managed to stop the underage participants. I had enough collateral to help people see that it was not in their interests to continue."

"You blackmailed your guests?!"

I'm finding the conversation hard to follow.

"Not at all. They never knew they were being filmed. I was persuasive without needing to resort to that."

"But you could have."

"Yes."

"So ... what's this? Is this blackmail real?"

He runs his hands through his hair.

"Oh, it's real alright. I began to suspect that the filming was being intercepted and relayed from the Farm to ... elsewhere. I'd always used a secure, closed circuit."

"And ... you suspected Van Sant?"

"He was the obvious candidate."

I fold my arms.

"Too obvious?" I ask, pressing the point.

"Possibly. I would have expected Aston to make a more direct approach. This cloak-and-daggers email doesn't feel like him."

"So all along you've been expecting something like this. Is that why you hired me?"

"That was part of it. But the other threats against me are real, too." He grimaces. "Wealth and success brings out the bastard in most people."

And I don't know if he's talking about himself or other people. What a mindfuck.

"Did you remove the recording devices, too?"

"Of course."

I'm hanging on to my temper by a thread.

"And you weren't planning on sharing that information with me or Mason's team?"

He cocks his head on one side.

"I needed to know that you weren't part of the conspiracy."

My brain is beginning to throb nicely when Howard reappears.

"Dude, that email was pinged halfway around the planet."

Probably not the planet Howard is on.

"Epic, like Forrest Fen! But, you know, without the Rocky Mountains."

"Howard, did you find where it was sent from?"

"Oh sure. Manhattan. Pretty boring."

I glance at Anderson, but his expressions is neutral as he stares out of the window.

"Send the coordinates to Mason's team."

"No, can do, Mr. T. He's set a trip. If you pick him up, he'll spam it to millions of networks. Dude is clever."

Anderson's head snaps around.

"Can you access his computer?"

"Not legally." Howard's eyes spin with excitement. "But I can be inside within forty minutes. I'll Trojan him and spike his circuitry. He won't know what hit him. It'll wipe out everything."

Howard cracks his knuckles as Anderson nods.

Without looking at me, he gives his next order.

"Have Mason's men pick up Aston in 45 minutes."

"Yes, sir."

Finally, something I can call action.

I'm halfway to the comms room when I get a call from Rachel.

It's odd. She normally just texts or I call her when I'm working so she doesn't interrupt anything.

"Rachel, honey, you okay?"

"Justin..."

Her voice is shaking.

"Fuck, what is it?"

"You need to tell Mr. Anderson to come home."

"What's going on?"

"Please, Justin! Right now! It's important!"

She sounds upset. She sounds *scared!* My pulse is racing but I need to manage this situation. The words are so tight in my throat that I can hardly spit them out.

"Okay, honey, keep calm. Just answer yes or no. Are you alone?"

"No."

Fuck!

"Is it a man?"

"Yes."

"Is he alone?"

"Yes."

"Is he armed?"

"Ye—"

I hear shouting in the background and the phone goes dead.

Chapter Twenty-One

HEARTBREAK RIDGE

My heart triple-times. It's a Marine's worst nightmare, the people you love in danger when you're not with them and there's nothing you can do.

I turn so quickly, an employee who was behind me in the corridor slams into my chest. I catch her elbow and set her upright against the wall, ignoring her squeak of surprise. Automatically, I check my Smith & Wesson as I run to the express elevator. Then I call Mason on my cell, cursing the slowness as I drop thirty floors.

"There's a lone male intruder at Wolf Point. Armed. And he's got Rachel!"

As I end the call, I can already hear him shouting orders.

Mason's team knows how to access Wolf Point and will get there faster than the police. Besides, I know Mason's men and I trust them to handle any situation. They can back me up because Rachel needs me and I'm not letting anyone or anything get in my way.

Then I violate every known traffic law on the way and screech into the underground garage.

I take the service elevator, pulling my Smith & Wesson from the holster as the doors slide open with a soft rumble. I duck down automatically, but there's no one there.

Moving silently, I make my way into the main living area. And that's when I see them.

Rachel is seated on Anderson's sectional, her ankles and wrists secured with zip ties, and standing over her, pointing a gun at my woman is Aston Van Sant.

Rachel's eyes widen when she sees me and she whimpers softly.

Van Sant turns and frowns.

"You're not him. Where's Devon?"

I swallow, my throat dry, but when I speak, my voice is calm.

"He's on his way. He'll be here soon. Why don't you be smart and put the gun down, man?"

He shakes his head slowly.

"No. He has to come. He has to. I didn't do it! He must know I didn't do it! I'd never do something like that! I'd never try to hurt Devon!"

I take a step forwards, but that's too much for him, and he swings the gun back to Rachel.

"Don't come any closer!"

At that moment, I hear the main elevator doors open and Anderson walks towards us cautiously.

"He's armed, sir!"

Anderson holds out his hand, telling me silently to keep back. Rachel looks like she's in shock, and the boss is only just reining it in.

We all stare at each other. I'm less than a heartbeat from pulling the trigger. If Van Sant makes a move, I'll take him down. If he touches one hair on Rachel's head, I'll take him down. If he even looks in Rachel's direction, I'll take him down.

But then the boss's face changes. The fear and uncertainty drop away, and his expression grows diamond hard.

His voice is a harsh whisper, an order cracking like a whip.

"Aston! Stop this!"

Van Sant hesitates, his arm wavering, then he lowers the gun and slumps onto the sectional.

He looks crazed. The Miami Vice-wannabe is a mess. His face is pale but blotchy and covered in stubble, his clothes are wrinkled and stained. He looks as if he's been sleeping in his car for a few days. His eyes are bloodshot, the pupils tiny points of black. He's high as a kite and desperate. A dangerous combination, but the boss seems to know how to handle him.

He's staring at Van Sant as if he's trying to calm a wild animal.

"Put the gun down. I know you don't want to hurt anyone."

Van Sant blinks rapidly, staring at the gun as if he's not sure how it came to be in his hand. Finally, he lowers his hands and lets it slip to the carpet.

I cringe when I see it's a Sig Sauer—known to fail drop tests.

Thank fuck it doesn't release a bullet this time.

Moving slowly and deliberately, grimacing with disgust, Anderson picks it up with the tips of his fingers and places it out of reach.

I holster my weapon and take Rachel into my arms as she sobs, terrified, her tears soaking my shirt. Gently, I untie her hands and feet, rage filling me when I see angry red marks on her pale skin.

"It's okay, sweetheart. It's okay," I murmur, quietly.

But it's not okay. It's really fucking not.

A soft whimper escapes her.

What can I say to comfort her? I've failed her utterly. And what do I do—pass her a fucking handkerchief to wipe her tears.

I hold her against my chest, reliving the terror of seeing a gun pointed at her head.

I carry her to a sofa in the corner of the room and hold her. I just hold her.

She can't speak, her sobs softer but just as desperate. And my battered heart breaks wide open.

I try to speak, to tell her how sorry I am again, but no sound comes out.

Her pain is judgment enough.

I'm filled with loathing and anger for Anderson whose fucked up life has put Rachel in danger, but also for myself, for my failure today. None of this should ever have happened.

I hear Anderson talking to Van Sant quietly and calmly.

"You're not well, Aston, but I'm going to take care of you. I'll do everything to help you get better."

"I didn't do it, Devon! You know that, right? I'd never hurt you! Never! I love you! Tell me you know that!"

The boss takes Van Sant's hands in his.

"Yes, I know, Aston. I've always known. And now I'm going to help you."

Van Sant collapses into the boss's arms, sobbing.

Anderson's eyes are wide and worried when he turns me.

"Is Rachel...?"

"Safe."

"Call Doctor O'Brien at Phoenix House. It's a rehab center on Long Island. Speed dial five. Get him here."

"Sir."

I don't know why the fuck Anderson has a rehab clinic in his contacts and I don't ask.

Keeping one arm around Rachel, I catch the cellphone that the boss throws to me, dialing the doc's number.

"Yes, this is Justin Trainer, I work for Devon Anderson. We have an emergency at Wolf Point. I need to speak to Dr. O'Brien immediately."

Seconds later, they call is transferred.

"Doctor O'Brien speaking."

"I'm with Devon Anderson at Wolf Point and we have a distressed man, some sort of mental breakdown, probably high?"

"Is he physically injured?"

"Negative. I'm no doctor, but he looks pretty out of it. His name is Aston Van Sant, mid-thirties."

"We have a private ambulance service in the city that can be there in twelve minutes."

I give him a temporary access code then call Mason so he can tell the armed response team to stand down. They're already in the building, so will check all the access points just to ensure that Van Sant acted alone.

I can't help wondering where Van Sant got the gun. But then again, I can only guess at the kind of contacts he's made over his years with Anderson.

A kernel of disgust hardens to stone in my chest. Van Sant is a casualty of the train wreck that is the boss's life.

"Go with him," Rachel whispers. "Just in case..."

"I'm not leaving you."

"I'm fine, Justin, I promise. But it's not right that they're alone. He could say anything ... later."

Even after all this, Rachel is still thinking of others. She's also right about the possible consequences. Reluctantly, I follow the boss.

Van Sant is a blubbering mess but Anderson is being ... tender. Is that the right word? I wonder if they were ever together, lovers. It looks more like Van Sant has some sort of unrequited crush on the boss, but I could be wrong.

I hear the boss saying that he should call Landon, but that makes Van Sant shake even worse, his eyes widening as if he's afraid.

Frederick Landon. He brought both Anderson and his godson into this fucked up lifestyle. And they've paid the price. And paid. And paid.

Christ, I hope the ambulance gets here soon.

Van Sant murmurs wordlessly. Suddenly he says, "What day is it?"

"It's Tuesday, Aston," Anderson says, quietly.

"No, no it's Saturday! You always come on a Saturday. What day is it?"

"It's Tuesday."

"But why? Why is it Tuesday?"

"It's going to be okay, Aston. I'll take care of you."

"Take care. Take care. Take care. What day is it?"

"Tuesday."

"Hmm. Mmm. Mmm."

Anderson looks at me helplessly.

"The medics are on their way, sir," I repeat, uselessly.

He nods and continues holding Van Sant.

When the elevator doors open, the boss jumps, Rachel cries out, and I nearly fucking shoot myself, but Van Sant doesn't even react. He's somewhere else, completely detached from his mind, and I can't help wondering if he'll ever find his way back.

Two male EMTs approach, taking in the situation quickly. The older of the two goes up to Van Sant.

"Hello. I'm Walter Hicks, and this is Ben Wroska. We're friends of Devon's and we're going to help you."

"Mmm. Mmm. Mmm. What day is it?"

"It's Tuesday. Do you like Tuesdays?"

"Mmm. Tuesday? Is it Saturday yet? I see him on a Saturday."

Hicks and the boss exchange a glance. Anderson looks tortured.

He fucking should be.

"I'm going to give you something that will make you feel sleepy. It'll help you to rest."

"Mmm. Mmm. Is it Saturday?"

Hicks takes a syringe out of his bag, rolls up Van Sant's sleeve and slides it into a vein.

And suddenly he turns to the boss and smiles.

"I love you," he says. "My Dark Angel."

Anderson looks utterly shattered.

We're all relieved when the drugs start to work and Van Sant's eyes close. He's still smiling.

Then the medics wrap him in a blanket and help Van Sant into a wheelchair, taking him out to the waiting ambulance.

I throw Anderson a look that should freeze his testicles, then I hold my hand out to Rachel. She stands shakily, and I put my arm around her as I take her to our room and we lay down on the bed together, holding each other.

She doesn't speak, but folds her hands into my shirt and eventually, she falls asleep.

My brain is whirling, wondering how Van Sant got in. He wasn't on the approved list, I know that much. Unless Anderson gave him access and didn't tell me. I need an update from Mason's team.

I ease away from Rachel, carefully loosening her fingers from my shirt, then covering her with a quilt. I close the door behind me softly.

As I walk into my office, I see the reassuring presence of John Evans, one of Mason's men who I've worked with before. We shake hands quickly and I explain the situation, who and what Van Sant is. He tells me that Anderson has gone to visit Van Sant in the rehab clinic but has chosen not to inform the police. I'm not surprised. We discuss the security implications, wondering how the fuck he got into Wolf Point when all the guest entry codes have been changed weekly since I came here, and to my knowledge Van Sant has never been inside. Me, Rachel and the boss all have fingerprint entry, of course. It would be a fucking nightmare remembering a new code every week. Yeah, I keep the intel in my phone, but a hacker as clever as Howard could get in. Fuck.

Anderson arrives home hours later, looking drawn and exhausted. My anger reignites and I want to hurt the fucker.

My expression makes it plain that he's not welcome in my office.

"Is Mrs. Smith ... okay?"

"No, she's NOT fucking okay!" I snarl at him.

He looks taken aback, but not angry.

"I have to ask you ... about what Aston said to her. Did he say why he wanted to see me? Anything to explain what drove him to this?"

"No. He wasn't very coherent, but he did say he hadn't done it. He could have been referring to the blackmail threat. The dude doesn't seem like he could have set it up, but he might know who did."

Anderson nods slowly.

"I don't know what could have precipitated this. I'm sorry that

Mrs. Smith has ... been affected. Security will be tightened up— we'll find out how he got in."

Yeah, pile the fucking guilt on my plate, Anderson. I fucking KNOW security is my job. I fucked up.

But I can't bring myself to look at him, and eventually he leaves.

Because I screwed up, the woman I love could have been badly hurt. I just want to hold her and hold her and never let her go.

Rachel doesn't sleep well. She thrashes about, muttering to herself. I've never heard her talk in her sleep before. The only word I can make out is, "Don't".

I keep running through the security arrangements in my head.

At four in the morning, I give up and get out of bed. Rachel is frowning in her sleep, and I'm fighting every instinct to pull her into my arms, but I don't want to wake her and she needs her rest.

I tug on a pair of jeans and a t-shirt, and start working my way through the building. I check every door, every window, every possible entry point except the balcony in the boss's bedroom. Van Sant would have to be fucking Spiderman to have gotten in through there.

The only conclusion is that someone let him in. Landon is my number one suspect.

I see a light on in the boss's study. Someone else who can't sleep. I don't feel like talking to him, so I head to the kitchen. But he's not in his study, he's sitting at the breakfast bar, still wearing the clothes he went to work in yesterday morning. He hasn't even tried to rest.

I start to back out of the kitchen, but I hear his low voice, speaking in a monotone.

"Howard's virus worked. The blackmailer is out of action. For now."

I nod, not particularly interested, even though I know I should be.

"How is Mrs. Smith?"

I sigh. Okay, let's do this.

"Sleeping. She's pretty shaken."

"I'm sorry, Trainer. I couldn't have guessed that Aston would do this..."

"Couldn't you?"

His head snaps up, breaking the weird trance, and his tone sharpens.

"What do you mean?"

But I don't need to answer because he gets it, and his head sinks to his hands, before he looks up at me again, pain and doubt and fear on his face.

"You think I made him as fucked up as I am."

It's the most honest conversation we've ever had.

"There's that ... and the fact he's in love with you. And the most likely suspect to help him gain entry is Frederick Landon."

I stare at him, leaving my words hanging in the air, meeting the darkness in his expression. Then I walk away, because if I say anything else now, one of us is going to really regret it.

The next day, we're all tired and edgy. The alarm technician arrives at 8AM to service all the systems, but I already know that there's nothing wrong with them.

I check the CCTV for the millionth time, but there's no recording of Landon or Van Sant in the garage or in the foyer. It's as if he just flew up to the thirtieth floor. I have my suspicions about one of the fire exits, but there's no sign of a forced entry and I know for a fact that the boss doesn't give out those access codes to anyone, not even Landon, he says. But even though all the codes have been adjusted to a rolling algorithm that now changes every few hours, just for my own piece of mind, I tape a small length of cotton over the door to each fire escape. If anyone tries to enter, I'll know about it.

It's an old trick, but sometimes the simplest solutions beat the high-tech shit any day of the week.

I really fucking hate shutting the stable door after the horse has fucking shit in the straw and bolted.

The rehab facility is being difficult about updating us on Van Sant's condition since none of us are related to him. Even Landon's access is restricted, or so he says. I don't believe him and I don't trust him.

And then like tragic opera that the boss is so fond of, things get worse after the interval.

"He fucking what?!"

Half of Manhattan can probably hear the boss yelling.

"How? I thought they were watching him around the clock?"

He listens intently, but my heart sinks. I can guess what's happened and Anderson confirms it.

"Van Sant absconded from the facility. He's missing."

"How long?"

"Could be hours! The fucking idiots weren't watching him!"

That is not good news. I want to take Rachel away from here and keep her safe.

My eyes follow Anderson as he paces up and down the main room.

He turns abruptly.

"Yes. Work. Twenty minutes, Trainer."

Fuck.

After I drop him off, I park the SUV and head to my office to call a meeting of all security team. There's a frisson of excitement because I've never done this before at DMA Tower.

"Gentlemen ... and Miss Jameson. We have a situation that you need to be aware of. This man, Aston Van Sant..." I flash up his photograph on the whiteboard, "has a personal grudge against Mr. Anderson. He attempted to enter his home yesterday." *No need to give them all the gory details.* "He is considered a medium to high level threat. Nobody, and I mean nobody, gets into DMA Tower without clearance through one of you. I don't care if it's a pizza delivery boy with a blind monkey on his grandmother's bicycle: no one gets in without being vetted first. Any questions?"

"Mr. Trainer, sir. Who is he?"

"We only know that Van Sant is a person who has a dangerous fixation—and he may be armed. Anything else? Back to work, people."

I make sure they're all jumping like frogs on a hotplate then head over to Wolf Point. I don't like leaving Rachel right now. Evans will drive Anderson home from work later. Rachel needs me, whether she admits it or not.

She's still arguing about that.

"Really, Justin. You don't need to fuss—I'm *fine*."

I won't be fine until we find Van Sant.

Rachel smiles weakly. But that's an improvement.

When the boss gives her the rest of the week off, I want to punch him. Is that supposed to make up for everything that she's been through? But then again, I don't know what would make up for having someone point a gun at your head. I've always been the one on the other side of the trigger.

She's going to Allison's later this evening, and I hate, *HATE* that she feels safer at her sister's than she does with me.

You didn't protect her.

She's in her bedroom, packing, and the sight of her suitcase on the bed makes me feel like a failure.

"How you doin', baby?"

She doesn't look at me as she replies.

"I'm fine, Justin."

I stand with my hands in my pockets, hating the distance between us.

"Anything I can do?"

"No."

And isn't that the truth?

I brush a quick kiss on her cheek, trying to push away the pain when her body stiffens at the contact.

"Supper will be at six."

She still isn't looking at me, but I feel like she threw me a bone, pathetically grateful for those words.

I head back to my office, wracking my lonely brain to come up with the answer of *how* Van Sant got in here and whether or not he's in cahoots with Landon, which the crafty old bastard is still denying.

By the evening, there's still no sign of Van Sant, and he hasn't tried to use any of his credit cards. And yes, I'm aware that I'm invading his personal files and violating privacy data. Do I look like I give a fuck?

Frustration turns to acute irritation when I see Landon entering the garage in his sleek Speed Six Bentley. The battleship gray color makes it look like a shark cutting through the darkness. Perfect for the predator that lurks beneath the polished surface.

His raptor smile is fixed in place when I meet him at the elevator. His eyes wander across my body, and I feel like roaches are skittering over my skin.

I'm also feeling pissed and incredulous that the boss has already given Landon the access codes.

"Hello, Trainer."

"Mr. Landon."

"You really are just the muscle, aren't you?"

What the fuck?

"I made the mistake of thinking that you were in charge of Devon's security, but obviously that's not the case—not after yesterday's fiasco."

He's goading me and he's fucking enjoying it.

Do not engage the enemy in a frontal attack. Retreat, regroup, and prepare.

I don't reply, instead turning on my heel and leading him to the boss's study.

"Mr. Landon is here to see you, sir."

He doesn't even look up from his computer.

"Now is not a good time, Frederick."

"You need help managing the Aston situation you've created."

He looks up sharply.

"The situation I created?"

"Yes, of course. If you hadn't treated him so peremptorily none of this would have happened. Have you learned nothing, Devon?"

He's talking to him like a first grader and Anderson fucking takes it.

I clear my throat, earning a venomous look from the viper.

"Should Mrs. Smith bring your dinner to the office, sir?"

It's a reasonable question, but you'd think I just detonated a bomb in the room, the silence is so shocking.

This job should come with free therapy.

At least the Landon creep decides not to stay. He doesn't need to. He's made his point and reinforced his waning control over Anderson.

With a sharp look at the boss, he turns on his heel and leaves.

After supper, Rachel is in the kitchen, staring out of the window. I didn't realize I was walking quietly, but when she glances up, she jumps and holds her hand to her heart.

"Oh, Justin! I didn't hear you."

A sob escapes her, and I scoop her into my arms.

"Oh, baby. I hate to see you like this."

We stand there, locked together, until her breathing calms.

"Did you finish packing?"

She nods.

"Sure you don't want me to drive you?"

"No, Mr. Anderson needs you. I'll be fine at Allison's. I just ... I just need to get away from here for a while."

Away from all this fucked up shit. Away from me? Does she blame me? I hope she does, because I blame myself, but I hate it, too.

I walk her down to the garage and put her luggage in the trunk.

"Call me when you get there."

"It could be quite late."

"I don't care, baby. Just call me. I won't be asleep—I need to know you've arrived safely."

I wish she'd let me drive her. I don't think she's in any shape to be behind the wheel of a car, but my woman is stubborn. Either that, or she doesn't want me around.

The thought kills me.

So I don't give her a chance to argue. I sweep her into my arms and kiss her hard, letting her know how much she means to me, holding her tight until she pushes on my arms.

"Justin, I'm fine. Don't worry about me."

Her eyes don't meet mine as she says it.

I watch her drive away and feel like a small piece of happiness has just dropped out of my life. I know she'll be back on Sunday evening but, fuck, I'll miss that woman.

I hope she'll be back on Sunday.

I trudge to my office and check through the CCTV footage one more time. There's still nothing to report.

I watch some dumb zombie movie on TV until my eyelids feel like small people are stamping on them. Rachel doesn't call but sends a text message to say she's arrived.

I drag my weary carcass into bed. It's too empty without Rachel, and with everything that's happened in the last forty-eight hours, my brain is too busy to allow me to do more than doze for a few minutes at a time.

Chapter Twenty-Two

DANTE'S PEAK

I'm missing Rachel.

Two days have dragged by, and even though I'm only getting four hours sleep a night while I work with Howard and Mason to track down the blackmailer and Van Sant—although perhaps they're the same person after all—the time passes slowly.

I want her back. I want her with me. And right now, I don't know if I'll have either of those things.

It makes me want to take Anderson out myself. You'd be surprised how many bodyguards end up shooting their employers—guess we get to know them too well, all their sordid little secrets. Or maybe I'll just give him a stern talking to.

Nope, shooting him would be more satisfying.

Howard is enjoying the hunt, pitting his brain against the best there is, or so he says, and as he's using words above my paygrade, I'll just agree with him. He's getting closer and even says that he knows who the other hacker is, a pay-per-play egghead who only takes on 'impossible' jobs.

"Dude, they don't call him 'The Ghost' for nothing. I've come across him before and he wouldn't care about crashing the entire internet and causing a fire sale."

"A fire sale?"

"Yeah, banks, utilities, air traffic, 911 calls—take those down and pow! Armageddon. Or what we call in the biz, a fire sale because..."

"Everything must go. Got it. So can you stop this Ghost?"

"Yeah. He's good, I'm better. Scored ten points higher than him on the MENSA test. It's pissed him off ever since."

"Wait, you know who he is?"

"Sure I do."

"Give me a name and I'll hunt the fucker down."

"No can do, T. He'll release the boss's porn to the news channels. It'll get messy. I can shut him down, it'll just take time—an epic battle, like Gandalf versus Saruman."

"In English?"

"I'm Gandalf, and Saruman doesn't make it to the end of the movie."

"Right. Thanks, Howard."

I turn to go, needing to update Mason's team.

"By Grabthar's hammer, by the suns of Worvan, you shall be avenged."

He looks serious, so I give him a salute.

"Carry on, Marine."

"Epic, dude! Like a real soldier of fortune!"

We're doomed.

Perhaps Howard's approach is subtle. For all I know it could be a nerd war with Thor's hammer as the weapon of choice. What I do know is that for 48 hours, no more threats have appeared and none of the other participants of Farm sex have been contacted.

Okay, 'farm sex' sounds bad, like really bad. Like some cowboy who's had a long, snowed-in winter and is getting frisky with a heifer. Oh hell. I've been working for Anderson waaaay too long.

Howard says he's close...

And then Armageddon comes to DMA Tower.

The first thing I know about it is when one of the security guards on duty in the lobby has pressed the silent alarm button.

My eyes snap to the screen and I see Van Sant waving a pistol around and shouting something.

Even on a tiny monitor, he looks bad—worse than when we found him at Wolf Point.

"Secure Anderson!"

The security guard on CCTV duty looks panicked and vacant.

"Make sure he's guarded at all times. Under *no circumstances* allow him out of his office—not even to piss! Got it?"

"Yes, sir! But Mr. Anderson has a private bathroom, sir!"

Give me strength.

"Do NOT let him leave his office! Vasquez, inform Pam Russo that Aston Van Sant is armed and in the lobby, then secure the elevators including the freight elevators. Move, people! Follow the Lockdown Protocol! This is not a drill!"

I make sure that everyone knows what they're doing and are securing their positions. Mason is already aware since he's got a direct link to DMA security systems.

"Murdoch, who's on duty in the lobby?"

"Benson and Khan."

I swear quietly under my breath as I pick up a headset and turn it on. Khan is solid, an older guy, ex-military. He'll be okay. But Benson is a rookie—he's the worst possible person to have in a situation like this.

Now is a fucking bad time to come to that conclusion.

"Mitchel, with me!"

I take the fire exit and we run down 29 floors, going slowly on the last set of steps. I tap my earpiece and speak quietly.

"Vasquez, report."

"Lobby is cleared of extraneous personnel, but the perp grabbed Heidi Burey, the receptionist, sir. But I got a call from NYPD: they received a 911 saying that there was a gunman onsite and a SWAT team is en route. ETA: three minutes."

That is not the news I wanted to hear. Having cops storm the place will not help. Which gives me three minutes to end the stand-off. Shit.

I can hear Van Sant screaming from behind the fire door.

"Where's Devon? I want Devon! I'm not leaving until I've seen him! Devon! DEVON!"

I open the door slowly and step through it.

Van Sant sees me immediately.

"It's you! Tell them that Devon will see me! Tell him I'm here!"

"Not going to happen, Aston."

For a moment, he's stumped, then he grabs Heidi's ponytail and tugs hard. She shrieks and tears pour down her face, her legs wobbling.

"I'll waste the bitch!"

"You're not a killer, Aston. Let her go."

"Stop saying my name like we're friends! Tell Devon I want to see him! Devon *always* sees me! He's the only one who ever did."

I lower my gun and take another step toward Van Sant.

"He's not going to come down."

His lip trembles.

"He'll come! He will!"

"Let Heidi go. She's not part of this. She's innocent."

He shakes his head, his eyes wild. One hand wraps tightly around the receptionist's long hair.

"I was innocent once! So was Devon. But he understands. He understands *me*. Devon! DEVON!"

Khan and Benson inch closer while Van Sant is distracted by me. I don't like the look in Benson's eyes. He's sweating and his gun hand is shaking so badly, he'll probably shoot himself.

"The police are on their way!" Benson yells out. "Drop your weapon now."

Fuck! He wants to be the big hero, but he has no clue what the fuck he's doing.

Van Sant pushes the gun into Heidi's cheek and this time she drops to her knees. He's holding her in front of him by her hair.

In the distance, I hear police sirens, and know that time is running out.

"We can end this quietly, Aston. Let Heidi go, put the gun down, and I promise that I'll arrange a meeting with Devon."

He blinks rapidly.

"You will?"

"You have my word."

He starts to lower the gun.

"That's right, asshole!" shouts Benson. "Put the gun down."

"Shut the fuck up!" Khan hisses at him, but it's too late.

And just when I think the situation couldn't be more fucked up, Anderson steps out of the elevator, cool as ice.

"Aston, I'm here now. Let the girl go."

Van Sant sags with relief, dropping Heidi's ponytail. She scuttles away and Khan moves her behind the large, heavy reception desk.

Anderson is now in the firing line, and Benson is a wildcard.

"Put the gun down, Aston, and we'll talk in my office. Just you and me."

I hear the SWAT team screech to a halt outside. So does everyone else.

Van Sant whips around, his gun dangling in his hand. And then Benson fires.

"No!"

Anderson shouts out and is already running forwards, but I football tackle him to the ground, covering his body with mine.

Van Sant is sitting on the floor, looking surprised at the blood leaking out of his belly. The SWAT team bursts into the room, and seeing Van Sant still holding his gun, they order him to drop his weapon.

Yells come from all directions: *Get down! Drop your weapon! On the floor, now!*

Van Sant stares around him, hopelessness and defeat in his expression.

He turns to Anderson and smiles sadly, then brings the gun to his head.

"Aston, no!"

Van Sant pulls the trigger.

Benson vomits.

The police are all over the scene, relieving me of my weapon until they've checked my ID, interviewing Khan, soothing Benson.

The guy is shaking and in shock. He's never shot a human being before. Never seen anyone die violently. You don't get over that. Ever.

Anderson stares at Van Sant's body, his expression unreadable, but I feel the weight of his sadness. I could have talked him down, so could Anderson.

It didn't have to end like this.

Chapter Twenty-Three

THE GRADUATE

The incident brought Anderson a lot of negative publicity, but in the end it was decided that Van Sant's actions were brought on by depression at losing his job.

Which is strange, because Anderson never fired him.

Heidi made an unreliable witness because she'd been so scared. Benson only spoke about the minute leading up to his taking the shot. Khan kept his mouth shut, so no one told the investigators about Van Sant's speech saying that he was innocent.

It seems like business as usual, but I notice some changes. For one, Anderson doesn't go for dinner with Landon like he used to; for another, there are no more parties at the Farm.

The boss 'meditates' more than usual, which upsets Rachel, but at least she's home again. And at least she's giving me a second ... or maybe a third chance.

She seems calmer now, as if being with her sister restored some balance in her life. I hate that I wasn't the one who could give her that, but all I have to offer is a strong arm and more craziness. Why would a woman like her want that? But at least she can meet my eyes again; at least I can be part of her life for now.

And then, a month later on a Tuesday afternoon, Ryan calls my cell phone.

"Mr. Anderson wants to see you, Justin."

"Just throw a raw steak into his cave and retreat thirty feet."

"Funny ... not. I'll tell him you're on your way."

Sighing, I drag my weary ass to the boss's office.

"Yes, sir?" *'Sup, dude?*

"Change of plan for tonight. I'll be visiting a club in the Village."

"Sir?" *Say what?*

He sighs, irritated at having to repeat himself.

"The Comedy Cellar, it's on MacDougal Street, eight o'clock."

I'm hearing it, but I'm not believing it. The boss is to comedy what nuns are to porn. Oh wait, there was that one time ... whatever, *it's not normal!*

I head back to my office certain that the world ended and no one told me.

"Relax, big guy," says Pam, catching up with me.

"What just happened in there? Is he on drugs?"

"Maybe, or just the oldest drug of all—sexual attraction."

I wait, count to ten, consider taking off socks to count higher, but no, Pam's still not making sense.

"He's turned on by crappy comics? Why doesn't he just watch *Saturday Night Live?*"

Pam gives a fake sigh.

"So young, so foolish. He's going to see a woman."

"A woman? A female woman?"

"Hark, it's an echo!"

"Fuck's sake, Pam!"

Eventually, she takes pity on me.

"Remember when he was interviewing interns a few weeks back and we got interrupted by news of the blackmailer?"

I scowl. I'm not likely to forget that in a hurry.

"Two females: IC1, IC2 and an IC1 male."

"How reassuringly pedantic."

I don't bother to reply.

"Well, the dark haired woman, Maria Alvarez, does a standup routine there..."

And a memory comes back to me.

"I'm funny on Tuesdays."

"Yeah, I remember. The boss wants to see *her?*"

"Possibly. Right now, he seems to be interested in seeing some up-and-coming comics."

I go home, irritated by the change of plans. I've downgraded the security around Anderson since Van Sant did a handstand over the great divide, and Howard seems to have chased off the blackmailer, although he's still looking for him in his spare time. I guess everyone needs a hobby.

Rachel is annoyingly upbeat.

"Oh, this is wonderful news, Justin! Mr. Anderson is interested in a normal girl in a normal way!"

"Not for long," I mutter under my breath.

"What do you mean?"

"Rachel, the moment she walks through the door and sees his 'meditation room', she'll do one of two things: freak or run. Possibly both."

Rachel's face falls.

"Oh dear."

I go to my closet and pull out a pair of jeans and a shirt. It feels strange to dress casual around the boss, but he wants to fly under the radar tonight. The Press have had enough kicks off of his buck this last month.

I drive us to the club and the silence is awkward. We're not buddies, we're employer and employee, but now we have to act like friends. I prefer it when the boundaries are firmly in place.

I enter the club first, peering through the gloom to find a table against the wall where I can guard the perimeter—or at least have one angle that I don't have to worry about.

I sit nursing a glass of mineral water while the boss sips on a white wine, not so patiently waiting for the star attraction.

Eventually, the girl shuffles onto the stage, blinking through her schoolmarm glasses and smiling timidly at the audience.

"Hi, me again. And you were hoping for Sarah Palin. But if you want to throw fruit at me, I make a great grapefruit salad."

She's dying on her feet out there.

A rush of pity washes through me. She's gripping the microphone like it's a lifeline.

"So ... I went for a job interview recently. It was awkward. And yet I'm such a relaxed person."

A couple of people laugh politely, but it seems to give her confidence.

"I wanted to make a good impression. Well, I made an impression when I showed up with two skinned knees, but the bleeding stopped by the time I got to his office and I didn't make any inappropriate comments about blowjobs on the Subway steps, so that's good, right?"

She grimaces, but flounders on. Oh boy, this could be interesting!

"The guy interviewing me was a billionaire and he says, 'So, why do you want to work for me?' Really? I'm supposed to lie and say, 'your ethical approach to agriculture and green issues makes your company a go-to agrichem company' instead of, 'well, gee, if you're smart enough to hire me, I'm definitely smart enough to be as rich as you if I work for your company'."

A few more people laugh and I sense that she's beginning to relax. She's not too bad now she's loosened up a bit. Or maybe the audience just feels sorry for her.

"He's a billionaire from the Hamptons, and I'm a Latina from the Bronx—you could call it a match made in Havana."

I glance at the boss, but he's watching her with a stony expression.

She goes on for another ten minutes about how awful her interview was and how she never even got a 'thanks, but no thanks' letter.

When she finishes, she gets a muted round of applause and leaves the stage looking flushed and happy.

Which is when the boss makes his move.

I stand behind him at a short distance when he follows her to the bar.

"Good evening, Ms. Alvarez. That was most entertaining."

She gapes, her hands limp at her sides.

"I ... I..."

"Enlightening too, I might add."

He's doing his best to sound charming, but he's not happy.

"OMG! Mr. Anderson! Oh wow, you're pissed. I'm really sorry. It's just comedy."

"Very amusing. And instructive."

She looks up at him sheepishly.

"I was kind of a mess and you were all dark and intimidating."

He stares at her, his head on one side.

"My mother's maiden name was Gloria García. She was from the Bronx, too."

Her cheeks turn red.

"I'm sorry. I didn't know. I didn't mean..."

"There's a lot about me you don't know," he says softly.

And guess what? He spends two hours with little Ms. Alvarez. *Two hours!* When a journo from the *New York Times* wangled an interview with him off the back of a charity event he was involved with last year, he was out on his ear within fifteen minutes.

But the look on his face when he saw Ms. Alvarez ... he's interested. I know that look: enthusiasm. He gets it when someone's telling him about a new work project, or a recent development at the UVM Agriculture Division. It's rare, but he's excited.

And I have a bad feeling about this. If the boss is excited about a woman, it can only end one way because he doesn't do relationships.

Hell, she looks about seventeen, although I know from her file that she's 24. There's no way she'd be into his twisted shit.

So far, that hasn't stopped him from being interested, because when we return to Wolf Point with Ms. Alvarez's number on the boss's cell phone, he orders an in-depth security check from Mason. And you know what, there's *nothing* to find. She's not overdrawn at the bank, she doesn't do drugs, she doesn't seem to drink much, she hardly ever goes out, she has a part-time job in a carpet warehouse store, for fuck's sake; and Mason can't find any evidence of a boyfriend.

And so we wait. What for is anyone's guess.

Since Van Sant, everyone at DMA Tower is tiptoeing around Anderson, waiting for him to erupt like Old Faithful, only less predictable.

In the meantime, the boss is working-out like it's the only thing stopping his brain from frying. He runs with me, trains with Basqiat, and works-out in his gym—it's Anderson's own version of Hell Week.

Every night, he wakes up screaming, and I'm so fucking tired of that. I'm thinking of buying ear plugs—except that paid security is supposed to be eyes and ears 24/7. I'm seriously thinking about looking for a new job, and I would, if it weren't for Lilly's tuition and Rachel.

She sees there's something up with Anderson, but despite what she knows about him, she thinks he's decent. Is that the word? It's partly true. I've seen the depth of his philanthropic projects, his lack of interest in publicity, how hard he works but ... and it's a big but, there's something behind his eyes, a barely contained violence. Rachel has never seen him come close to losing it. I have, and Krakatowa waiting to blow has nothing on him. And then, of course, there's the meditation room, and Anderson's demons are beaten into submission.

But Maria Alvarez ... totally different story.

"Justin, do you really think Mr. Anderson would hurt this girl, the one he went to see last Tuesday?"

Rachel is frowning at me. I know a way to bring a smile to her face. I try to wrap my arms around her waist and pull her into my lap, but she laughs and steps away.

"Oh no, let's try and have a conversation that doesn't end up with me wondering where I've left my bra."

"Those are my favorite sort of conversations."

"I've noticed. But you'll have to take a rain check. I'm cooking supper, and Mr. Anderson will be finished with the gym soon."

She frowns as she says this. *Jeez, she's actually worried about him.*

"No problem. I like to watch you cook, woman."

She swipes at me with a spatula. I manage to duck just in time.

"Good reflexes."

"I can show you some better ones."

"Justin! Do you ever stop?"

"Never, baby. Twenty-four/seven. That's what I'm paid for. But if you agreed to marry me, I'd be all yours, 24/7."

She sighs.

"We've been over this. The answer is still no."

"One day you'll say yes, Rachel."

"If I did, you'd have a heart attack!"

"What a way to go."

She shakes her head and sighs, an exasperated sound, but even though she's got her back to me, I know she's smiling.

Her question eats away at me: would Anderson hurt the girl? Only if she saw his meditation room or he decided to start things up at the Farm again. So, yes, I think he would hurt her, given the chance. After all, that's his only way of having a relationship. *Sick fucker.* And I'm still surprised that he's interested in females.

Whether this girl would agree to it, that's something else entirely. I know that Anderson is charismatic; he's also persuasive and manipulative. I've seen him in action often enough, and I've seen the way men and women respond to his looks—I've seen him despise them for it. He's not vain, although he likes to dress well, but that's a uniform, part of the image, the Anderson brand. So would a naïve, young-looking college girl from the Bronx fall for the handsome billionaire? You do the math.

If I don't like the way things go, I'll have to leave—with or without Rachel. The thought makes me sick as fuck.

I wonder if girlfriends are a tax break. Executive-stress toys, maybe? I bet if his accountant put their expenses as 'massage therapist', the taxman wouldn't look twice. You never can tell with rich people.

And you know what? There *are* different rules for the rich.

You don't want to wait? *Head on over to the front of the line.*

You want a table in a fully-booked restaurant? *Some other sucker gets kicked to the wait list.*

You don't like the squalor of flying first class? *Buy your own jet.*

You want someone to dance to your tune? *You pay the piper.*

And if you want someone to look the other way, *everyone has a price.*

Even me.

My price would be the safety of my daughter. She's my weak spot—her and Rachel.

Rachel smiles gently.

"He likes her."

"You think?"

She sighs heavily, obviously thinking my question is dumb.

"Justin! It's obvious. He's fallen for this girl, in a nice, normal way!"

I'm not so sure, but I don't want to argue. I just want to take my woman in my arms and forget all about Anderson and all about his fucked up, twisted world. We're in his life, but Rachel is my sanctuary, and right now, I just want to feel her soft, warm body. I want home.

"You look very stressed, Justin. I think I have something that could ease your tension."

And my eyes willingly follow her as she walks into the bedroom. A second later, the rest of me follows.

I don't see the message from Howard on my cell phone until the next morning.

. . .

The blackmailer posted more of the boss's home movies on a porn site. I got it taken down, but it's a threat. And the price just went up: three hundred million.

TO BE CONTINUED...

Read the Prologue and first chapter of *Saving the Billionaire* now!

SAVING THE BILLIONAIRE

Prologue

Hope.

Small word. Big meaning.

When I started working for reclusive billionaire Devon Miguel Anderson, I had no idea what a screwed up son-of-a-bitch he was, but live and learn.

He has more money than just about anyone on the planet, except maybe Bill Gates and God, and I'm not sure about God. That doesn't mean he's happy though. As a matter of fact, Anderson is not a happy guy: just miserable in Armani suits.

I'm not his friend, I'm not his drinking buddy, but I am the guy who knows him better than just about anyone else, and that includes his shrink.

I'm a close protection officer: that's 'bodyguard' to you. And when the shit goes down—which it will—I'm the one who'll take a bullet for the billionaire. I really hope that doesn't happen, because I've kind of got a thing for living. Who knew?

But Anderson? He has a lot to learn.

So if you want to know why this fucked up dude in Tom Ford shoes gives me hope, well, read on.

SAVING THE BILLIONAIRE, CHAPTER 1

Pretty Woman

This has been one of the longest weeks of my life, and that includes the winter tour I did in Afghan, up to my balls in mud in a shit-hole of a town called Now Zad. A place that put the hell in Helmand Province.

The boss is in a vile mood. So what's new? It's a good thing the hanging of employees has been banned, otherwise several who breathed out of turn would be dangling from the yardarm right now.

Everyone is tiptoeing past his office, and I wouldn't be surprised to see some of them on their hands and knees to stay out of sight. We're all waiting for the dam to burst and everyone is praying they're not in the firing line when it happens. Do I care that I'm mixing my metaphors? Not this week. Although the boss hasn't actually fired anyone today—that I know of—it's come close.

And when I say 'fired', the only reason that's not literal is because Anderson doesn't believe in the right to bear arms. Luckily for him, I do. My Smith & Wesson M&P never leaves my side.

Tessa, the assistant to Anderson's assistant and a woman who's been making her mascara run on a daily basis since I met her, nearly got her marching orders when she dropped a cup of coffee on the boss's Bauhaus table, her hands were shaking so much. Although with Tessa, I can never tell if it's nerves around the boss or the fact that she's panting for him. He should have chosen her as his new submissive.

Huh, guess I should explain that.

The boss is into a load of kink: threesomes, foursomes, orgies, whips, canes, belts, voyeurism, sadism, masochism, and a ton of other 'isms' that I can't even spell. His weekend home in the Hamptons, the Farm, is a den of inick ... inikwit ... inquity ... vice. It's also the play pen for the well-connected and unashamed of Manhattan. I've seen politicians getting it on with judges while the wife masturbates in the corner; I've seen a state attorney (Democrat) jacking off while a lobbyist fucks him in the ass (Republican). The breaking down of political barriers—it's almost heartwarming.

Anderson is more of a mystery. I thought he was gay, then I thought he was bisexual, now he's playing it straight. So I'm not sure, and he's undecided.

Today, there are two reasons that the boss isn't his usual sunny, happy-go-fucky self. First, there's the threat of blackmail that will bring his orgy-shaped secrets to public knowledge. So far, his IT geek, Howard, has out-nerded the blackmailer and hacked his way through cyberspace ending the blackmailer's plans *for now*.

Howard is enjoying the "epic battle", his words, but with a potential three hundred million dollar price tag, the boss is putting a lot of faith in a man MENSA can't categorize.

But there is a second reason that the boss ain't a happy dude.

He's interested in a woman.

Yep, I'll have to say that twice just to make sure *I* believe it. *A female woman.*

This is new. I've never seen him date, his family have never seen him date: all he does is BDSM shit to people he knows from a distance. He's never wanted anything approaching a relationship.

Until now.

He's interested in a woman who is separate to all the nasty shit that goes down at the Farm. The object of his undying lust is a dark-haired, dark-eyed girl from the Bronx: Maria Alvarez. How this will play out is anyone's guess. The boss doesn't do waiting: that he's left it ten days before taking further action or heading to the Bronx to see the object of his obsession is the only surprise. Well, Ms. Alvarez, you're over twenty-one, so the choice is yours. Will a black-hearted billionaire make you an offer you can't refuse?

Have I ever been tempted by any of the offers I've gotten from the boss's fuck farm buddies? That would be a *HELL NO!* Besides, I have a thing with the very intriguing and delectable Mrs. Smith, whose name I'm working on changing to Trainer.

She's the boss's housekeeper at his Tribeca mausoleum mansion. And she cooks.

I'm blessed.

But back to this long-ass day.

Both Tearful Tessa and the table survive, thanks to Ryan, PA extraordinaire, saving the day with a handful of paper towels for the table and a bottle of Valium for Tessa. The man deserves a medal, although I think this week has aged him. Maybe he needs a vacation. Tessa spent most of the day in the ladies' room crying, so she wasn't doing much assisting.

Pam is the boss's right-hand, the most senior exec, and a double-hard I'm-calling-the-shots-and-you're-gonna-like-it kind of woman. She rolls with the punches and Anderson is smart enough not to yell at her. She'd probably lay him out cold if he tried. One punch. Plus, she's the Yoda of the thousand-yard stare, and as a former Marine, I know what I'm talking about.

By Thursday, I'm not the only one at DMA Tower desperate for the weekend. When a senior exec screws up a deal in South Korea and the bellows can be heard all the way to Pyongyang.

Stability in a CEO is so important, doncha think?

Saturday morning and this weekend already sucks ass.

First, Rachel, the love of my life and woman who will one day be persuaded to change her surname to match mine, has gone to stay with her sister. I only met Allison that one time at Thanksgiving, and that was more than enough. She doesn't approve of me: divorced, a kid, no home of my own, ex-military with the temperament to match. I don't know what Rachel sees in me either, but when I look into her sister's eyes, I know exactly what's there—and it's not good.

And second, the boss has turned into a stalker.

Let me recap—and I'll put this in words that even I can understand:

- The boss interviews for an intern
- He meets aforementioned brown-eyed girl (cue Van Morrison)
- He doesn't give her the job and blows her off, but weeks later tracks her down on a Tuesday evening to a club in the Village where she does a (really bad) standup comedy routine
- He decides it's a good idea to go visit her at her part-time job with *Value Carpets & More* on a Saturday morning.

Like I said: *stalker.*

Or maybe Anderson has decided that he needs to buy new carpets. Maybe a nice Paisley for his meditation room; something that says 'dungeon, but homey'.

At 8:15AM, I drive Anderson to the dismal carpet warehouse, a flea on the backside of New York in a dead-end industrial estate at the edge of the Bronx. I thank God that I hated my hometown so much I joined the Marines, because otherwise I could have ended up working somewhere like this.

Anderson is edgy, anxious, and if I didn't know better, I'd say excited, maybe even nervous. *Nervous?*

Ms. Alvarez is hovering at the entrance to the store, waiting for the manager to open for the staff. Her face shuts down when she sees Anderson. Poor kid. Poor, poor kid. The boss isn't a bad guy, but this is wrong.

"Wait in the car, Trainer."

Yup, wasn't planning on watching this disaster movie.

But just in case the boss needs a witness, I crack the window an inch.

"Good morning, Ms. Alvarez."

"What are you doing here? First the club, now where I work!"

He blinks, surprised by her hostility.

"I don't want to interrupt you."

"I don't want to break my back hauling carpet swatches all day," she snips out, "but we don't always get what we want."

Anderson folds his hands across his chest.

"What do you want?"

"For real?"

"Yes, tell me what you want."

She stands up straight.

"Fine. I'll tell you. I want to get a job where I can use my degree in business and environmental science and earn enough money to get my family out of the shitty apartment we live in and move somewhere decent. I want to enjoy my work and spend my time meaningfully; I want to contribute to the world somehow. I want to conquer my fears, I want to travel the world. And..."

"That's quite a long list, now there's more?"

He glances at her and he's got that look: you see it on wildlife shows when the lion is about to pounce on the little baby zebra who got separated from the herd.

She thrusts her chin out.

"I want to make people laugh at the comedy club because I'm funny, not just pity-applause because my routine is pathetic."

"I didn't think it was pathetic, Ms. Alvarez. I actually found it rather incisive wit."

She smiles for the first time.

"You like my routine about going for a job interview with a famously reclusive billionaire?"

Anderson almost smiles.

"It had a certain ring of authenticity."

She laughs out loud.

"I like a guy who can take a joke." Then her cheeks flush as she realizes what she's said. "I don't mean you. Not that you're awful or anything..."

Her words trail off and I gotta tell you, I really feel for the boss. He's getting shot down big time.

He takes a step back.

"I'd like to offer you an internship with my company."

The girl gapes, then her jaw shuts with a click and she crosses her arms.

"Why?"

"Because having reviewed your résumé," he says slowly, "I believe you'd be a good fit for my company."

"And it's taken you this long to figure that out?"

Anderson doesn't reply.

"I'm not going to sleep with you," she says quickly.

Anderson's expression becomes glacial, and I see Ms. Alvarez inch away from him.

"That would be most inappropriate. I have no desire to ... sleep ... with you."

The boss is telling the truth. He'd like to fuck her, probably beat her or have her watch him beating himself, but sleeping wouldn't be part of the trifecta of delights.

"I'm sorry," she says. "It's just weird, you coming out to the club, then out here."

"I'm not like other employers," he says starkly.

I can definitely vouch for that.

"So ... if I say yes, I mean *if*, it would be just like a regular job? No funny stuff?"

Ms. Alvarez has balls.

Anderson leans toward her, his dark eyes glittering.

"Ms. Alvarez, if you come to work for me, I can guarantee that there will be nothing regular about it."

"Show me a contract and I'll think about it."

"You can read the contract in my home office now."

"Email it to me."

"No."

"Why not?"

"Confidentiality. My last offer, Ms. Alvarez. Take it or leave it."

She sucks her teeth, thinking about that. She's talking tough but her eyes are saying something else. She's wary, excited, nervous, and yeah, flattered. The GQ billionaire has followed her to the Bronx—of course she's flattered. She's also right to be wary.

"Fine, but I'm bringing someone with me."

"I beg your pardon?"

"Dude, I'm not getting into your car with you and the Rock, and going to your home without having someone with me!"

She's comparing me to a guy who's known for his limited facial expressions while pretending to act? I'm wounded.

"Come back when I finish work. Six o'clock. *My* last offer."

She turns her back to Anderson as the lights go on in the carpet warehouse and the door opens. She walks away without a second glance.

Anderson watches her, bemused, and as far as I can tell, impressed as hell.

She's nothing like the scared, mousy woman that he interviewed two months ago.

Nope.

The rest of the day is spent with the boss's attempts to ignore the seconds and minutes ticking by. We go for a longer run than usual, twice around Central Park and back to Wolf Point. I'm ready to kick my feet up and watch a ball game on TV, but the boss heads to his pool, swimming laps until his arms fall off.

Yep, the boss is suffering from a lil ole slice of sexual tension. I'm waiting for the slam of the door to his meditation room, but the mausoleum is silent as the grave.

The traffic report says it will take 34 minutes to drive the 14 miles to the Bronx, but at 1700 hours, the boss is wearing a hole in his Italian marble flooring as he paces up and down.

It's weird to see him in jeans and a leather jacket. Maybe he thinks that will help him fit in at Value Carpets. I don't know, can you get designer nylon? 'Cause that's what Ms. Alvarez's uniform is made from.

At least the Rover will fit in with the drug dealers' rides of choice.

The drive to the Bronx is tense, and when the lights go off in the warehouse at six, the boss is on his last nerve, although you wouldn't know it unless you were me.

The girl pokes her head out of the door and seems surprised to see us.

"I'll open the door for Ms. Alvarez," the boss says quietly.

I watch them in my rear view mirror. They're staring awkwardly at each other like a couple of teenagers on a first date. It's weird to see the boss acting this way.

"Good evening, Ms. Alvarez," he says.

She smiles and nods politely, "Mr. Anderson."

When she sees me watching her, she smiles warily, "Hi."

"That's Trainer, my driver."

Jeez, demoted to driver. I'll complain to my union.

"Hello, Mr. Trainer."

"Good evening, Ms. Alvarez. And it's just Trainer."

Another girl approaches, a short woman wearing a poncho and heavy glasses. *The 'Ugly Betty' look is still in. Who knew?*

"This is my friend Dolores Quinlan. She's coming with us."

"Ms. Quinlan."

I open the door for the second girl who's trying not to be impressed by the boss, the Rover, or yours truly.

I nearly pass out when the boss offers his hand to Ms. Alvarez as he helps her into the SUV. And I try really hard not to listen to their conversation but I can't help myself. I have *never* seen the boss hold a woman's hand—not even his sister or his mom. *What the fuck is going on? When did the world stop turning and why did nobody tell me?*

"How was work?" he asks.

"Dull."

"That wouldn't happen if you worked for me."

"I'd like to see that contract now."

"I told you—it's at my house."

She glances at her friend.

"I texted Auntie Vera with the car's license plates. We're good."

Anderson raises his eyebrows but doesn't comment.

The sass that was there this morning has been replaced by something else, making me feel like a third wheel, or possibly a fourth wheel, which makes no sense. Dolores looks equally uncomfortable and is staring out of the passenger window, ignoring her friend, me and the boss. I get the feeling that if I wasn't here, Anderson would jump on Ms. Alvarez right now. Or maybe the shy and not-so-retiring Ms. Alvarez would make the first move. Pigs are flying in formation and all bets are off.

I slide further down into my seat and act deaf and dumb for the rest of the drive. I'd close my eyes, too, if it wasn't for the fact that I'm driving. I can't get to Wolf Point quickly enough.

Finally, I cut through the Saturday night traffic and we're there. I open the door for Ms. Quinlan, and then for Ms. Alvarez. The boss slides out behind her, as if he can't bear to be more than touching distance away from her.

"Trainer," he nods at me curtly.

I nod and get back in the Rover.

Ms. Alvarez—you are on your own.

REVIEWS

Reviews are love! Honestly, they are! But it also helps other people to make an informed decision before buying my book.

So I'd really appreciate if you took a few seconds to do that.

Thank you!

MORE BOOKS BY JHB

Series Titles
The Education Series
An epic love story spanning the years, through war zones and
more...
*The Education of Sebastian (Education series #1)
*The Education of Caroline (Education series #2)
*The Education of Sebastian & Caroline (combined edition, books
1 & 2)
Semper Fi: The Education of Caroline (Education series #3)

The Traveling Series
All the fun of the fair ... and two worlds collide
*The Traveling Man (Traveling series #1)
*The Traveling Woman (Traveling series #2)
*Roustabout (Traveling series #3)
*Carnival (Traveling series #4)
*Gypsy (Traveling series #5)

The Justin Trainer Series
The bodyguard and the billionaire

Guarding the Billionaire (Justin Trainer series #1)
Saving the Billionaire (Justin Trainer series #2)

* The EOD Series
Blood, bombs and heartbreak
*Tick Tock (EOD series #1)
* Bombshell (EOD series #2)

*The Rhythm Series
Blood, sweat, tears and dance
*Slave to the Rhythm (Rhythm series #1)
*Luka (Rhythm series #2)

Standalone Titles
Contemporary Romance
The Lilac Cadillac
Battle Scars
One Careful Owner
*Lifers
At Your Beck & Call
The New Samurai
Exposure

New Adult
*Dangerous to Know & Love
Dazzled
Summer of Seventeen

Paranormal
*The Dark Detective: Venator (Book #1)
*The Dark Detective: Paukúnnum (Book #2)

Novellas
Playing in the Rain
*Behind the Walls

Anthologies of Short Stories
*The Year Book Volume 1
*The Year Book Volume 2
*The Year Book Volume 3

Audio Books
One Careful Owner
(*narrated by Seth Clayton*)

On the Stage
Later, After: Playscript
Trailer

With Alana Albertson
Father Figure

* These titles are published in languages other than English.
Please check Jane's website for details—and receive **a free short story every month** when you sign up for her newsletter :)

QR code for Jane's website

ROMANCE WITH STUART REARDON

Books written with my lovely co-author

Two book series - contemporary romance

*Undefeated

*Model Boyfriend

Three book series - romcom

*Gym Or Chocolate?

*The World According to Vince

*The Baby Game

Standalone

Survivor Love Island *(romcom)*

*Touch My Soul *(novella)*

WRITING AS BERRICK FORD

Police Thrillers, UK

Dead Water
Dead Man's Dive
Dead Reckoning
Dead Shore

www.berrickford.com

www.ingramcontent.com/pod-product-compliance
Lightning Source LLC
Chambersburg PA
CBHW070835250626
47159CB00003B/792